CRAZY HOT

"A cast of memorable characters in a tale of fast-paced action and eroticism." —*Publishers Weekly*

"Edgy, sexy, and fast. Leaves you breathless!"
—Jayne Ann Krentz

CRAZY COOL

"Wild nonstop action, an interesting subplot, a tormented-but-honorable-and-brilliant bad boy and a tough girl, and great sex scenes make Janzen's . . . romance irresistible." —*Booklist*

CRAZY WILD

"While keeping the tension and thrills high, Janzen excels at building rich characters whose lives readers are deeply vested in. Let's hope she keeps 'em coming!" —*Romantic Times*

CRAZY KISSES

"The high-action plot, the savage-but-tender hero, and the wonderfully sensuous sex scenes, Janzen's trademarks, make this as much fun as the prior Crazy titles." —*Booklist*

CRAZY LOVE

"Readers [will] instantly bond with [Janzen's] characters. Driving action and adventure laced with hot passion add up to big-time fun." —*Romantic Times*

CRAZY SWEET

"Exciting and adventurous suspense with nonstop action that will keep readers riveted. I highly recommend it, and can't wait to read more."
—*Romance Reviews Today*

ALSO BY TARA JANZEN

CUTTING LOOSE

TARA JANZEN

A DELL BOOK

CUTTING LOOSE
A Dell Book/January 2008

Published by Bantam Dell
A Division of Random House, Inc.
New York, New York

Dell is a registered trademark of Random House, Inc., and the
colophon is a trademark of Random House, Inc.

ISBN 978-0-440-24385-4

Printed in the United States of America
Published simultaneously in Canada

www.bantamdell.com

OPM 10 9 8 7 6 5 4 3 2 1

CUTTING LOOSE

CHAPTER ONE

Friday, 2:00 P.M. —Langley, Virginia

Alejandro Campos slowed the black Mercedes to a crawl, and carefully negotiated a serpentine series of heavy gray concrete pylons leading up to the security checkpoint at the entrance to CIA Headquarters. The positioning of the barricades looked haphazard.

It wasn't.

NASA's astrodynamics lab in Huntington had designed the maze. At four miles an hour or less, traffic flowed smoothly through the pattern. Anything over four mph guaranteed smashing a quarter panel against a pylon at an angle guaranteed to put a vehicle broadside to a guaranteed line of fire from the armored guard station at the end of the serpentine.

The CIA liked their guarantees.

They liked them double-downed hard.

Peeling a couple more antacids off the roll he'd been working since Dulles, Campos gave the mirrored third-story windows in the main building a quick visual once-over. Behind the windows was another NASA-designed product, an array of computer-directed weaponry with a broad range of capabilities, from putting a bullet neatly through a single driver's eyeball to turning an armored vehicle into a smoking tangle of twisted metal, or doing anything in between, depending on the perceived threat level. In terms of firepower, the imposing guard station at street level was mostly for show, but it was a damned convincing show.

When he reached the last of the pylons, he pulled the Mercedes to a stop, popped the antacids in his mouth, and shoved the rest of the half-eaten roll back in his pocket.

Yeah, it was good to see the old place.

Sure it was.

The security officer at the checkpoint was hard and lean, about thirty-five years old, with a layer of Kevlar soft body armor just visible inside the open collar of his uniform shirt, and Campos didn't doubt for a minute that he was capable of handling most situations without third-story assistance.

Approaching the driver's window, the officer

pressed a switch on his multifunction communications device. Campos knew everything that happened during the guard's contact with the vehicle, both audio and video, would be transmitted in real time to the control center's computer inside the main building.

To smooth things along, he rolled his window down to the bottom stop and deliberately placed both hands, palms open, on top of the steering wheel.

"Good morning, sir," the officer said pleasantly. "Could I see your entry authorization?"

"Certainly," Campos said, taking a business card off the dash and handing it over.

The guard entered the numeric sequence written on the back of the card into a PDA and viewed the response on the screen. He was carrying a custom single-action .45 caliber sidearm in a tactical SWS polymer holster with four spare magazines on his duty belt. The pistol's rosewood grips showed wear marks, an indication of the amount of use it got—plenty, probably at one of the agency's off-site high-tech qualification ranges.

"Look directly at me," the guard instructed, then aimed the lens of the PDA's digital camera toward Campos. He compared the image with whatever else was on the screen. "Is there anything more you would like to tell me, sir?"

"Zachary," Campos said, just loudly enough for the officer to hear him clearly.

Zachary Prade—the name he'd used the first time he'd come to Langley, and, according to his orders, the name they were giving back to him, at least for a while. Alejandro Campos had served his purpose.

It was the way of things, whether he was ready or not. He knew it. He just didn't know if he was ready or not.

He had a feeling he wasn't.

Dammit.

The guard nodded and handed him a visitor's pass.

"I'm clearing you for building entry, but not through security screening. Park your vehicle in the Alpha Two section on your right, proceed inside the main entrance, and wait outside of screening for your escort. Should pick you up within ten minutes. Any questions?"

"No," Campos said, and put the Mercedes in gear.

A few minutes later he was heading for the building, and it occurred to him that in all his years with the CIA, this was the first time he had ever, literally or figuratively, walked in through the front door.

Four sublevels down, his escort swiped a key-card through the cipher lock reader on a door marked "Forensics." The temperature inside the room was a good ten degrees cooler than the hallway, which made his suit jacket almost comfortable.

Campos noted three rows of what appeared to be oversized stainless-steel filing drawers set into the wall on the left, an assortment of analytical instruments along the remaining walls, and a steel examining table in the center of the room.

Perfect. A morgue.

He wasn't surprised.

Given his involvement in a recent debacle in El Salvador, and his report, he could even guess who the guest of honor would be. *Hell*.

There were three individuals already in the room, two men and a woman. They were standing close to the table and the thick black body bag lying on top of it, unzipped. He recognized the woman and one of the men immediately, then recognized the other man, but only just barely. Despite an active—some might say *hyper*active—history of correspondence between the two of them, conducted through various cutouts, intermediaries, and back channels, he hadn't actually seen the man who had recruited him in over eleven years.

"Hello, Zach," the man said, turning to face him, but leaving both hands inside the deep pockets of his lab coat. Short and stocky, with steel gray having replaced his once dark hair, Alex Maier looked like he'd lived every one of his thirty-odd years with the agency.

"Alex," Zach said, acknowledging his case officer. "Are you planning on telling me what's important enough to terminate my cover?" On the flight up from San Salvador, he'd compiled a pretty good shortlist of reasons for Alejandro Campos to disappear, and his partner, Joya Molara Gualterio—Jewel—could probably add, oh, a million or so even better reasons why it was time for his butt to be pulled out of Central America. Past time, actually. He had no problem with that part, not really, despite eight years of damn hard work and a damn near perfect record as a Salvadoran cocaine kingpin with more connections than a South Central bookie.

Okay, "no problem" was stretching things a bit. He had a couple of problems with it, all of them personal, all of them still living in his villa in Morazán.

Ex-villa, he reminded himself. *Dammit*.

But this little trip to Langley had required a catalyst beyond any reason to pull him out of deep cover, and that's what really had been eating at him since he'd gotten the call. A lot of shit had hit the fan in El Salvador three weeks ago; and suddenly, after eleven years, he was face to face with his boss. It wasn't a coincidence, not in his business.

"Yes, of course," Alex said, his words measured, his tone tired, reflecting the lines of strain in his face. "But, as always, first things first."

"And what exactly might that be?" Zach asked, already knowing at least part of the answer. Hell, it was stretched out on the table.

"First of all, Zach," Alex said, "allow me to introduce Charles Kesselring and Amanda van Zandt. Charles is Deputy Director, Operations, and Amanda is Deputy Director, Intelligence." The woman was blond, of medium height and build, the man taller, about six two, with a pale complexion and narrow shoulders. The two senior officers each gave Zach a polite nod, which he returned.

The introductions were required by agency protocol, but were completely unnecessary. Zach knew perfectly well who the current DDO and DDI were, and he knew that having the two of them in the same place, especially this place, at the same time, probably meant a situation serious enough to have foreign policy implications.

"And," Alex continued, "may I regretfully direct your attention to the body of Mark Devlin, recently killed while on assignment in Central America." The body bag. The guest of honor, literally.

Zach recognized the dead man as one of the agency's contract aviators, a hard-core former Marine who had been a frequent visitor at Alejandro Campos's plantation in northern El Salvador. He had known the man by another name, a name that would never again be spoken by anyone inside the agency.

"Your most recent field report included a videotape of Devlin's death at the hands of CNL guerrillas after his Cessna was shot down in Morazán," Alex said. "This tape was filmed by one Lily Robbins, an American schoolteacher from Albuquerque, New Mexico, whose return to the States you expedited at the conclusion of the Morazán incident. We are here to discuss Robbins's possible connection with the flash drive from Devlin's downed aircraft."

Well, there it was, his worst-case scenario rearing up and biting him in the ass, the catalyst, the reason he was standing in a morgue with the DDO and DDI—Lily Robbins.

Geezus. Her name was the last damn thing he'd wanted to hear in this place, the absolute fucking last. But he'd known, so help him God, he'd known he hadn't put the mess in Morazán behind him, no matter how brilliantly he and Smith Rydell, a Department of Defense operator on the scene, had performed their missions. All by himself, he'd saved the agency over a million dollars and gotten their stolen courier's pouch back for them. Rydell had recovered the classified flash drive from the CIA's downed Cessna, but by the time the DOD operator had been brought on board, the critically injured Devlin had already been captured by the CNL. No one on the U.S. side had been aware of the pilot's fate until the guerrillas, in an uncharacteristic gesture of decency, had delivered his body to the Catholic mission in San Cristobal for transport back to the States. After that, the entire incident had exploded into a violent tangle of conflicting agendas involving more actors and intrigue than an Italian opera, including cocaine smugglers, arms dealers, international assassins, and Salvadoran insurgents, not to mention deep-cover CIA intelligence assets and a New Mexico schoolteacher. The agency had, at first, suspected Lily Robbins of being an agent for at least one of the players in the drama, but had eventually agreed with Zach's assessment that she had simply been in the wrong place at the wrong time.

At least they *had* been in agreement, but now—well, hell, now it looked like Lily Robbins was riding shotgun in his handbasket.

"What kind of connection are you thinking?" he asked, keeping his thoughts to himself and wondering if a couple more antacids might help the situation.

Probably not, *dammit*, and only years of hard training and even harder experience kept him from giving in to a weary sigh.

Van Zandt picked up the conversation, speaking with a clear, refined eastern accent. Zach guessed Vassar, or maybe Yale, definitely not Albuquerque.

"We have downloaded and analyzed the contents of the flash drive," she said. "The files are extensive, mostly routine field reports and other regional data. The largest file, however, initially downloads as an overwritten area of the device's memory, appearing to contain only random bytes with no recoverable data."

"I'm guessing 'appearing to contain' is the operative part of that sentence," he said when she paused, but there really wasn't any guess about it.

"Correct," she continued. "Using the appropriate algorithm, the file can be reordered into random character strings. That, by itself, doesn't accomplish anything of value. When paired with the proper literal key, however, the file becomes readable. In this case, the encoded file was created using a true random one-time literal key."

Zach knew about literal keys. The cryptographic method was centuries old, and had fallen out of favor in the computer age. The technique involved mapping plain-text characters through random characters to create encoded text. If done properly, the only thing a cryptographer could tell from the encoded text alone was that each character was somewhere in the alphabet from A to Z, with each letter being equally probable, assuming that the plain text had started out as English. A computer could make the encoded text mean anything at all, with equal odds of success for each decryption version. Zach knew systematic computer codes, including computer-generated pseudo-random keys, could eventually be broken by other computers. Codes using true random keys, however, could be broken only if the same key were used repeatedly. If the key was only used once, computer analysis could not recover the plain text.

"Normally, of course," Kesselring interjected, "both the originator and the recipient would possess the same literal key. In this case, for reasons that are not pertinent to this discussion, the only copy of the key accompanied the encoded file. One of Devlin's transport options for such data was a macramé bracelet with a polymer strand containing a series of microdots woven into it. Very low tech in this modern age, but still quite effective, especially since so few examiners even look for it." He activated a laptop computer screen on a table next to Devlin's body. "Our medical examiner scanned Devlin's wrists and found a pattern of hemp fibers embedded into the skin on the left one. Here's a color-enhanced image of the pattern." Kesselring paused to let Zach take a close look at the purplish chain-link outline. "Your report states that Ms. Robbins was in physical contact with Devlin just before he died. Her tape shows clearly that Devlin had nothing on his wrist at the time of his death. The report also states that she was wearing various items of personal adornment when she arrived at your residence. Could a fiber bracelet such as this have been one of those items?"

Oh, hell, yeah.

Lily Robbins had been wearing all sorts of jewelry the night she'd shown up at his plantation, including a macramé bracelet. She'd been soaking wet from a rainstorm, packing a guerrilla *capitan*'s engraved pistol, and obviously in more trouble than he'd thought, and he'd thought she'd been in plenty.

"Yes," he said evenly. "It's entirely likely Ms. Robbins has your key." Though he'd be damned if he could think of a reason for an innocent bystander to steal a cheap bracelet off a dying man.

On the other hand, he didn't have any trouble coming up with a thousand and one reasons for a not-so-innocent bystander to steal the bracelet. Neither would the CIA. Hell, they probably had a couple of thousand reasons, any one of which could bury Ms. Lily Robbins.

"Likely enough to send you to find her and look for it," Kesselring agreed. "There are a few more things you need to be aware of, though. First, the only individuals on this end who know of the key's existence are the four of us in this room. Second, we consider it entirely possible that Devlin was photographed after he was captured. Third, there are some pretty clever folks who serve—ah—other interests, and those folks just might figure out that he left without something he arrived with. If we can guess what it is and where it is, then so can they. Best case, you locate Ms. Robbins, recover the bracelet, it turns out to be what we think it is, you return without incident, and that's the end of it. Worst case . . ."

"I get it," Zach said. And he did. Worst case was going to make Lily Robbins wish she'd never left Albuquerque.

"You'll maintain your current identity and use your existing resources for this, at least to begin with," Van Zandt said. "Alex will brief you on the risk assessment, operational details, and options. Do you have further questions for Charles or myself?"

"No, ma'am," he said, not even considering asking what was in the file. Everything he'd ever been tasked with recovering had come under the heading of Top-Secret, None-of-Your-Business Trouble. He doubted if the bracelet was any different.

With another short nod, Van Zandt left the room. Kesselring was close behind her, leaving Zach with Alex and what would undoubtedly become an hours-long briefing.

His boss gestured toward a door at the other end of the room, and Zach followed him out into another hallway.

"Report only to me on this," Alex said.

"Yes, sir." It was an order, not a request.

"And this was sent down from State for you." The older man handed him an official-looking sealed envelope.

Zach opened it while they walked, and pulled out the single sheet of paper. There were six words on it.

Six unfuckingbelievable words.

Geezus. A fleeting grin curved his mouth. *How in the hell?* He read the note again, twice, then refolded it into the envelope and stuck the whole thing in his pocket.

Geezus.

"I don't know why you're getting letters from State," Alex said, a note of disapproval in his voice, "but they're in this thing up to their neck, right along with us. They're the ones who pulled the DOD operator, Smith Rydell, in on the Salvadoran deal, so be careful, and don't forget that you work for me. When Amanda spoke about 'existing resources,' she meant everything. You've got ties to Rydell's team in Denver, Special Defense Force, SDF. Use them. Shake these guys down, find out what they know about this mess, names, dates, orders, everything, and make sure we come out on top."

He stopped in front of an unmarked door and swiped a keycard through the lock. When the lock released, he opened the door, and Zach followed him into another hallway, more of the Langley maze.

"I'll be damned if we take the fall for State's mistakes," Alex continued, "and the last thing we need is the Defense Department on our back. After our briefing, you will leave immediately for Colorado. Find out what you can. If this is going to go bad, I want SDF going down first, then State. When you're finished in Denver, go pick up the woman. I expect you to be in Albuquerque by tomorrow afternoon at the latest. The clock is ticking on this thing."

Of course, it was. The clock was *always* ticking. It had been ticking for Zach for eleven years, and sometimes it wore the hell out of him, but all he said was "Yes, sir."

He didn't have a problem with going to Denver. He understood interagency politics, and he also knew the bad blood between the chop-shop boys of Steele Street and the CIA went back over a decade, to an incident in Moscow involving Dylan Hart. Regardless, he sure as hell didn't think he'd be shaking down the SDF team, at least not as his first order of business. Later, though, if Lily Robbins didn't pan out, he'd do whatever it took to get the job done. That's what he did, get the job done, every time.

But going to Denver was a good idea. He'd been considering it since he'd landed back in the States, and the letter clinched it.

His grin returned for another fleeting second. Going to Denver was a damn good idea, but not for any reason Alex would understand, because for all his Ivy League education and brilliance, Alex was no mechanic.

CHAPTER TWO

Lily Robbins leaned over the side of the bed and checked to make sure her incredibly annoying and incredibly effective wake-the-hell-up alarm was set for five A.M. It was. Falling back on her pillow, she stared at the ceiling and took a deep breath. The FedEx envelope she'd found on her doorstep two days ago was lying next to her. It was the craziest damn thing. She'd opened it right off the bat, and then spent the last two days wondering what it all meant.

Oh, hell, she knew what it meant—trouble.

Pure, unadulterated, a-good-girl-wouldn't trouble.

She was a good girl.

Maybe too good.

Silently asking herself what in the world she

thought she was going to do, she picked up the envelope, belled it open, and dumped the contents onto her duvet: a plane ticket to Tahiti, a politely phrased, anonymous invitation written in a stylized hand on twenty-pound bond, and ten thousand dollars in cold cash.

Ten.

Thousand.

Dollars.

And Tahiti.

She lifted her gaze to the far wall and the travel poster framed and matted and hanging next to her bedroom door—Tahiti at sunset, palm trees, white sand, a thatched bungalow, and a sailboat silhouetted against a soft blue and pink sky. Tahiti, the poster said, Island of Dreams.

Certainly the island of her dreams. She'd been dreaming about Tahiti since she'd been twelve years old, after seeing *South Pacific*. Bali Hai hadn't existed, but Tahiti did, and it was exotic, tropically colorful, bounded by an endless ocean of water, and full of early morning mists and wild, lush greenery, the absolute opposite of everything in Trace, Montana, where she'd grown up, which she knew was the whole point of her fixation. She had a bookcase full of books about French Polynesia and not a cowboy poster in sight.

And now she had a plane ticket to Tahiti and ten thousand dollars.

Either someone had gotten lucky, or someone had gone to a whole helluva lot of effort to find out what she liked. Only one name came to mind, only one person with that level of cool sophistication, that many resources, and that much cash on hand: Alejandro Campos, the drug lord who'd saved her butt in El Salvador three weeks ago.

Drug lord, she reminded herself, looking at the pile of money. Cocaine smuggler. Criminal. Bad guy.

At best, it was an interesting way to ask for a date.

At worst, it was an interesting way to ask for a whole lot more.

Ten thousand dollars—she picked up a taped stack of bills and ran her thumb over the top. She could sure use the cash, but nothing inside her could accept the illicit invitation, and she most definitely didn't need the trouble. She already had more trouble than she could handle, all of it coming out of nowhere, just like the damn envelope.

Today had been the day—last-day-of-helping-out-at-school day, last-day-of-blackboards-and-books-and-lying-about-why-she'd-come-home-from-her-sabbatical-early day, last-day-in-Albuquerque day. She was going home.

At least that's one way to put it, she thought, dropping the stack of bills back onto the rest of the pile. Running away was another way to put it, and in her heart, she figured that was actually closer to the truth.

She slanted her gaze toward the bedside table, and to the .45 caliber semiautomatic Colt lying next to the alarm clock. She'd already packed her suitcase for tomorrow's early morning departure. All she needed to add was her toothbrush and a couple of books to read on the road, and she'd be ready for three months at her family's ranch in Trace.

She wouldn't need the Colt once she got there. Any varmint running loose and up to no good on the Cross Double R was better gotten after with a rifle than a handgun. Pistols were for killing people, and that was exactly why she had one by the side of her bed and why it was going with her on the road.

Life had taken a few unsettling turns since she'd come back from El Salvador. She'd gone to Central America to film a documentary on a group of Catholic nuns running an orphanage near the Honduran border. But what she'd gotten was in over her head. Within days of her arrival, she'd found herself in the middle of a bunch of guerrillas and drug runners, with far too many people dying on the sidelines. She'd gotten out in one piece, thanks to Campos, the biggest drug dealer in the Salvadoran province of Morazán, but staying that way was proving to be more of a challenge than she would have imagined possible in Albuquerque.

Her house had been broken into three days ago, at least according to her. The police thought she was imagining things. Nothing had been stolen. Nothing had been left out of place. No one had seen anything or anyone strange in the neighborhood. No burglary, no robbery, no sign of any breaking and entering; therefore, no crime, just a jittery woman's imagination.

Bull.

Someone had been in her house, touching her things, searching through her rooms.

They.

Two guys.

She would put money on it.

One tall, older guy with a gray ponytail and a paunch; the other guy with buzz-cut, white-blond hair, dark sunglasses, of average height, with a better-than-average build. They drove a silver Aston Martin, a car so unusual in her usual haunts that seeing it and the guys who drove it more than a couple of times had set off a warning bell, especially when she'd seen the sports car leaving the high school parking lot on Tuesday with the gray-haired guy at the wheel.

Coincidence?

Maybe.

But her daddy was a sheriff's deputy in Chouteau County, Montana, and a former United States Marine, and he didn't believe in coincidences. Neither did she, not enough to take even a long-shot chance, and in the last three days, she'd put her plans in place, gotten her stuff packed, and mapped out her route—the interstate, all the way, straight north. Home.

She'd also started sleeping with her pistol cocked, locked, loaded, and well within reach. If she was imagining things, great, perfect, all for the better, and if she wasn't, she had the Colt.

She didn't blame the police for not believing her, not really. She hadn't exactly told them where she'd been and what she'd been up to, or anything else about what had happened or what she'd witnessed in Central America. The whole surreal experience had ended with a luxurious trip back to the States on a private jet, compliments of the mysterious Alejandro Campos.

No, she'd decided, telling the police everything hadn't seemed like her best bet, so she was going home instead.

Of course, she hadn't exactly told her dad

everything either. The last thing Deputy Grant Robbins wanted to hear was anything even remotely resembling trouble getting within spitting distance of his youngest daughter. It made him cranky, bearish. It brought out the Marine in him. It made him overbearing, Lily's ex-husband, Tom, had said repeatedly, and ridiculously overprotective, and since her dad had thought her Italian husband was nothing but trouble, he'd been bearish through the whole six years of her marriage.

Rightly so; by the time she'd filed for divorce from the spoiled, exotically foreign, philandering Tomaso, Tom, Bersani, Lily had felt a little bearish herself.

And now she felt in the need of some deputy sheriff overprotecting.

Maybe she was only imagining things, seeing danger where there were only a couple of guys with an expensive car who happened to be driving around her part of Albuquerque.

But her instincts said something was up, something that said maybe she should call the phone number she'd been given on the private jet. The one she kept in her backpack. Though exactly how Campos could help her was a question she hadn't been able to answer, at least not well enough to get her to actually dial up a known drug dealer.

She wasn't that crazy, not yet, Tahitian invite or no Tahitian invite. She had three months of summer vacation, four thousand acres of Montana high country, and her father to stand between her and anybody who might be after her. There was no reason for her to go looking for more trouble, and Alejandro Campos really was trouble, dangerous trouble, criminal trouble, and, for reasons she didn't want to admit even to herself, personal trouble. She'd known it the instant she'd looked up into his eyes and felt the world shift under her feet.

It was the stupidest thing in the world, and she wasn't going to think about it, let alone pursue it, plane ticket or no plane ticket. If she'd had any sense at all, she would have thrown his phone number away three weeks ago.

But she hadn't.

Instead, she'd casually jotted it on her kitchen calendar—just in case she lost the piece of paper he'd given her.

Then she'd written it in her homework assignment notebook at school, the one she kept in her desk—in case she lost the piece of paper and her kitchen calendar spontaneously combusted.

And she'd put it in her computer, under a file named ACES—Alejandro Campos El Salvador—

in case she lost the paper, her calendar com-busted, and somebody's dog broke into the school and ate her homework assignment note-book.

It was all precautionary.

It was all so ridiculous.

It was all just in case—just in case she lost every ounce of common sense she had and gave in to calling him, just to touch base, maybe to thank him again for saving her butt, maybe just to hear his voice.

Yes, it had all been just in case, and now she had ten thousand U.S. dollars in taped bundles staring her in the face.

"Stupid girl," she muttered, rolling onto her side and wrapping herself around her pillow. What she needed was sleep, not another night of fantasizing about Alejandro Campos, and most definitely not a night of fantasizing about Alejandro Campos in Tahiti.

Friday, 10:00 P.M.—Denver, Colorado

Some things a guy never forgot.

The first woman he'd ever loved. He'd been seventeen.

The first man he'd ever killed. He'd been nineteen.

And how to break into the first place he'd ever called home.

Zach stood in the alley and looked up at the thirteen stories of steel-reinforced brick at 738 Steele Street. The old building in the heart of lower downtown's historical district, an area affectionately referred to as LoDo, had started life as a car dealership back in the forties. A few economic booms and busts, and half a dozen reincarnations, had passed before it had become the most notorious chop shop in a tristate area, run by a fifteen-year-old mastermind with a handpicked crew of boys who'd made an art form out of juvenile delinquency and grand theft auto.

She was in there: Charlotte, a 1968 Shelby Mustang Cobra GT500KR, the first car he'd ever rebuilt from the frame up—Charlotte the Harlot, in Candy-apple Red with white panel stripes on the lower body and white Le Mans stripes going up over the hood and down the deck. She'd done 0 to 60 mph in 5.5 seconds for him every day of the week, taking the quarter mile in 13.8, and on some days, she'd done better than that. One cool autumn night, a lifetime ago, he and Dylan had clocked her at an even 5 seconds and a 12.9 quarter mile out on the Doubles, a strip of abandoned highway east of Denver. Hawkins had been in and out of prison by then, and the other chop-shop boys had gone their own ways, most of the core group going into the military, a few of the stringers melting back into the streets, and him disappearing off the face of the earth.

He'd been good at it, disappearing. A couple of times, he'd been too damn good at it, getting in so deep his handlers had lost track of him. Those had been some strange years—the Asian Years, he called them, the four years in Laos and Cambodia, the months spent going in and out of Thailand and Indonesia before he'd been reassigned to the Panama country office and ended up in El Salvador.

He slid his gaze down the night-darkened alley, until it landed on an iron door with a grid pattern of bolts across its face. Seven thirty-eight—the numbers were painted on the brick above a stone lintel. A large metal sign with the word "WEATHERPROOF" had been secured to the wall next to the door.

A grin curved his mouth. *Weatherproof. Geezus.* He'd forgotten about the chop-shop boys' weatherproof theory of sex. Hell, they all should have forgotten it by now, but there was the damn sign, still in place.

And there was the door.

And three blocks to the north, there was an iron grate in the street.

He took a long draw off his cigarette before dropping it onto the pavement and grinding it out with his boot. The streets were quiet—for now. Once he fired Charlotte up, he'd have about two and a half minutes to pull this damn thing off and get out, or he was going to have a helluva lot of explaining to do. Days of it. Weeks of it. Except to Dylan.

Dylan would understand how it all had come down, about why he'd left the way he had, without a word. Quinn wouldn't. Creed would understand why he'd left, but not why he'd stayed away so long. And Hawkins, *fuck,* he really didn't want to have to explain himself to Superman.

He'd kept up with them, Special Defense Force, SDF, a group of black-ops warriors birthed in the shadows of the Pentagon and the Potomac. The team skirted the edge of the Department of Defense, the State Department, and sometimes Posse Comitatus, the act forbidding the use of federal troops inside the United States. But their roots were here, in the grease and iron of Steele Street. Lost boys, every damn one of them, and he'd been the most lost of all.

Dylan knew. Dylan knew everything, had known it from the start and still taken him on, made him one of the finest car thieves ever to survive on the streets of the Mile-High City.

Charlotte running fifteens. Needs a mechanic.

The letter he'd been handed in Langley hadn't had a signature. It hadn't needed one, or any more of an explanation. Six words had said it all.

A mechanic. *Fuck.* Another quick grin curved his mouth.

He owed Dylan Hart, and later, after he finished the Lily Robbins deal, he'd come back. At Steele Street, he could put Charlotte back on twelve-seconds-plus-change quarter miles.

Or else he'd take the Mustang and keep going, the way he always kept going: away. The eight years in El Salvador were the longest he'd ever spent anywhere, but he'd been there as Alejandro Campos, not himself, and Campos didn't have a history before his arrival in Central America. Zach Prade did, in spades, and there was no hiding from it here, not at Steele Street, not with Dylan, and probably not with Superman either.

Hell. He'd come for Charlotte, not to get his life back. Not to pay overdue debts—but he did have one stop he had to make, one person up on Seventeenth Avenue he had to see before he left Denver.

He raised his left hand and touched the side of his face, the gesture almost unconscious, but not quite. The narrow line of his scar ran from above his temple down to his jaw, and being back in Denver made it impossible to be unconscious of it, of how he'd gotten it, or of the man who'd put him back together.

Yeah, he had some debts in Denver.

Lowering his hand, he lifted his gaze and followed the lines of Steele Street's open freight elevator where it crawled up the side of the building. All girders and cables, steel plate and ironwork, the whole of it looked more like an upended suspension bridge bolted into the brick than anything else—bolted deep, Gothic and sweeping, with a garage door opening onto it at every level.

He'd left Charlotte in her bay on the ground floor, pulled her in one long-ago summer night and said good-bye to everything he'd known. Patriotism hadn't exactly been his motivation, and even from the start, he'd been pretty damn cynical about making a difference in the world.

But the challenge—oh, yeah, that had grabbed him hard. Could a nameless kid from the American heartland survive in the farthest-flung reaches of the world as an agent of his government? Could a street rat from Denver take his skills into the underbelly of the world and come out in one piece, time and time again?

The answer was a resounding yes. He'd not only survived, he'd thrived, and sometimes he wondered what that said about him.

Not tonight, though. Tonight all it said was that he was going to get his car, and then he was driving to Albuquerque, New Mexico, and taking a small macramé bracelet from a sweet-faced schoolteacher who, if he did his job right, and he always did, would never have a clue how close she'd come to the edge of his world.

CHAPTER THREE

Saturday, 5:00 A.M.—Albuquerque, New Mexico

At exactly five A.M., Lily's incredibly annoying alarm clock screeched, and at five A.M. plus two seconds, she whacked it, unerringly hitting the off button. The damn thing could wake the dead, which was why she put up with it. Not that she'd needed the extra incentive lately. She hadn't had a decent night's sleep since she'd gotten back.

Sitting up, she swung her legs over the side of the bed, turned on her lamp, and reached for the Colt .45. She flipped off the safety and press-checked the chamber, making sure the first round was still loaded. Then she flipped the safety back on and headed for the bathroom, taking the pistol with her.

It was a crazy way to live, armed and dangerous for her morning shower, but that's the way life was going to be, crazy, until she was back on the Cross Double R...or unless she ended up lying under the French Polynesian sun with a beach drink in her hand.

Yeah, she'd dreamed about Tahiti, a warm-water blue sea washing up on white sand, a thatched hut and a slow-moving fan—and yeah, a dark-haired man. But that's all it was, a dream. The FedEx envelope and all the goodies stuffed inside were headed to Trace, Montana, and the Cross, right along with her, without a Tahitian island in sight.

From where he was parked half a block down on Somerset Street, Zach saw a light go on in Lily Robbins's house. A minute later, another light came on.

Early riser, he thought around a long yawn, reaching for his cup of gas station coffee. He'd made record time, he and Charlotte all but flying over Raton Pass and sliding into Albuquerque just before dawn, the hour of the barbarians, of which Lily Robbins was obviously one.

Five A.M., *geezus.*

Choking down a swallow of bitter brew, he set the Styrofoam cup aside and reached for his

pack of smokes—cold coffee and a hot cigarette, a perfect combination for the ungodly
hour. He lit up and settled in to wait. Charlotte
was hardly the ideal stakeout car, a Shelby
Mustang with racing stripes and headers, but
he wasn't planning on staking out the Robbins
place for very long. He and the pony had glided
into place at a discreetly low and slow rumble,
and once the lovely Lily left for the day, he was
going inside. With luck, he'd find the bracelet
and be on his way without her ever being any
the wiser. It was a long shot, but he'd played
worse odds and come out ahead more than
once.

That was Plan A. Plan B, if he didn't find the
bracelet, entailed paying Ms. Robbins a more
personal visit; shorter odds, but infinitely more
complicated.

He preferred simple.

And food.

Yeah, food would be nice, he thought around
another yawn. Real food—croissants, chèvre,
scrambled eggs, smoked salmon, fresh-squeezed
orange juice with a thin slice of lime, maybe
some papaya.

Maybe not.

His gaze locked on a low-slung sports car
slowly turning the corner onto Somerset Street.
Sitting up a little straighter, he took a last drag

off his cigarette before stubbing it out in the car's ashtray.

Lily lived in a nice neighborhood, but not Aston Martin nice. She had a ten-year-old Ford short-bed pickup parked in her driveway, and her next-door neighbor's truck looked older than that. The expensive import was out of place and showing up at an odd time of day. In the morning, people were usually leaving their homes and neighborhoods, not arriving.

When the Aston Martin stopped in front of Lily's house, Zach reached into the gun bag he'd put on the passenger seat and withdrew a suppressor for the Para .45 semiautomatic pistol he carried in a shoulder holster. Somerset was a quiet street, and Zach planned on keeping it that way, no matter who parked in front of her house, and no matter what they had in mind. He could imagine a few things, any number of which could end quite poorly for someone, probably not him, and to the best of his ability, not Lily Robbins.

Van Zandt and Kesselring had played coy with the contents of the flash drive Devlin had been transporting, but during their briefing, Alex had laid enough information on the line to keep Zach's stomach in knots until the Fourth of July. "Russian Nobel Laureate Gone Bad in Iran" was a crappy headline in any language.

When the laureate was an eminent nuclear scientist, and the bad part was her collusion with the Iranian government to expedite their enrichment of significant amounts of uranium, and the whole mess was documented on a flash drive whose encryption key had quite possibly ended up on a New Mexico schoolteacher's wrist—well, that's where Zach's stomach had started to knot up. Foreign policy issues aside, the loss of that kind of data was enough to get a senior station chief killed, let alone an expendable civilian like Lily Robbins. The problem being that she didn't feel at all expendable to him.

Reaching back in his gun bag, he pulled out a cool little tracking device he'd found attached to Charlotte's ammeter gauge when he'd stopped for his coffee. He dropped the tracker in his pocket, and threaded the suppressor onto the Para, and kept his eye on the Aston Martin, hoping for the best, but preparing for the worst.

He got the worst.

Both doors on the sports car opened at once, and two guys got out, *dos pendejos,* one with a thick gray ponytail, the other with buzz-cut white-blond hair. They didn't look like carpool buddies, or a couple of cousins dropping by for an early morning visit, and they sure as hell didn't look like they'd stopped for directions. No, the men looked like they knew exactly where they were and exactly what they wanted. They didn't hesitate when they got out of the car; they fanned, as in "fanned out," each one taking a different side of Lily's house and heading toward the back.

Fuck them.

Zach didn't hesitate either. He rolled down the passenger-side window on the Shelby, moved the gun bag, and silently slid out of the car, no lights, no opening and shutting doors, no nothing, only him on the street and heading toward Lily's house with a suppressed .45.

Three weeks—that's how long it had taken the CIA to come back around to Lily Robbins, obviously long enough for other interested parties to draw the same damn conclusions about the American woman's involvement in the Salvadoran incident. He knew exactly what kind of people would have been sent after the literal key, and he knew who would have sent them: half a dozen governments, another half a dozen big-name dealers on the international black market, and a handful of shadow organizations that made their way in the world by straddling the line between legitimate and rogue. They would all have sent men like him to find the bracelet and retrieve the code, except, unlike him, those men wouldn't give a damn about Lily Robbins. Her death, if it came to that, would be one of those unexplained murders that no New Mexico cop shop would ever unravel. The guys who did his kind of work wouldn't leave a trace. They were covert, and they were good. Lucky for Lily, Zach was pretty sure he was better than the Aston Martin boys.

Coming up on the sports car, he quickly knelt down, activated and attached the tracking device, and memorized the license number. Nevada plates only meant one thing to him— Vegas wiseguys. He'd have names and sheets on them before noon.

Yeah, he was pretty damn sure he had the upper hand on Somerset Street this morning, but he never took anything for granted. Never. That was what made him better—an acute sense of paranoia and a fear of dying. Not death. He didn't have any fear of being dead. But, man, he'd seen the results of some very bad dying. The Far East, the Near East, all over Latin America, it didn't matter where he'd been, people were butchers, and he wasn't going out in pieces. No fucking way. He'd take a bullet to the back of the head any day over some of the things he'd seen.

J.T. had gone out in pieces—yeah, pieces. John Thomas Chronopolous, J.T., one of the original chop-shop boys of Steele Street. Zach had heard all about how the Special Defense

Force operator had died in Colombia, and how J.T.'s youngest brother, Kid Chaos, had brought him home. Zach had even seen the photographs and wished so goddamn badly that he hadn't.

He came to the corner of Lily's house and snuck a quick look at her back door. It was ajar, and there was no movement anywhere around it.

Fuck. The Aston Martin boys were already in the house.

In half a dozen steps he was beside the door and took a quick look inside—a laundry room, leading into the kitchen, one step up. Even before the last piece of information snapped into place, he was moving forward, the safety on his Para flipped off and his finger on the trigger. Two guys from Las Vegas fanning out and sneaking into a woman's house in New Mexico through the back door at five o'clock in the morning just about sealed their fate as far as Zach was concerned.

Just about. He was always open to last split-second decision making, because once he pulled the Para's trigger, there was no coming back.

The kitchen was clear, the house quiet, except for the sound of a shower, which he hated. She might as well have put up a neon sign— "Naked, vulnerable woman in here." *Fuck*. He followed the sound, moving silently, swiftly, every sense on alert. A door on his right was open onto a flight of stairs leading into a basement. Light from her bedroom showed a large footprint pressed into the carpet at the top of the stairs. At least one of the Aston Martin guys could be in the basement, maybe both. He wasn't hearing any movement on the main floor. He sure as hell wasn't making any noise. When he'd been taught "swift and silent," his instructors had meant exactly that.

Checking each door, each room, each opening, he finally reached the bathroom at the end of the hall. His mission, of which he was well aware, was to get the bracelet. That was it. Get the bracelet and get it to Alex—a simple, straightforward, closed set of commands. "Save the woman" was way down on the CIA's priority list, and honest to God, it might not even have made the list.

Okay, there was no "might" about it. "Save the woman" was not on the list.

But here he was, and there were men in her house, and she was in the shower, and he was going to open her damn bathroom door and scare the holy fuck out of her, just so he could "save the woman," and then he'd get the bracelet.

So now he was up to Plan C, and the sun hadn't even broken the horizon yet.

Aligning himself flush with the door frame, he reached over and turned the knob—and in the next instant, something crashed in the basement.

CHAPTER FOUR

Inside the bathroom, Lily's heart jammed into her throat and the cup of water she'd been holding landed in the sink, along with a flurry of aspirin tablets out of her other hand.

Holy crap. What in the hell was that?

She lunged for her pistol and barely got her hand around it before the door swung open and a man stepped inside.

"Let go of the gun," he ordered, his voice low and harsh.

Let go?

No way.

There was a man in her bathroom, and he had a gun leveled at her chest.

"Lily, let go of the gun. *Now.*" It was a

command, but she could hardly breathe, let alone move.

He knew her name. Dark hair, broad shoulders, gray suit jacket over a black T-shirt, and stone-cold green eyes freezing her in place—she knew his name, too, and her heart was racing like a freight train. His gaze was fierce, direct, compelling, the scar running down the side of his face unmistakable. Her heart beat once . . . twice.

Out of the corner of her eye, she caught a flash of movement behind him, and life slid into a time warp, where every second lasted and lasted, where the length of a breath hovered in one endless moment after another—plenty of time, an eternity to process it all: the crash from her basement, the man with the gray ponytail bursting out of her stairwell, a cold, blank look on his face, a gun in his hand, how he brought the pistol up, pointing it at her, or possibly at the man in front of her, who was dropping to his knee and swinging around, his gun firing at the same time as hers.

The sound was deafening, the blast of her .45 in a small, confined space and the clack of Alejandro Campos's pistol cycling a fresh cartridge into the chamber.

Campos had a silencer on his gun.

"Get—" He started to say something over his

shoulder, then whirled around and grabbed her instead, jerking her out of the bathroom and all but throwing her onto the hallway floor. She heard it, too, the sound of someone pounding up the stairs. The white-haired man came out of the stairwell firing, and the time warp shattered at light speed.

No more orders were necessary. She understood perfectly. She was scrambling, one gun blast after another following her down the hall, tearing through drywall and two-by-fours, and Alejandro Campos was hot on her tail, returning fire.

Oh, my god. She kept moving, scrambling, crawling, ducking, making a beeline for the door into her garage. At the end of the hall, without missing a beat or standing up, she wrenched the knob, pushed the door open, and tumbled through. Campos was with her. She could feel his energy, and his heat, and feel him moving, the brush of his shoulder, the strength of his arm when he pulled her to her feet and pushed her toward the door leading to the outside.

Even in early June the air was crisp and cool before dawn, the grass wet with dew, and she was barefoot, in her summer pajamas, and running—running through old man McCready's backyard, trampling azaleas and tearing through his prizewinning lilies. *Goddamn.* He already thought she was a blight on the neighborhood, and if he caught her, there'd be hell to pay, absolute years of endless nagging, but catching her dead was worse, so she ran, keeping up with Alejandro Campos—*so help her God*.

When they came out of McCready's yard onto Somerset, it suddenly hit her just how barefoot she really was—completely. And they were running down the street, hell-for-leather, heading toward a Fastback Mustang. Campos had taken her hand as soon as they'd left McCready's yard, and when they reached the car, he opened the door and swung her into the passenger seat. She hadn't even righted herself, before he was sliding in behind the steering wheel.

Not three minutes had passed since she'd been calmly getting ready to down her routine morning dose of aspirin to counteract her routine morning headache.

Maybe not even two.

But she hadn't really been calm in the bathroom. She'd been nervous, on edge, which was still eight hundred steps down the chart from the visceral panic she currently had churning through her veins—*crash, guns, shots, run*. Everything was happening so fast.

Or so she thought until Campos slipped the key into the ignition and gave it a twist. Suddenly, the term "fast" took on a whole new meaning. She had a feeling "fast" wasn't her running for her life. "Fast" was the Mustang, coming to life with an earthshaking, rumbling roar of headers and horses, a lot of horses, and a finely tuned set of headers.

She slid a glance across the interior of the car and instantly understood. There were cobras everywhere, embedded in the dash, on the shifter handle and the steering wheel, and embossed on the console armrest.

"Sweet Jesus," she breathed. She had her butt tucked into the bucket seat of a Shelby Cobra GT. *Oh, my god.*

Well.

This was so perfect.

He was sitting next to a half-naked woman and going fifty miles an hour in under five seconds down Somerset Street.

Black stretch sports bra and a pair of black, low-rise, boy-cut short shorts with lace trim—he'd thought women only wore those in his sex-with-the-gym-teacher fantasy. Or was that his sex-with-the-underwear-model fantasy?

Regardless, the girl could run like a freaking gazelle, and he was grateful—at least for that.

The rest of the morning so far had been an un-qualified disaster.

Clandestine, Zach reminded himself, shifting Charlotte up through her gears. He was a clandestine operator, not an overt operator, or a covert operator. Overt meant both the act and the actors in an operation were known. Covert meant the act was known, but not the actors.

But clandestine, which had been his personal fucking goal this morning, meant being invisible: Slide in, do the deed, slide out. Clandestine meant no one even knew anything had been done, let alone who had done it.

Leaving a faceless, gray-ponytailed corpse in a suburban bungalow with five of his tactical handloads buried in the walls broke all the rules of clandestine operation.

Zach didn't particularly like rules, and he didn't particularly live by them, but he had a couple he didn't screw with, two to be precise, both of them tested in the crucible of the back alleys of half the damn Third World countries on the planet. Suburban Albuquerque was not a damn Third World country, but that didn't mean the two rules didn't apply.

He glanced over at Lily and noticed her hair was coming all undone, whole swaths of silky dark strands slipping out of an already loose braid and trailing down over the tops of her breasts.

If he remembered correctly, and he did, her cleavage had kind of riveted his attention the first time they'd met. Which, as he remembered, and he did, had been under circumstances only nominally better than their current circumstances.

Perfect.

He was sure he was making a good impression.

He shifted his attention back to the street. Fifty-five miles per hour, sixty, sixty-five, another second gone, and then it hit him. Something was wrong.

He glanced at her again, his gaze going from one of her wrists to the other. *Sonuvabitch*.

"Where's the bracelet?" he asked.

"Wh-what?" Sapphire blue eyes cut him a terrified glance.

"The bracelet, macramé. The one you got off the pilot who died at St. Joseph's."

"The macramé bracelet?"

"Where . . . is . . . it?" He said the words succinctly, trying to get them to sink in through the shock plastered all over her face.

She'd killed the guy with the ponytail, beating the bastard on the shot, beating Zach, too, and he wondered if she knew it, if she'd had time to realize her bullet had been ahead of his by the merest fraction of a second. It wasn't something he was going to tell her any time soon.

"It's . . . it's in my suitcase, in my bedroom."

And now things were absofuckinglutely perfect.

He slammed on the clutch and the brakes, pulling Charlotte to the left side of Somerset as she rocked to a stop. Rule Number One: Don't assume anything. Ever.

Yeah, that one was chiseled in stone, and he hadn't assumed she'd be wearing a dead guy's cheap bracelet, not for three solid weeks. Actually, he'd thought it pretty damned unlikely, up until he'd opened the bathroom door and kind of forgotten about the bracelet. Yeah, for a minute or two there, it had all been about saving the woman, which brought him to Rule Number Two: Don't fuck with the mission. Ever.

Reaching over with both hands, he took hold of her wrist and disarmed her, twisting the Colt out of her hand. It was a short, sweet move meant to save them both a whole boatload of trouble. In quick order, he released the magazine, emptied the chamber, dropped the magazine in his pocket, and stowed the pistol in his gun bag. If she'd been a little quicker herself, she might have been able to use the Colt to influence current events. Not now, though, which was just as well, because he wasn't in the mood to be influenced.

Really not in the mood—and she was absolutely dumbfounded at how badly the last few seconds had gone for her. He could tell by the way her mouth had fallen open.

Cranking the wheel hard to the right, he threw the Shelby into reverse and gave her some gas. When Charlotte hit a ninety-degree angle, he threw her back up into first and slammed down hard on the gas, cranking the wheel hard left—a classic bootlegger's turn executed at the low end of the Thrill-a-Minute scale, smooth and fast, and without waking the neighbors.

With one hand on the wheel, he opened the top of the console and pulled out one of his cell phones with the other. He left the console open and keyed in a code while he drove.

"Can you drive a stick?" he asked.

"Y-yes."

Good. Then there was the plan.

He had five minutes max, before Somerset was crawling with cops. Five minutes to get back in the house, get her suitcase, and if necessary, kill the other son of a bitch from

Nevada—Plan D, and the goddamn sun *still* wasn't up.

It wasn't aesthetics that had given him the opinion about dawn being the time of barbarians. It was fact, cold and simple. It was an offensive time of day, as in attack, and that's exactly what he was doing.

He finished with the code and tossed the phone into the backseat. The screen was blinking.

"You are going to take the car and park two blocks east of your house," he told her, "at the first intersection on the north end of that street. Do you understand?"

She nodded once when he looked over, and he got the feeling that despite the rather alarming sequence of recent events, she really did understand. If not, he could track her through the cell phone, not that he was going to tell her that.

"Do you remember me?" he asked her.

Again, she nodded once.

"And do you remember what I do for a living?"

Yes, she nodded silently.

"Good," he said. Knowing what he was would help her understand what happened next. People expected the worst from drug runners, and the worst was what he was going to give her, at least from her point of view. He could guarantee it.

Without further ado, he lifted a pair of handcuffs out of the console, slapped one cuff on her left wrist before she even had a clue what he was doing, and locked the other to the steering wheel. Then he pulled Charlotte to a rumbling stop half a block behind the Aston Martin and got out.

He couldn't protect her, if he didn't know where in the hell she was, and now he knew she'd be with the Harlot, come hell, high water, or a horde of barbarians.

He shut the door solidly behind him and leaned down to the window.

"You need to get on this side and drive," he said, reaching for a fresh magazine off his belt clip and slamming it up into the Para. "I'm going back to get your suitcase."

"You . . . you—" She finally got a couple of words out.

Bastard was probably the other word she was looking for, and he couldn't fault her for that. He'd be angry, too, if someone had handcuffed him, so he made sure his promise to her was very clear.

"If you are not on that street corner when I get there, I am going to key a code into my cell phone that will detonate a small block of C4 hidden inside the cell phone in the backseat. There will be an explosion. You will not be happy. Do not mess with me on this, Lily. Get to the corner and stay put."

"You *bastard*."

Yeah, he'd thought that was the word she was looking for.

"Don't flood the engine," he advised, and without another word, turned and headed back toward her house.

CHAPTER FIVE

Saturday, 5:20 A.M.—Denver, Colorado

"What's this? The Bad Girls Breakfast Club?" Dylan Hart asked, stepping off the elevator and onto the roof of the SDF building at 738 Steele Street. The SDF crew called the roof retreat "The Beach," but that was being kind. Two lawn chairs and a wooden crate bolted on top of a patch of Astroturf did not make a beach. It did make a helluva place for a private conversation, though, and The Beach hosted plenty of those, including the one obviously in session.

"Skeeter says something's up," one of his operators said, rising to her feet. Five feet five inches of sleek and lean in a pair of cowboy boots, skin-tight jeans, and an olive-drab tank top, Gillian Pentycote was the strangest, and probably the most deadly, of all the people on Dylan's team.

Without a doubt, she was the most danger-ous, with a reputation that had been made on the long gun as Red Dog, a code-name takeoff on the wild mop of auburn hair she kept profes-sionally disheveled. Dylan deployed her fre-quently, on a short rotation, but never alone. Whatever the assignment, he teamed her with one of the guys: Hawkins, who had practically built her from the ground up; Kid Chaos, who wouldn't hesitate to shut her down if things got out of hand and she couldn't do it herself; Rydell, who had enough years under his belt to make sure things *didn't* get out of hand; or Travis, her lover, a.k.a. the Angel Boy, and prob-ably the only person on the planet who really knew what went on inside her head. Dylan had never yet let her loose with just SDF's jungle boy, Creed Rivera, holding the leash. Creed knew where the lines were, and he'd never crossed them. But he pushed them. He pushed them hard, and Gillian pushed them even harder.

She was a case history in experimental psycho-pharmaceuticals, highly classified: the drug—XT7, a real mind-bender, a memory destroyer straight out of Thailand; the means of delivery—injection during torture, two and a half years ago; the results—a physically and mentally en-hanced human being with an infrequent but statistically measurable tendency toward sud-den instability.

That's what made her dangerous.

That's why Dylan never deployed her with Skeeter.

Yes. He most definitely played favorites, and his most favorite was the baby-faced blond bombshell standing on the rooftop wearing combat boots, black-and-white-striped leggings, and a dark pink satin bustier. Her legs went on forever, and not having them wrapped around him in bed is what had woken him up.

Dawn was barely breaking the sky, and for some reason, all the Steele Street girls cur-rently in residence were on the roof, including the newest little bit of millionaire heiress fluff to wash up on SDF's shore—Honoria York-Lytton, also known as Honey York, no code name, just one of those things.

Dylan knew her. They'd met in Washington, D.C., at a State Department reception for the Prince of Brunei a few years back. She was easy to remember, warm, funny, and drop-dead gor-geous—usually. This morning she looked like someone had put her through a blow dryer backward. He never would have guessed that her hair could stick out that far, or that it kind of had a life of its own.

And he never would have guessed that Rydell would have landed himself a blue-blooded, Harvard-educated, East Coast socialite with markedly feminist leanings, let alone put a ring on her finger. As he recalled, Rydell's first marriage had cost him everything, down to and including his socks.

But there it was, an engagement ring, on Honey York's left hand.

"Something good, or something bad?" he asked the group at large, but his gaze had definitely strayed to the satin bustier. Skeeter hadn't been wearing it, or anything else, when he'd gotten in about midnight and crawled into bed with her.

"We don't know yet," Honey said around a yawn. "Gillian and I just got here. Her brother called an hour ago and is on his way in from the airport, and I . . . I don't know. I've got a flight out later, but for now I just needed some air."

"Which brother?" he asked, his gaze going from the piece of blond fluff curled up on one of the lawn chairs next to Gillian. Red Dog had two brothers; one was an Army Ranger who'd just come off a tour of duty in Iraq, and the other was—

"Gabriel," Gillian said.

The other was Gabriel Shore, a pencil pusher and data analyst with an obscure division of the Commerce Department, whose office wasn't too far down the hall from General Richard "Buck" Grant's in a hell-and-gone annex east of Washington, D.C. Buck Grant was Special Defense Force's commanding officer, a job no one had expected to last longer than SDF's first mission. Eleven years later, Grant was still in the hell-and-gone Marsh Annex, next to the boiler room, and the SDF team was busier than ever. Gabriel was the one who had helped Gillian get her job with Grant after her divorce, the job she'd been doing when she'd been kidnapped and tortured.

Everyone who'd been involved on SDF's end of that mission felt responsible for what had happened to her, none more so than Dylan himself. He'd been the boss, and he'd been the target. But he doubted if the facts of that night set very well on her brother's conscience either.

Still, visiting Red Dog couldn't be on too many people's list of fun things to do. The girl didn't "visit" well. She was better at just "doing," and the tougher the doing, the better she was at it.

"I didn't know you were expecting family," he said.

She gave him a clear-eyed look. "I wasn't."

Dylan held her gaze, waiting for more of an explanation. He didn't have to wait long.

"He called from the airport," she said, giving him what he wanted, which was the way things worked best. She'd learned that lesson the hard way, but she had learned it. "He came in on the red-eye from Washington and is on his way to see me."

Dylan checked his watch. It was five-thirty now; an hour ago would have been four-thirty in the morning, technically the middle of the night. Personally, he wasn't much of a family guy. All the family he had, he'd created here, at Steele Street. Even so, brothers coming to visit in the middle of the night seemed odd, even for Red Dog. Maybe the red-eye flight was all he could get.

"Is everything okay with your parents?" he asked.

"Yes, sir."

"And our other situation?"

"Copacetic."

Good. He'd called her from Tokyo two days ago with an odd rumor he'd picked up from some of his most trusted Japanese assets, and he trusted her to stay on top of it. The two of them had a meeting scheduled for later in the day to evaluate the information.

As for Honey, he knew what her problem

was, and it wasn't air. Rydell had left yesterday for a mission in Afghanistan. It was his first deployment since El Salvador, and she was nervous and wearing his clothes, trying to stay close to him with an old gray T-shirt and a pair of black running shorts, both five sizes too big. Dylan wouldn't say it didn't help, and she wasn't the first woman he'd ever seen cling to whatever was on hand, but from a guy's point of view, the outfit's only redeeming quality was the lacy black bra strap revealed by the T-shirt falling off her shoulder.

Not that he was looking. But he did remember a time, not so long ago, when there had been no women in the building. Skeeter had been the first, and the whole idea of women living at Steele Street had just snowballed since then, absolutely snowballed.

Dylan shifted his attention to his wife. She was standing with her back to the rest of them, looking out across the city to the south.

"Skeeter?" he asked.

"The Harlot is gone," she said without turning around. "Poof. Unlawfully Absent. No longer on board. AWOL."

The Harlot is gone . . . Charlotte—a slow grin eased its way across his mouth.

He'd been right.

Zachary Prade was alive and well, and three

weeks ago he'd been in Denver, standing on the tarmac in the shadows of a private jet.

Goddamn.

Prade.

Rydell had called him by another name, Alejandro Campos, a name Dylan and everyone else who had ever worked Central America knew well. Campos was connected in a hundred different directions, from governments to cartels, guerrillas to mercenaries—and one look at him had been enough for Dylan to understand why he hadn't heard from Zachary Prade since he'd bailed out of Laos eight years ago.

So he'd sent a message, going through SDF's State Department connection to try to access a deep-cover agent for the CIA. It had been a long shot, but Zachary Prade had been a long shot from the beginning—and it looked like Dylan had succeeded. His message had gotten through.

"Since when?" he asked.

"Sometime last night."

"Who was on security?"

She hesitated, and he thought he knew why.

"It's okay, Skeet." Prade knew Steele Street inside and out. She wouldn't have known he was in the building, not even while Zach was snatching Charlotte, which couldn't have been complete stealth, not with four hundred and twenty-eight cubic inches of Cobra Jet displacement under her hood.

"I never heard or saw a thing," she said, finally turning around. "No breach was noted on the security grid. I didn't even know the car was gone until about an hour ago, when I woke up thinking something was wrong and that I better go find out what in the hell it was. I never expected to be missing a car, a whole damn car." And she wasn't happy about it. He could tell by the cool, measured tone of her voice and the stance she'd taken at the edge of the Astro Turf. Forget the bustier; she was all about the combat boots this morning. "Dylan, Charlotte and Charlene are the only Shelby Mustang Cobra GT500KRs we own, and the Harlot is currently running her ass off in Albuquerque, New Mexico."

"Albuquerque?" What the hell was Prade doing in Albuquerque? And it had to be Prade. Only a chop-shop boy could have gotten past Skeeter. Prade had been one of the very best— an exemplary thief.

"Albuquerque," Skeeter confirmed. "I had a SAT tracker on her. After I realized she was gone, I booted up my system, and that girl has been running at over a hundred miles per hour since late last night, all of it heading south. I lost the signal for about half an hour, but it's back up now, and still in Albuquerque."

Albuquerque. There was something about Albuquerque, something recent.

"What's in Albuquerque?" he asked.

"Lily Robbins," Honey said.

"Robbins?" He turned back to the little blonde wearing her fiancé's clothes. She'd either get used to Rydell's job, or she'd get out. There was no in between. "The woman from El Salvador?"

The SDF report on the incident in Morazán Province had been detailed and complete, inasmuch as Rydell had been involved—and Honey was right, it had mentioned a woman named Lily Robbins, a schoolteacher from Albuquerque who had been taking a sabbatical in Central America and filming a documentary.

Yeah. That was right. She'd been making a movie about nuns, which, in terms of the current situation, meant . . . what? A schoolteacher was definitely not Prade's type, so Dylan was crossing love affair right off the top of his list, and that left business, but what possible kind of business could Prade have with a schoolteacher?

"She was visiting the orphanage where my sister works," Honey added. "St. Joseph's."

Where the CIA's pilot had died.

There were no coincidences, and it never

took more than the three letters C, I, and A in a row to set off Dylan's alarm. They'd been after his ass for years, and twice they'd almost gotten it. Skeeter was right. Something was up—and the one guy who might be able to fill in the blanks, Smith Rydell, was gone, incommunicado, out of sight, out of contact, out of the country, hell-and-gone to Afghanistan, and not just Rydell, but Creed and Travis, too, on a reconnaissance mission to set up a missile strike near the Pakistani border. The American government, of course, was not involved.

Johnny Ramos was in Iraq with his U.S. Army Ranger regiment out of Fort Benning, Georgia, on his second tour of duty. Kid was conducting a training mission at a Defense Department camp west of Steamboat Springs, and Hawkins, hell, Superman had packed up the wife and kids and hauled all their cute little butts to Disneyland.

Which left Dylan with the girls, two of whom could kick major ass, and one who . . . honestly, he wasn't sure what Honey York was good for, other than the obvious.

Not that he was too worried about getting into an ass-kicking situation. Prade could handle himself, and Albuquerque wasn't known as a hotbed of international intrigue.

It was just the CIA thing, that faint connection tying Rydell, and therefore SDF, to Albuquerque through the Morazán incident—which had been more about a downed Cessna carrying top-secret documents than the original orders for a Personal Security Detail had implied, or even hinted at—and then the Cessna had ended up belonging to the CIA instead of the State Department, which had called SDF in on the job, and then the pilot had died in a chapel where a schoolteacher from Albuquerque had been filming a documentary on nuns.

And now, after eleven long years of being someplace else, anywhere else, Prade had shown up in the middle of the night and reclaimed Charlotte for a midnight run to New Mexico.

Screw it.

"Do you still have your SAT connection up and running?" he asked Skeeter. Prade could fill in the blanks, if he was so inclined, and Dylan understood that he might not be. The chop-shop years were far behind them, and Zach's loyalties would have changed. He'd be a "Company" man. Dylan not only understood that, he respected it.

But he also understood Prade, and he was making the call.

"Yes."

"What else besides a tracker did you put in the Shelby?" He knew Skeeter, too, and it would have been something. An exquisitely cherry GT500KR or not, one lone tracking device did not create a home base communication link in her book. She would have bolted something else onto the car, or built something into it. She liked to know where people were, her people, who were everybody who belonged to 738 Steele Street, and by whatever means necessary, be they devious, convoluted, or out-and-out just grabbing onto them, by God, she kept in touch. She was actually pretty damn pushy, and pretty damn nosy that way. He knew for a fact that she'd broken into every deep-sixed confidential file in SDF's database, including all the juvenile records.

It wouldn't matter to her that she'd never actually met Prade. She'd know him inside and out, up until he'd disappeared off the map, and she'd think of him as one of Steele Street's, and she definitely knew his ride, so, yeah, she would have tagged Charlotte the same way she'd tagged Charlene, Jeanette, and Roxanne, and Nadine, and Angelina, and Mercy, and Corinna, and Coralie, everyone except Trina. She'd never tagged Dylan's 1965 AC Cobra 289. Even in the rare iron realm of Steele Street, Trina was untouchable, more than a car.

"A Bazo VJX-UZ468 700 series PC," she said.

Okay. That sounded great, a Bazo VJ whatza widget, whatever the hell that was.

"With always-on high-speed Internet and full PDA capabilities, including cellular communications."

And she'd gotten all that in the Shelby? Without leaving a trace? It was her trademark, not leaving a trace. Her first electronic installations in a few of the cars had been pretty crude, but she'd refined her techniques over the last few years and prided herself on leaving the dashboards and consoles absolutely pristine, without a mark or a telltale sign of her work anywhere.

"You got all that in the Shelby?"

"I stuffed it in the tape deck slot, just below the radio. Mustangs had an eight-track option that year, and the Bazo fit it like a dream."

Excellent. He'd known from the get-go that he'd married a certifiable geekazoid nerd. Between her and Kid and a stringer they kept on contract, Cherie Hacker, there didn't seem to be anything that needed doing that couldn't get done—the cost be damned.

"Is this the rig everybody has in their cars now?" He was almost afraid to ask.

The look she gave him said it all, but she

went ahead and gave him the answer he'd hoped he wouldn't hear.

"I'm a techie. Updating SDF's electronics is my job," she said, her hands going to her hips, "and I stay busy, especially since you hardly *ever* let me do anything else. Don't think I haven't noticed."

He'd hoped she hadn't noticed. He thought he'd been very clever, very subtle with the job rotations.

"I haven't been out of Denver in over six months," she added, and it was definitely a complaint.

Tough. He was going for twelve.

"And during these last six months I have replaced all the original laptops I bolted into the cars with brand-new Bazo VJX-UZ468 700 series PCs, for the low, low cost of only seven thousand, two hundred and forty-eight dollars each, including custom fabrication and installation of every unit."

A not-so-small price to pay to keep her close to home.

"We do work on a budget," he reminded her.

"You work on a budget," she said. "I work on computers and cars."

They were having a fight.

How unusual, he thought, and how annoying.

They'd been getting along great until she'd gotten out of bed.

"And nobody does it better," he said. "Thank you." He wasn't a complete idiot. "So you can raise Charlotte whenever you want?"

"Almost."

"Almost?" What was with the "almost"?

"Cherie and I have been working on a small glitch on this end. It's strictly a transmitting situation in our system. All the Bazo PCs in the cars are transmitting just fine."

He was glad to hear it, but his plan was to contact Prade, not to wait until hell froze over and Prade decided to contact them.

"Get Cherie on the horn and get her over here. I want Charlotte's Bazo transmitting and receiving within the hour."

He didn't give her a lot of orders, but that had definitely been one, and she was shaking her head at him.

"What?" If she didn't like something, he'd rather find it out sooner than later.

"I've got a stolen car and an unknown perpetrator who was in my building last night, and I am not at all inclined to let this carjacking jerk know Charlotte is loaded. I say we track him down and apprehend his butt."

Well, when she put it like that, his plan

sucked. But she didn't quite have all the facts; and he was pretty sure he did.

"I think the carjacking jerk is Zachary Prade, and the connection is Albuquerque, Lily Robbins, and whatever went on in El Salvador."

She shook her head again, not so subtly telling him his plan still sucked. "There wasn't anything about Zachary Prade in Rydell's report on the mission in Morazán."

"No, but I got a look at Alejandro Campos when he dropped Rydell and the women at DIA, and . . ." His voice trailed off. He dragged his hand back through his hair. *Geezus*.

"And?" she prompted.

Lifting his gaze to the southern end of the city, he let out a short laugh. It was a fairly amazing turn of events, no matter how he looked at it.

"I think Zach has been in El Salvador for the last eight years," he said, "working deep cover for the CIA. I sent a letter down through State to Langley, to see if I could get a bite, and suddenly Charlotte goes missing to Albuquerque."

"What exactly are you saying, Dylan?"

"What I'm saying, sweetheart, is that I think Alejandro Campos is Zach, the last lost chop-shop boy."

CHAPTER SIX

Saturday, 5:30 A.M.—Albuquerque, New Mexico

Parked two blocks east of Somerset at the intersection of Pike Street and Lawrence Avenue, in front of John and Shirley Brock's house, Lily came up with a great idea—honking the horn. That way, John and Shirley could come running out to save her . . . and see her half naked and handcuffed just before they got blown up.

Crap. She slammed her hands down on the steering wheel.

Even in her neighborhood, there were probably only a handful of people who would think twice about detonating a small block of C4 to stop some idiot from blowing their horn at five o'clock in the morning. She could guarantee Alejandro Campos wasn't one of them. The minute she pressed the Shelby's horn, he'd know it was her, and that would be it, the last it, ever.

Dammit.

She was shaking just a little, even in the warmth of the car. She probably needed a drink. Something stiff. Something on the rocks, like whiskey, or a straight shot, or two—and a shirt would be nice, maybe some pants, shoes, a handcuff key.

She'd seen *The Dukes of Hazzard,* and she knew a bootlegger's turn when she was in the middle of one, but she'd never been in the middle of one before, and her head was still spinning. One hundred and eighty degrees of lightning-fast turn with her stomach already in knots and the sheer mind-frying panic of the last five minutes had frayed her nerves to a razor's edge, and she was afraid she was going to come undone.

Right here.

Right now.

Handcuffed to a steering wheel in a sports bra and her jammie panties.

She tried to steady her breathing, tried to stay calm, but the facts of the situation were too horribly grim. She could see the blinking light of the cell-phone bomb in the backseat, every small green flash reflecting in the windshield, one right after another, like a countdown.

She could be blown up any second, and the fact was nearly incomprehensible—like having Alejandro Campos drag her out of her bathroom in a hail of bullets.

Oh, God.

A very unsteady breath left her on a long, shuddering sigh.

He'd saved her in El Salvador. She would never forget it, but she wasn't going to forget what he was, either—a drug lord, the dregs of the earth, the kind of man who handcuffed women to cars and profited from other people's misery. And if people weren't miserable enough, he lured them into it, for money, so he could live in his highland villa, surrounded by servants and—*oh, geez*, she'd killed the man with the ponytail.

She tightened her grip on the steering wheel to keep her hands from shaking, to keep her whole body from shaking. She'd killed him. She knew it beyond a doubt. She knew exactly where her shot had gone—center chest. The man's face had been missing in the next split second, and that must have been Campos's shot, but she'd fired first, and the guy with the ponytail was dead.

And in her house.

There had been blood everywhere.

Another shuddering breath left her.

Blink . . . blink . . . blink—the green light flashed over and over, pushing her closer and closer to the brink of . . . of she didn't know what, but it wasn't going to be pretty.

And then things got worse.

Parked on Pike Street, she saw the Aston Martin go screaming past her down Lawrence Avenue, doing about a hundred miles an hour, and then she heard sirens, police sirens, but they weren't chasing the silver sports car.

Cold dread washed down her spine. Where was Alejandro Campos? Had he been captured at her house? Killed? And what were the odds, really, of some cop picking up Campos's damn cell phone and accidentally hitting the button that blew her to smithereens?

She was going to be sick.

As best as she could manage, she hung her head out the window and coughed, but nothing came up.

Fuck. She all but collapsed in the seat, her cheek resting on the door frame. Someone would find her. Everyone would notice the car. As soon as people got their butts out of bed and started seizing the day, they would notice the

Candy-apple Red Shelby Cobra and the not-quite-dressed woman handcuffed inside.

Oh, God. Oh, God. She brought her free hand up and covered her face. *Oh, G—*

"Move over, babe." The order was growled at her, and the door came open.

She would have fallen out, except for Campos's taking hold of her.

"Come on, hurry it up. Hustle. Hustle." He kept pushing her back toward the passenger seat, and being none too gentle about it.

And he'd taken her gun.

She hadn't forgotten.

She'd sat there like an idiot and let him take her gun. No matter what she finally ended up confessing to her dad, she was *not* confessing that part.

The handcuff slid around the top of the steering wheel, and her suitcase was shoved in over the top of the driver's seat, and her butt was in the air, and he'd taken her gun.

Goddammit.

By the time she got in her seat, she was strung from one side of the damn car to the other, and they were moving, which all but demanded that one of them pay attention. She'd kept the Shelby rumbling and rocking in neutral with her foot on the brake, but it was rolling now, rolling and picking up speed with the two of them playing Twister in the front seat.

"Step on the brake," she said, swiping her hand across her cheek, wiping away the only tear that had gotten away from her. "Or find a goddamn gear." *You . . . you bastard. You mealy-mouthed, drug-running sonuva—*

He glanced at her, and her silent tirade screeched to a stop, derailed by a wave of mortification.

She was *so* in her underwear.

"I—I want my clothes." All of them, every stitch in her suitcase.

He shifted into first, and his gaze came back to her, sliding down her body in one long sweep, before coming up and meeting her eyes.

"Good idea," he said. "As soon as I go through your suitcase, you can have all the clothes you want."

The bastard, the mealy-mouthed, drug-running sonuva—

"Oh, my god," she said, her gaze falling on his shoulder. "You've been shot."

Of course he'd been shot. He was always getting shot. This was the second goddamn time this month.

"Skinned," he said. "Just caught me across

the top." But it hurt like hell. Blood had soaked through his T-shirt and was seeping through and staining his favorite, ruined Hugo Boss suit jacket, the charcoal gray one with the shredded, ragged-ass tear across the shoulder. *Christ*. He probably needed stitches. He was always needing stitches.

On the upside, that's all he ever needed, a few stitches. No matter how knocked around he got, or how many damn times he'd been shot, a couple of stitches here and there had taken care of the problem. The worst thing that had ever gotten ahold of him had been dengue fever.

"If you unhandcuff me, I-I could put pressure on the wound."

How sweet.

"Nice try." He had enough experience to know he wasn't going to bleed out from getting nicked across the top of his shoulder, and truthfully, he wasn't absolutely sure it was a bullet that had gotten him. It could have been any one of a hundred pieces of crap that had been flying through the air as he and Lily Robbins had dodged bullets and death trying to get out of her house. No shots had been fired during his last sortie onto Somerset. However he'd been skinned, he'd been skinned during the first fiasco.

But he'd gotten the suitcase.

Which didn't really mean he had the bracelet. Not yet. Not according to Rule Number One.

Crossing Lawrence at just under light speed, he slid Charlotte up into fourth. There was no traffic at five-thirty in the morning, but the sun had finally edged up over the horizon into BMNT, Beginning of Morning Nautical Twilight, a clearly defining moment for the barbarians of the world. BMNT was their hurrah.

Spilled coffee was his. There was no way to hit fifty miles per hour in under five seconds and have a cup of coffee stay put on the console. It was back there somewhere, in the backseat, probably in his gun bag, running out of the cup and sloshing through his ammo and spare magazines.

Dammit.

The blocks whizzed by under Charlotte's wheels, one after the other, taking them west through the neighborhoods and past half a dozen strip shopping malls. At five miles out, he felt they had enough distance from her house to make a stop. He either had the bracelet secured, or he didn't, and if he didn't, he was going to have to go back, cops or no cops.

Yeah, he was one of the good guys, too, but chances were, he wouldn't show up as a good guy in any database used by the law enforcement community of New Mexico.

Actually, there was no chance in that equation. His prints would have the Albuquerque chief of police doing a happy dance in the streets. Apprehending a notorious Central American drug dealer would just about make the guy's whole year, maybe even his whole career. Not that the good chief would get a conviction, but it was best to avoid the whole mess to begin with by not getting arrested—also known as Rule Number Three.

Yeah, he lived by that one hard.

Pulling over, he parked the Shelby on a tree-lined avenue. It might be a nice gesture on his part to take the cuffs off Lily Robbins, and he would, as soon as he had what he'd come for—Mark Devlin's macramé bracelet.

Stretching back between the front bucket seats, he popped the catch on her suitcase. It was quickly growing light enough to see, and what he saw did not make him happy.

"Do you always pack in a wind tunnel?"

"Wh-what do you mean?" She twisted around as best she could, which wasn't very much.

This wasn't right, he thought, staring at the contents of her suitcase. Her clothes were a mess, jumbled up, some of them folded, but most of them not. They looked pushed around . . .

like somebody had pushed them around. Like maybe somebody who was looking for something.

He lifted a white blouse up—and swore under his breath.

"What?" she asked, trying to see over the seat.

Blood, fresh, a long smear of it, stained the blouse's sleeve. Buzz-cut Boy must have gotten hit by something, too. Zach hoped it had been one of his .45 caliber, 230-grain, full-metal-jacket, flat-point tactical handloads clocking in at nine hundred feet per second.

That would have hurt.

And it would have definitely slowed the guy down, which was exactly what Zach needed, because he had a sneaking suspicion he was going to have to go find Buzz-cut Boy real damn quick if he wanted that bracelet.

Dammit. He started going through her clothes, piece by piece, carefully checking each item, shaking it out, taking his time in order not to make any mistakes, and hoping to hell Buzz Boy had made a mistake, rushed through the job, and left empty-handed. He hoped the bracelet would fall out of something, like her underwear. She had a lot of it, a lot of colors, a lot of styles, and she obviously liked lace.

He did, too—black, red, white, purple. Her

suitcase definitely had its share of lace underwear. He picked up a demicut lace underwire bra, lime green with hot pink ribbons slinking across the tops of the cups.

Very nice, he thought, setting it aside and moving on to the next piece of clothing—the matching lime green panties with a hot pink ribbon slinking around the waistband.

Very nice.

She had jeans, and yoked shirts with pearly snaps, a tooled leather belt with a silver buckle, and an honest-to-God pair of chaps, brand-new, cream-colored with buff inserts.

Well, that had been a while, since he'd had the sex-with-a-cowgirl fantasy. He'd never actually had sex with a real cowgirl, but he had a feeling he had a real one handcuffed to his steering wheel. It was enough to make a guy think—make a guy think he better keep his mind on his business.

A pair of boots came next, slant-heeled, suede, and looking like they'd seen better days. She'd packed them inside a plastic bag, and after shaking them out—and getting nothing—he checked the bag.

And got nothing.

Then things got interesting—too interesting.

Beneath the bag with the cowboy boots was a taped stack of fifty-dollar bills. He moved a tie-dyed aquamarine tank top and found another taped stack of bills. A little more careful moving of clothes, including a yellow-flowered shirt stained with blood, revealed a FedEx envelope with another taped stack of bills poking out of it. There were two more stacks inside. He didn't need to count the bills, or even run his thumb over one of the stacks. He dealt in cash, and he was looking at five short bricks of two thousand dollars each.

Ten thousand dollars in a FedEx envelope packed inside the suitcase of a woman in possession of an internationally volatile encryption code only said one thing to him: trouble. If anyone was going to get arrested in Albuquerque this morning, it might well be Lily Robbins, and it just might be him doing it.

He belled open the envelope, looked over the airline ticket, skimmed a very short letter written on expensive paper, and dropped it all back inside the suitcase.

"Wh-what are you doing?" she asked.

Wondering who in the hell you really are, he thought. *And wondering who in the hell made you that offer.* There'd been no signature on the letter, and the return address on the mailing label was a Ship and Go Store in New York City.

The cash was preliminary at best, nothing

more than traveling expenses. The bracelet was worth millions on the open market.

"I need the macramé bracelet you were wearing at my villa the night of the rainstorm," he said. Ten thousand dollars in cash, and Buzz-cut Boy had left it untouched in the suitcase. Considering what the real prize was this morning, Zach would have done the same thing. "That's the one you still have, correct? That's the one you put in your suitcase? The pilot's bracelet?"

"Yes. But . . ." She was straining to see into the backseat, but with the lid up on the suitcase, he doubted if she could see much.

Tahiti?

And ten thousand dollars in cash?

Who in the hell made that kind of deal? And what was going to be that guy's next move?

He had a feeling those were questions with answers he wasn't going to like. He and Alex had gone over Lily Robbins's dossier before he'd ever left Langley, and even to the world-class analysts at the CIA, she'd looked to be precisely what she presented herself as—a schoolteacher in Albuquerque, born and raised in Montana on a ranch called the Cross Double R that had been in the Robbins family for nearly a hundred years, some of them damn lean, including most of the years since she'd been born. High-country, hardscrabble ranching was not for the faint of heart or will.

He figured that's where she got her grit—and she did have grit, and impeccable aim under pressure, two things he tended to like in a woman. Considering how many people were already on to her, it couldn't hurt for her to have plenty of both, even with him on her side.

And he was on her side. For now.

"Once I've secured the bracelet, I'll take you someplace where you'll be safe." All he had to do was figure out exactly where that might be. He had one idea, and it wasn't in Albuquerque.

"H-how did you know about the pilot's bracelet?" she asked. "That he gave it to me?"

Gave? He stopped with his hand around a charcoal gray T-shirt and looked up from the suitcase.

That was his first mistake. He should have kept his attention on her clothes, not let it stray all over the place and get caught in her cleavage. Big mistake.

Mistake number two was not catching himself in time to keep from glancing up into her eyes.

He knew blue, but he'd never seen anything as blue as her eyes, crystalline sapphire blue, with dark rims and light shot through the middle—and with him stretched back between the front seats, and her leaning over the passenger seat, trying to see in the back, they were quite close to each other. Quite. Much closer than he'd actually realized.

He cleared his throat and went back to sorting through her clothes. Mark Devlin had never given a woman anything except grief and more inches than Zach personally believed—but the rumors were rampant.

"Why don't you tell me why he gave the bracelet to you. Did you know him, at all, even just casually?" That was what he needed to know, not "How did your eyes get so mother-loving blue?"

"No."

"He hadn't stopped at St. Joseph's while you were there? Maybe you spoke in passing?"

"No. I never saw him until the soldiers dragged him into the chapel."

"Then why did he give you the bracelet?"

"I—I don't know. I think he knew he was dying. Sister Theresa and I ran over to help him, and when I knelt down next to him, he grabbed hold of my hand. He . . . he held it so tight. I was surprised at how tightly he held me. He was . . . he was . . . so . . ." Her voice gave up, and she slid back into her seat, facing forward, her free hand coming up to cover her face.

Broken up. That's what Devlin had been—so

broken up. After seeing the body, Zach's respect
for the guy, which had already been high, had
skyrocketed. That Devlin had lasted as long as
he had was a testament to how tough he'd
been—tough enough to do the job for a dozen
years, and tough enough to die for it.

Dei gratia. He crossed himself, the action
nearly unconscious—nearly. He knew the risks
of what he did. He knew how easily and how
quickly he could end up just like Devlin. *By the
grace of God.*

"Did he say anything to you? Anything at all?"
He'd asked her that question before, the night
at his villa, and she'd said no.

By the slow shake of her head in the front
seat, he guessed she was saying it again. For her
sake, he hoped she was telling the truth. Even a
New Mexico schoolteacher would be tempted
by the kind of money in her suitcase, let alone
by the fortune promised by the bracelet. If
Devlin had told her what he was giving her, he
figured Lily Robbins was smart enough to figure out what to do with it.

Which made him wonder again about what
in the hell was up with the FedEx envelope. If
she'd worked fast, and if she'd been connected,
she'd had three weeks to put wheels in motion
and get her name and product out into the marketplace. Plenty of time for an interested buyer

to make an offer, and if the deal was to be final-
ized in Tahiti, well, then he had a believable
scenario that put her at the top of the U.S. government's Most Wanted List.

But nothing in her file had pointed to the
kind of person who had the kind of connections
necessary to put together a piece of high-order
espionage in under a month. Hell, it would
have taken *him* three weeks, at least, and he
was connected from Manila to Mazatlán to
Mozambique.

He went back to the suitcase. Closer to the
bottom, things started looking more promising—
and less promising. Her jewelry and whatnot
and makeup bags had been dumped, and lots of
small stuff had settled in the bottom. He'd
found the mother lode, but he was afraid the
true treasure had been lost.

"Did you put the bracelet in one of your jewelry bags?"

"Yes." The word was spoken quietly, but
firmly.

He liked that in a woman, too, being on the
verge of tears, and still being able to pull it together.

He sifted through everything—every earring,
every eye shadow box, every necklace, every
teeny brush and doodad—and got nothing.

There was no macramé bracelet.

Fuck. Buzz Boy and the Aston Martin had just locked in the top spot on Charlotte's chase it, shake it, and eat it for lunch list—and there was only one way for her to do it.

Sliding back into the front seat, he pulled his phone out of his pocket and started to dial. The audible intake of Lily Robbins's breath stopped him in mid-number.

He looked up, and immediately felt like the bastard she'd accused him of being.

"Th-the, the...the—" She was stuttering, and her face had gone deathly pale. Rightly so. And truly, he was a bastard.

"There's no bomb," he said, the look of terror in her eyes more than enough clue to remind him of his threat. He went back to dialing his number. "I lied about the cell phone."

"Y-you . . ."—she took a breath—"you *lied*?"

He nodded. Yep, he sure had, and considering how effective that little bit of subterfuge had been, he'd do it again in a heartbeat.

He finished up with the sequence of numbers guaranteed to get him what he needed. Alex was his best bet for a quick communications patch anywhere in the world. This morning, he only needed to go about three hundred miles due north.

"Lied?" she repeated. "There was no bomb?"

"No." He brought the phone to his ear and

waited for his coded entry to route through to Langley. When Alex answered, he got straight to the point.

"I need a secure line to SDF, Steele Street in Denver. Can you put me through . . . Albuquerque . . . yes, sir . . . no . . . I've got a tracker that belongs to SDF on a car I need to find, an Aston Martin, silver, Nevada plates, 01B-4381. One of the guys from the car is now dead in Robbins's house . . . yes, sir. I've got her . . . Yes, sir. Scorpion Fire. I'll wait for your call. Thank you."

He pressed the "end call" button on his phone and checked his watch.

"And I fell for it?" she asked.

He slid her a glance. He was pretty sure the question was rhetorical, especially since the answer was obvious. So he didn't say anything.

But she did, muttering something under her breath over on her side of the car.

He didn't quite hear the words, but it had definitely sounded derogatory, and might have had something to do with his lineage or the lack thereof. He wasn't offended. He was impressed. She had a real theme going with the bastard business, and in less than fifteen or so minutes of hanging out together this morning, she'd nailed his lineage dead-on.

CHAPTER SEVEN

Saturday, 6:00 A.M.—Denver, Colorado

Six oh freaking clock in the morning. Cherie Hacker flicked her smoked cigarette into the alley ahead of her and mashed it into the pavement with her next step. Her boots were speed-lace, lug-soled, desert tan, and tactical with sidewall traction. In her hand, she carried a pair of spike-heeled sling-backs in gold leather with gossamer chiffon bows. Dior had made her cocktail dress—white silk, ruched, and strapless. The backpack slung over her shoulder was desert camo, expensive, and complicated, holding everything from her powder brush to her canned air and screwdrivers.

Her jacket was black leather.

With zippers.

Dylan Hart owed her for this.

Behind her, she heard the limo pulling away from the curb, and her dream of waking up on the warm sands of Cabo San Lucas pulled away with it.

Hart *really* owed her for this.

She was *supposedly* on vacation this week, waiting for the final phase of construction to finish on Hacker International's new luxury offices, and she'd almost—*almost*—made it out of town.

Yawning, she adjusted her grip on her small piece of carry-on luggage and kept walking.

The opening she'd attended at the Toussi Gallery last night had spilled over until morning, with a group of die-hard Rocky Solano fans deciding to move the party south to Cabo for the weekend. The plan was going forward, with the limo heading to the airport, but she wasn't heading anywhere except the seventh floor of 738 Steele Street and a late-breaking disaster of untold proportions, which Skeeter had not exactly explained in those terms, but why in the hell else would everyone be up at six oh freaking clock in the morning, calling her?

Cherie stopped in the alley, set down her carry-on bag, and rustled through one of the smaller pockets on her pack, looking for another cigarette. When she found one, she flipped her windproof lighter and bent her head over the flame. She inhaled, got the darn thing going, and snapped the lighter shut.

The sun was barely up.

At one end of the alley known as Steele Street, dawn was lighting the sky and bringing on the day. At the other, night still ruled the streets.

Hefting her bag, she blew out a long stream of smoke and continued walking.

She passed the ironclad door next to the "WEATHERPROOF" sign and kept walking. Steele Street had a main entrance set back into the corner of the building and a rather elegant lobby, but she was the only one who used it. Everyone else came and went through the garages.

Well, hell. She wasn't going through the garage in Dior, and she wasn't slopping through the alley in her gossamer-bowed Blahniks to get to 738's front door. Age-darkened brick, with a huge, mechanical, neo-Victorian freight elevator crawling up its outside wall and looming over the narrow stretch of pavement that was its namesake, the thirteen floors of SDF's home base were—

Wondrous.

Steel-reinforced.

Hardwired and softwared to within an inch of their lives.

The building hummed for her. It breathed with information, digibytes, code, encryption sequences, and a million interlocking highways into cyberspace. She, and Kid, and Skeeter had made it so—but it was mostly hers. She was its creator. She'd had the vision of what it could be, and she'd made it hers. The once-infamous chop shop, home of a wily crew of teenage car thieves, had been transformed into a world-class computer-geek playground, with a BCH-designed state-of-the-art firing range. BCH, an acronym affectionately referred to as "Bitch," stood for Bang, Chaos, and Hacker. There were a lot of Bitches in the building, and more security goodies than Fort Knox.

At the front entry, she keyed a ten-digit personal identification number into the lock, and a massive set of mahogany doors opened in near silence. As she passed through to the marble-tiled foyer, she noted the extravagant bouquet of fresh flowers on a delicately proportioned console set against the wall.

The flowers were always fresh. If they weren't, she was supposed to step back outside, key a lockdown code into the door, and disappear off the street. Those orders were straight from Dylan, the big boss. In the eight years that she'd been doing contract work for him, the flowers had always been fresh.

The elevator on the ground floor only went to the offices on the seventh floor, and she rode up with the familiar winding clacks and clangs, trying not to think about Cabo. She was due a little downtime, a little fun, instead of facing Saturday night alone.

Again. Hell. She let out a sigh and then took another long drag off her cigarette.

She needed a new habit.

Sex would be nice.

She leaned back against the elevator and thought that idea over a bit—then wished she hadn't.

Damn. Cabo had looked promising. She'd been getting along pretty well with this guy from one of the big law firms up on Seventeeth, a guy named Henry Stiner. He'd been cute and blond, a little pudgy, but with that whole surfer-boy thing working for him, except surfer boy in a Burberry suit. He was also on his way to Cabo San Lucas for the weekend with everybody else from Toussi's, including Suzi Toussi's new gallery girl, Wanda.

Cherie swore under her breath, watching the floor numbers light up, one after another. Wanda and Henry—oh, yeah, she could see where that was all going to end up.

She swore again, and sucked another long drag off her cigarette.

Dylan owed her.

The elevator came to a grinding stop on the seventh floor, and the doors opened to a familiar scene: Red Dog prowling, pacing a stretch of turf in front of a bank of television screens, each turned to a different news channel, half of them foreign.

The auburn-haired woman gave her a laser-sharp glance when the elevator opened, a look capable of unnerving even the hardened guys who worked with her.

Cherie wasn't fazed.

She exhaled and entered the office in a cloud of smoke. To her credit, it did cross her mind to spend a little more time at the gym.

Yeah, like that was going to happen. One totally ripped redhead in the office was probably enough.

"Hey, babe," she said, heading for a desk she'd long claimed as her own. It was off in a corner, all by itself, and had a fabulous view of the mountains through one of the floor-to-ceiling double-hung windows lining the north wall. It was also the only place in the office where a girl had a chance of sneaking a smoke.

"Hey, Hacker." Red Dog's amber-eyed gaze softened for a moment, and a brief smile curved her mouth, before she went back to monitoring the news.

A smile, Cherie thought. *Good.* Red Dog didn't always smile, but she was damn good at saving people's asses, not that Cherie ever ended up in those my-ass-needs-saving situations. She was definitely of the office-support-staff, part-time-contract-employee variety, not the save-the-world-or-die-trying operator-type employee.

"Hack, over here," a tall blonde working on a keyboard said.

"Hey, Baby Bang."

Anything could be up when Skeeter was working a keyboard. The girl could jack a hard drive's innermost secrets almost as quickly as Cherie could herself.

"Come check the download off that Bazo number eight, the one we've been having trouble with. We need to get it up and running ASAP."

The Bazo? Cherie lifted her eyebrows. She'd been called in at six A.M. for the number eight Bazo? She and Skeeter had been working on the compact PCs for the last couple of months, and the number eight had been giving them fits. She'd figured it out, though, last night between the champagne and the canapés.

But still, *geez,* the number eight Bazo was in a car nobody even drove—and Henry Stiner was on his way to Cabo San Lucas with Wanda the gallery girl.

There was no justice.

She dropped her carry-on next to her chair and set her backpack on top of the desk. *Crap.* No justice, and technically, no smoking in the office, so she inhaled a last drag and looked for the damn soda can she kept for these occasions. When she didn't see it anywhere, she knelt down to sort through the papers in her trash, thinking she might have accidentally thrown the empty can away.

"Hi, Cherie," the not-so-tall blonde on the couch behind her said. "Love the Dior."

Cherie had noticed Rydell's fiancée when she'd gotten off the elevator, and the cute thing was half buried in newspapers spread out around her on the couch and lying on the table in front of her—*The New York Times, The Washington Post,* and *The Christian Science Monitor.*

"Thank you, Honey. Nice, uh, gym shorts." Honoria York was from back East, very smart, very connected, and obviously getting off to a rough start today. A baggy old gray T-shirt and University of Wyoming basketball shorts? Those had to be Rydell's from way back.

Spying the soda can, she reached a little farther under her desk, wondering how it had gotten so far away, and then, once she was under there, decided to take an extra drag off the cigarette, before she ground it out in the can.

God, it was six o'clock in the morning after an all-nighter. She should be going to bed with somebody, not going to work. This was painful. Getting on a plane to Cabo and sleeping her way through the flight had been her plan for the morning.

Black combat boots and a pair of long legs laminated in black-and-white-striped leggings came into her line of vision, and the next thing she saw was Skeeter's face, peeking under the desk. A long fall of platinum blond ponytail fell over the girl's shoulder and pooled on the floor.

"Dior? At six A.M.?" Skeeter said. "Did you forget to go to bed last night?"

Cherie shook her head. "It was a conscious decision."

"Do you need—"

"Hacker!" a male voice called her name out, and Cherie groaned.

"Coffee?" Skeeter finished, her sweet face like a ray of sunshine breaking through the black cloud Cherie felt heading her way, a black cloud named Dylan Hart. The man was ruthless—thank God. The cold calculation of Dylan's mind was the reason Steele Street existed, and the reason she'd come back after getting Hacker International up and running. She trusted him implicitly, respected him the same.

Dropping her cigarette into the soda can, she stifled a yawn and nodded her head.

"Double-shot latte?" Skeeter asked.

"Triple." She backed out from under the desk and rose to her full five feet eight inches in height. She was going to need all of it, plus the stilettos, if she was going to face Dylan Hart eye to eye—which was the only way she ever did it.

Using the desk for support, she toed out of her tactical boots and eased into her Blahniks, making sure the bows didn't get stuck beneath the vamps.

Dylan was still in his private office. She could see him standing next to his desk and checking something on his computer. He was hard and lean, with dark hair, choirboy looks, and a street-toughened edge—an impeccably dressed enigma in gray slacks and a black polo shirt. With Dylan, it was all in the eyes, and his were pure arctic gray ice.

"Don't worry about that problem with the Bazo, Dylan," she said, leaning to one side and running her finger around the back of her foot, slipping the back strap up onto her heel. "I've got it covered."

"Covered or fixed?" he asked without looking up. "I need it fixed."

Okay, boss-man.

"Gillian," Skeeter said. "I think your brother's taxi just pulled up in the alley, if you want to go downstairs and do the security check."

Cherie watched Red Dog nod and head toward the door into the stairwell.

Back at the communication console, Skeeter keyed a code into the computer she was working on while simultaneously reaching for the landline phone. It rang just as her fingers touched the handset.

"Uptown Autos. We only sell the best," she said into the phone, then looked up at Dylan and nodded.

"After Gillian IDs him, she can take him up and show him the firing range," Dylan said. Everyone wanted to see the firing range. Cherie was particularly proud of it herself. "She's free to visit, until I need her. But she needs to stay here. No going back to the garage in Commerce City until after our scheduled contact with the team in three hours."

Skeeter nodded and turned back to the phone. "Yes, sir, Mr. Shore. Gillian is on her way down."

Red Dog's brother—Cherie's interest was definitely piqued. She wondered which one, the

Army Ranger or the brilliant geekazoid from the Marsh Annex? She'd love to meet the geek. *Really* love it. Good Lord, a guy from the Marsh Annex. She'd been there a few months ago at General Grant's request, but other than her meeting with the top brass, she'd only been introduced to a girl named Rhonda, who had shown her around. All the actual tech boys had been behind closed doors.

Perhaps the morning would shape up to be far more interesting than Cabo San Lucas.

"And you," Dylan said, and somehow Cherie knew he meant her. She shifted her attention back to his office door. "How long to get the Harlot's onboard PC up and running to receive?"

"Half an hour," she said. "I think we've still got a dedicated pair of SJV80s. I'll switch them out of the computer in the car and here in the office, and—"

He was shaking his head.

"No?"

"No," he said. "Switching parts out of Charlotte is no good."

Yes, it was.

She opened her mouth to explain in layman's terms how it would work, something she did an awful lot of, but he beat her to the punch.

"Somebody broke into Steele Street last night

about ten o'clock and stole the Shelby. Skeeter tracked her down in Albuquerque this morning."

Broken into? Her building? Not very bloody damn likely. She and Kid had done a security review just last week, and they hadn't missed a brick.

But Dylan was staring straight at her, and he'd said "broken into," which meant she needed to think—fast.

All right, sure, the building had been breached once, two and a half years ago. An Indonesian warlord, Hamzah Negara, had sent a bunch of his goons to bust into Steele Street and kill all its occupants. Not a good idea.

They'd gotten in using a code they'd tortured out of Dylan, but Denver had been the last place the Indonesians had ever used their frequent flyer miles, with three of the assassins hunted down in the building and killed by Creed and Hawkins. The fourth had been kept alive for interrogation.

Cherie had not asked for the details of that particular encounter. But she wanted all the damn details of this incident.

"Charlotte is in Albuquerque?" she said, starting with one of the worst details. One of Steele Street's rarest pieces of iron had been stolen, and that black mark was all hers.

"Running hard, and I want to know why."

She thought that over for a full second and a half. "And you want me to get you set up with the Bazo PC so you can call the thief and ask him what the hell he's doing in Albuquerque?"

"Exactly."

She gave that another half a second of deep contemplation.

"You got it. Give me thirty minutes and I'll hook you up." The rest of the damn details, finding and fixing the security breach, were going to take longer. Because frankly, she didn't have a clue how in the hell someone had gotten into her building and stolen a damn car without everyone from here to Timbuktu knowing it.

"Make it fifteen," he said.

She slanted him a skeptical look across the main office, but he just held her gaze, cool and steady.

He wasn't kidding.

Of course he wasn't. She knew a gauntlet when one was thrown down, and the only acceptable response was "Yes, sir."

He wanted fifteen? He was going to get fifteen.

She turned to unzip her backpack, her mind still working over the disturbing fact of a security breach—when all of a sudden, it hit her.

Her hand stilled on the pack, and her gaze shot back to Dylan.

"It was an inside job," she said; she knew it down to her pink-pearl-polished toes. "And you know who did it."

His only answer was an indecipherable glance in her direction.

Somewhere in the office, a phone rang, and she heard Skeeter answer it.

"Do you know *how* they did it?" she asked Dylan.

Again, she got nothing but the look, which didn't deter her for a minute.

"Are you going to tell me?"

At that, he shook his head, and she pursed her lips, looking at him hard, thinking, and trying to read his mind.

He arched an eyebrow in her direction, and the little moue she'd made of her mouth slid into a true grin.

"No, you won't," he said, reading her mind like an open book, which was way farther than she'd gotten with him. "You won't find this breach, Cherie."

The hell she wouldn't.

"That's an order, Hacker."

Her eyebrows rose at that. What the hell? Finding security breaches was her job.

"Dylan," Skeeter interrupted. "A Mr. Alex

Maier is on the line, asking for you, and I am definitely showing CIA encryption on the call and a point of origin in Langley, Virginia."

Dylan didn't miss a beat. "Record and trace," he said through his open doorway, reaching for a pad and pen. "And put it through to my office."

He moved around the corner of his desk to his chair. The "incoming" light on his console came on almost immediately, and he picked up the phone.

"Hart," he said.

After a minute of listening, a look of satisfaction crossed his face, and he started writing.

"Skeeter," he said, still making notes. "I need you to make a call. This name, this number." He tore a page off the pad and handed it over his desk.

Baby Bang crossed into his office, took the paper, and headed back toward her communications console.

"Yes. We can patch you through and keep the line open for as long as you need," he said into the phone. "And I can guarantee the signal on the tracker will hold."

When the conversation ended, he hung up, and his gaze went straight to Skeeter. "Get Charlotte's tracker up on a screen. I want to be able to transmit that location back to the Harlot in a matter of minutes, not hours."

Skeeter gave him a nonplussed look. "So the guy who stole Charlotte, the one still running her tires off in Albuquerque, doesn't know where he is?" She paused for a second. "He's in Albuquerque, Dylan, running Charlotte's tires off. How can he not know that . . . unless he—"

"Found your tracker and put it on something else. Something he needs to catch," Dylan said.

Skeeter grinned. "Gotcha."

"Cherie?" Dylan's attention came back to her.

And it was funny, but she didn't have any trouble reading his mind this time. "Yes, sir," she said. "Fifteen minutes."

CHAPTER EIGHT

Saturday, 6:15 A.M.—Albuquerque, New Mexico

Spencer Bayonne stood on the edge of Somerset Street, milling with the crowd of half-awake people who had spilled out of their houses to gape at the police cars and the fire truck parked in front of Lily Robbins's bungalow.

Robbins's truck was in her driveway, but according to the rumors running up and down the street, she was nowhere to be found.

There had been shots, quite a few, resulting in one dead body, again according to the chatter on the street—and Spencer was not happy.

Whoever in Sir Arthur Kendryk's London office had decided to put two wiseguys from Las Vegas on this job needed to be cut out of the chain of command. Spencer would be happy to perform the service for Kendryk himself, the way he'd performed a number of services for the English lord over the years, literally and most recently with a seven-inch Recon Tanto blade. It was a great knife, a prize he'd won off a girl Kendryk had been keeping at his estate in Weymouth, England, a while back. Red Dog had been her street name, though Kendryk had preferred to call her Gillian. He also preferred to call her "his," and in Spencer's opinion was going to dangerous lengths to get what he wanted.

Gillian Pentycote, Spencer recalled; a Yank like him.

The woman here in Albuquerque was a Yank, too, born and bred, and if the Vegas boys had iced her without getting the bracelet, Spencer was going to ice them. Paul Stark and Jason Schroder had been given a clearly defined job— surveillance; get to Albuquerque and keep an eye on the woman until Spencer arrived on the scene.

The Vegas boys had overstepped their orders, having gone so far as to break into Lily Robbins's house, looking for the bracelet and probably to make a name for themselves, and now Spencer had a mess on his hands.

The sound of another siren approaching had everybody on the sidewalk straining to see down the street, everybody except him and a guy standing on the other side of Somerset, about twenty yards down from one of the cop cars. That guy was watching Lily Robbins's house like a hawk.

Spencer pulled his phone out of his pocket, took a photo, and sent it to his partner, who was waiting in their Lincoln Town Car a block away. It took about two minutes for Mallory to text him back, during which time an ambulance pulled up in front of the bungalow.

GRIGORI PETROV, Mallory wrote, ONE OF IVAN NIKOLEVNA'S LIEUTENANTS.

Petrov, The Chechen, Spencer thought. He'd heard of the man, and this thing had suddenly turned into a horse race. The potential had been there from the start. A multimillion-dollar piece of CIA-generated Russian/Iranian intelligence going down in the Central American highlands and disappearing off the map became a world-class bargaining chip for whoever came up with it. Sir Arthur Kendryk had hired Spencer to make sure he was that man.

A wolfish smile curved the corners of Spencer's mouth. If Nikolevna was throwing his weight into this international game of pickup sticks, the stakes had just gotten higher. He liked high stakes, and Russian Mafia godfathers played for some of the highest on the planet.

One of the few who played for higher was his current employer.

Nikolevna and Kendryk, he thought, now that was a black match. But Petrov versus Bayonne—Spencer's grin broadened even more—that was no contest.

Moving deliberately, he separated himself from the onlookers and headed across the street. He needed to know what had happened in the Robbins house. With his phone to his ear, he fell in behind the medical technicians from the ambulance and kept up a one-sided, low-volume, cop-shop-style conversation. One of the policemen they passed in the front yard had his thumb on his mic and was talking into the walkie-talkie on his shoulder.

"Yeah, an Aston Martin," the cop said. "The guy is positive, and get this, after the shots, he swears the *Bullitt* car tore down the street . . . no, not a 'bullet' car, the car from *Bullitt*, the movie . . . yeah, a fastback Mustang."

Not quite, Spencer thought, checking the guy's name tag as he passed. Whittington.

The *Bullitt* car was a Shelby Cobra—a fastback, sure, but far more than a Ford Mustang.

"Gonzales is getting a statement from the neighbor now," Whittington said.

Spencer catalogued the information and kept walking, keeping up with the guys from the ambulance. Jason Schroder drove an Aston Martin, and Spencer wasn't happy that the car had been tagged. The Vegas boys had just become a serious liability.

When the paramedics went through the front door of the bungalow, he stopped. He didn't need to go inside. Somebody's viscera were all over the far wall in the living room, a real mess. He checked the floor, where a hallway began, and saw everything he needed to see, a gray ponytail stringing out across the carpet, still attached to what was left of Paul Stark's head. The guy had a hole in his chest, too, which opened the possibility of a classic Mozambique—two to the heart, one to the head.

Somebody was a shooter. It was damned unlikely that Schroder had shot his partner, and even more unlikely that some schoolteacher in Albuquerque had pulled a Mozambique on a Las Vegas wiseguy.

So now he had a fucking mystery on top of a royal screwup, and what he needed was a bracelet. The woman was a negligible pain in the ass—unless getting the bracelet from her proved to be too difficult, for whatever reason. Then she was dead.

But he had to find her first.

It was just too damn bad Robbins hadn't

taken Mallory's offer. Then he'd know where in the hell she was, and she could have at least seen Tahiti before her life took a bad turn. His Mallory was such a romantic, such a softie beneath all her razor-sharp edges. When she'd heard about the poster and all the books in the woman's bedroom, she'd gotten a sweet idea, and the two of them had laid down a private bet.

It looked like he'd won. There wouldn't be any little side trip to Tahiti. The ticket hadn't been redeemed, and all hell had broken loose.

He noticed one of the cops inside the house heading in his direction, looking very official and in no mood to be messed with. He lifted his hand, making a point of catching the guy's eye.

"I'm looking for Whittington," he said. "Is he in here?"

"Outside," the cop said, his voice gruff, the accompanying gesture he made making it clear the word was an order, not an answer.

Spencer obeyed immediately, turning away from the door and heading out across the lawn. The day had gotten off to a rough start for the Vegas boys, and an even rougher stop for Paul Stark.

His phone vibrated in his hand, and he held it out to look at the screen.

GAZPROM, Mallory wrote, naming the giant

Russian natural gas monopoly, having obviously come up with the same question he'd asked himself when she'd given him Petrov's name, mainly "What in the hell connected Kendryk and Nikolevna?"

UKRAINIAN GAS LEASES. He'd buy that. Everybody wanted in on Gazprom's gas leases.

KENDRYK WANTS SHARES IN THEM. NIKOLEVNA WANTS SHARES IN THEM. THE RUSSIAN SECRET SERVICE CONTROLS A HEFTY PORTION OF THE LEASES AND HAS PUT THEM ON THE BLOCK IN EXCHANGE FOR THE DATA THE CIA COMPILED AND ENCODED ON THE BRACELET. WINNER TAKE ALL. LOSER GO HOME. Spencer's grin widened. His girl was good. Ukrainian gas leases in exchange for the retrieval of an extremely damaging piece of Russian intelligence proving collusion with the Iranians on their nuclear program was a world-class trade.

Kendryk had warned him the playing field might get broad on this thing. Spencer had to agree. The future of Ukrainian fuel supplies being decided on Somerset Street in Albuquerque, New Mexico, U.S.A., was proof positive of a very broad marketplace, even the black marketplace. It was also a testament to underworld intelligence assets. In that arena, Spencer was dividing his bets straight down the middle between Nikolevna's Russian *reketiry* and Kendryk's far-flung global network.

He grinned again.

This party had definitely started, and possibly, the price on the CIA information had just gone up. Way up. Billions of dollars were going to change hands before this was over—and at the middle of it all was one small bracelet and one insignificant woman who didn't have a rat's chance against the forces arrayed against her.

Mozambiques, a dead body, the woman snatched or fleeing, gross-national-product-altering amounts of cash, Vegas wiseguys, Russian Mafia, and the infamous tag team of Spencer Bayonne and Mallory Rush. Lily Robbins was in so far over her head, she'd be lucky to survive the day.

He crossed Somerset on his way back to the Town Car, keying in a speed dial to Mallory's phone.

"Hey, Kitten," he said when she answered. He called her Kitten because of her claws, literal and figurative. "Call London. Let them know we're here, and find out what hotel Stark and Schroder are staying at in Albuquerque."

He was betting Schroder was going to pull a grab-and-scram, as in grab his goodies and scram back to Las Vegas. With the police already onto the Aston Martin, Spencer didn't think he'd get too far, which made him more than a serious liability. It made him a dead serious liability. But Schroder would have seen something this morning. Spencer didn't have a doubt, and whatever little piece of information the guy had tucked into his brain somewhere, Spencer was going to get it out, one way or the other. He really wasn't too particular about the method of extraction, only the results, and once he finished with Schroder, he was going after Lily Robbins.

Poor thing. Mallory's Tahiti deal had been her last chance for a few moments in the sun. Nothing could save her now—absolutely nothing.

Hell, she'd be lucky if she lasted until lunch.

CHAPTER NINE

Albuquerque was a nice place, Zach decided, a few birds singing in the morning, the soft hush of dawn before everything from the pavement to the traffic started heating up, Johnny-on-the-spot cops, and the city's schoolteachers had incredible legs.

At least the one trying to get dressed in Charlotte's front seat did.

He kept his gaze forward, mostly, but there was no way not to be aware of Lily Robbins barely a foot away, shucking into her pants. He'd picked her outfit for the day, kept it simple—button-fly jeans, tie-dyed tank top, the suede cowboy boots, and a pair of socks.

"I've got ten thousand dollars in my suitcase,"

she said. "You must have seen it, and you can have it all if you let me go."

She finished with the buttons on her fly and reached down for one of her boots. She'd moved damned fast to get into her clothes once he'd taken off the handcuffs, and he had a feeling that as soon as she got her foot in the second boot, she was going to try and make a run for it.

She wasn't going to get far. He could guarantee it.

"I can have the money whether I let you go or not," he said around a yawn. That much was so damn obvious, he wondered how she'd missed it.

He slid her a glance. She was on that second boot, jamming her foot into it, tugging it on.

He checked his watch.

Come on, Alex, he thought. Every minute spent parked on the street, musing about Albuquerque and Lily Robbins's legs, was one more minute the Aston Martin spent speeding away.

"I'm just saying that kidnapping me isn't going to help whatever the hell this mess is all about, and ten thousand dollars is about nine thousand more than you could get out of my family in a good year, which this one hasn't exactly been."

She got her foot all the way into the boot, jerked the pant leg down over the top of it, and sure enough, her hand went for the door handle.

"That's all I'm saying," she said, her face still pale, her words a little rushed. "Whatever this is all about, you're better off without me."

He noticed her fingers slowly curling around the handle.

"Where did you get the money?" he asked.

"You were in my suitcase. You saw the envelope. No name, no address. I thought it was from you."

Well, that set him back a bit.

"And why would I send you ten thousand dollars and a plane ticket to Tahiti?"

Her mouth tightened ever so slightly, more a sign of distress than anger, and a warm blush of color came into her cheeks.

Oh.

This was sweet.

Damn sweet.

"I would have sent more than ten," he said, and the color in her cheeks deepened. "We'd be heading for the Maldives, not Tahiti, and I would have signed my name. I'd want you to know what you were getting into."

She dropped her gaze, and he saw the

muscles in her arm flex, felt her fight-or-flight system kick into "flight" mode and settle into a holding pattern. She was actually trembling, and he wondered if she ever played poker, or if he could talk her into it. Her deception skills were—well, they were nonexistent, which absolutely fascinated and appalled him in equal measure.

"Don't," he said.

It was an order, and his tone shouldn't have left a doubt in her mind, and still she was weighing her options. He could almost see the wheels turning in her mind—*Could she make it? Was she quick enough? Would he shoot her, if she wasn't?*

The answers to those questions were no, no, and no.

"Don't," he repeated, something he wasn't used to doing. He was used to being obeyed, but considering that she was the only one currently available for him to order about, he figured his compliance ratio was about to hit an all-time low.

That would not be good.

"If you want to leave, you can. I won't stop you." Personally, even by his own standards, which were damn high, he was an exceptional liar. "And I'm certainly not going to hurt you."

And that's how it worked for him: Every layer of out-and-out fabrication came with a layer of truth, albeit a thinner layer.

Much thinner.

He was quite capable of hurting her to some extent, if that's what it took to keep her where he needed her. And if it turned out that she wasn't a New Mexico schoolteacher inadvertently overtaken by events, and was actually an international thug out to make a few million selling the bracelet on the black market, appropriate measures would be taken no matter how blue her eyes were.

"But there are a couple of things I want you to consider," he continued. "The first being that it wasn't my house that got shot all to hell this morning."

It was an incredibly salient fact, but he still wasn't sure if she'd catch the significance of it right off the bat.

Her answer suggested that she did.

"I-it was mine," she said.

"And I don't live in Albuquerque." An equally salient fact.

"I do." Her trembling increased, which had not been his intent.

"And when the shooting started, I was—"

"Standing in front of me."

Yeah, she was getting the picture.

"This isn't about me, Lily. This is about you and the bracelet the pilot gave you. I'm only here to help." In a manner of speaking. Help his country and his agency get what they needed. Helping her was a secondary consideration. No matter what it looked like so far, this was not a PSD, a personal security detail. "Do you know who those men were this morning at your house?"

Her gaze lifted to meet his. "Do you?"

He stared at her for a second. That was it? A question? No movement of her head to aye or gainsay his inquiry?

Oh, she was quick, and the only thing that saved her from his "I'm the one asking the questions here" speech was the ringing of his phone.

Thank God.

"Yes?" he said, answering his cell.

"Good morning. I'm calling from Steele Street at the request of Scorpion Fire. This line is secure."

"Go on," he said. The voice was female, which surprised him. He didn't remember there being many, if any, women at Steele Street, at least on the operational end.

"The car you're looking for has stopped on Santa Ana Drive between Seventeenth and

Eighteenth streets. I'm cross-referencing that address now to see what's on that block, if it's a residential or business area. If you can give me your location, I'll map your route."

He looked out Charlotte's window. "I'm on Linden Place, at nine twenty-eight." He gave her the address of the house across the street.

There was a pause, before the woman came back on the line.

"Continue east for three tenths of a mile and turn north on Whedbee. I'm also tracking down the license plate of the Aston Martin and will have that information shortly."

"Good." He tucked the phone between his ear and shoulder and started the Shelby.

"You'll stay on Whedbee for two miles and turn left on Thompson Avenue. Let me know when you get there, and I'll give you your next direction. Until then, be informed that the Aston Martin is stopped at"—there was another slight pause—"the Sunrise Motel. I'm looking that up now and will give you whatever description I can, which will hopefully include a layout of the building. If I can access their computer, I'll give you a room number for... Jason Schroder. The Aston Martin, Nevada license plate number 01B-4381, is registered to Mr. Schroder. His address is three two two zero

Klamath Street, Las Vegas. I'm running him through my databases now...and he is most recently affiliated with Thomas Banning's organization. Mr. Banning, as you may know, is a mob figure, with a base of operations in Las Vegas. I'll have a photograph of Mr. Schroder up in a moment."

Uh, okay, Zach thought, beginning to wonder who was on the line with him, and how many computers she had running.

"Schroder is registered with a Paul Stark in room number two seven six at the Sunrise Motel," the voice said in a matter of seconds, and he wondered, really, could anyone hack that fast? On the other hand, how secure could the Sunrise Motel's system be?

Obviously not very.

"Schroder is thirty-four years old, five feet ten inches tall, one hundred and eighty-five pounds, white-blond hair, brown eyes, looks to me like he's pumping a lot of iron."

Okay, that information had to be coming up on a different screen than the one she'd used to jack into the motel's system.

"He checked into the Sunrise four days ago and is paying with a Visa card. If you need that number, I can give it to you."

"Uh, no." Who was this girl? She sounded

kind of young, but how young could she be to be running Dylan's communications console?

"In about five ... make that two minutes, I'm going to have you onboard with the Bazo PC concealed in Charlotte's tape deck, and all this information will be streaming to you."

His gaze went to the eight-track slot on the dash. Well, that was an unexpected upgrade, a Bazo.

"I'll set the PC to automatically open a file and save everything I send," the voice continued, "so you can access it at any time. In one minute, your tracking map will be in the upper right-hand corner of the screen."

A small, hardly bigger than palm-size computer slid silently out of the eight-track opening. It tilted itself upright, then came on, lighting up with a stream of data scrolling across its screen.

"Thirty seconds," the voice said. "Your speaker will be on, with two-way secure communication with me here at Steele Street, and I will terminate this call. The PC has a camera, which will also be turned on. Anything you want turned off, just let me know. Scorpion Fire has requested that we be of service to you. If you need something, ask."

As a matter of fact, he did have a question.

"What can I call you?"

"SB303." She no sooner spoke than a stream of pixels washed down the small PC screen—and there she was, in living color, in real time.

An odd, unexpected emotion gripped his heart. *SB303*. He didn't know her, but he did. It was in the chopped blond bangs and the platinum-blond ponytail. It was in the tattoo he saw snaking over the top of one of her shoulders. It was in the hot pink bustier, in her soft mouth and her button nose—and it was in her eyes, pale, silvery blue eyes looking straight through him.

SB303. Street girl. She'd been there. A long scar coursed diagonally across her forehead and cut through one of her eyebrows.

She'd been hurt.

"Hi, Zach," she said, a warm, surprised smile curving her mouth, her voice coming through the speaker in the onboard computer system.

The odd emotion intensified for another second, then another, before he was able to put it aside, compartmentalize it, and move on.

"SB303." He nodded once. It was a street name, a tag, her initials and the Denver area code.

"Here comes your tracking map on the Aston Martin," she said, and the map appeared in the upper-right-hand corner of the small screen.

He heard the phone call get disconnected, and he pocketed his cell.

"You should know that as long as your Bazo PC is up and running, I'm tracking you," she said. "If you want the signal terminated, I can give you the code, but we would prefer to stay with you and provide support."

"We?"

"The team."

The team. She meant SDF, and SDF meant Dylan, and he didn't doubt for a moment that if Dylan wanted to track him, he'd be tracked—unless a direct order to the contrary was forthcoming from Alex. The same went for voice communications. If he determined it was in the best interest of the mission to disappear off the grid, his call to Alex would be the last one Steele Street monitored.

He checked the map and made his next turn. The Sunset Motel wasn't far now, only a couple of miles.

"Can I use the Bazo as a secure line anywhere?"

"Yes."

Good.

Any line of communication could be intercepted. The advantage of using the Bazo lay in its distance from him. No one would be listening for Alejandro Campos on a line routing from a 1968 Shelby Cobra, through Denver, to wherever he called—except, for now, SDF and SB303.

And Lily Robbins. She was listening to every word.

"Keep the signal on." If something happened to him, it wasn't a bad idea for someone to know how to find her. "I have a passenger."

"Lily Lamont Robbins?"

Yeah. Lamont. That was right. He gave the computer screen a quick glance. *Christ*. What didn't the woman know? The name had been in Lily's dossier, sure, along with her married name of Lily Bersani, but how had SB303 known she was with him?

"Sorry about the . . . uh—" the blonde said, giving her head a small shake, knowledge of her mistake written all over her face.

"Yeah," he said. She shouldn't have used his name. The line was secure, yeah, but Charlotte's passenger seat wasn't. He should have said something himself.

He checked the screen again, turned onto the next street, and came up with two answers to his question. Rydell could have told her about Lily Robbins. The SDF operator knew Lily had been in El Salvador and knew she lived in Albuquerque. Zach had in no way leaked any information about Lily being with the pilot and filming his death, but it was known that they'd both been at St. Joseph's. His second answer was that, quite possibly, the baby-faced blonde in the pink bustier simply knew everything. Dylan would like that in a girl.

He'd like it a lot.

She'd known Zach's name, and he wasn't sure what in the hell to think about that.

He gave SB303 another look. Sure enough, there she was, looking like jailbait and sliding her way through cyberspace with all the skills of a world-class interface pirate. Still, no one at SDF could know anything about the bracelet or his mission.

Hell, *he* hadn't known about the bracelet until yesterday in Langley.

"I'm at the motel," he said, pulling Charlotte to a rumbling stop on Santa Ana Drive, halfway between Seventeenth and Eighteenth. "I don't see the Aston Martin."

"Try following the parking lot around to the back of the motel. Schroder's room is on the flip side of the Sunrise," SB303 said, and the screen filled with the L-shaped layout of the motel. The girl had highlighted room number 276.

God, she was good.

"Thank you. Later." He reached over and hit the off button on the PC, the controls being clearly displayed in a row down the side of the Bazo, a Bazo VJX-UZ468 700 series, according to the lettering under the screen. In one smooth move, the computer folded itself back into the eight-track tape deck slot. He was impressed. The PC was damned handy to have, but he wasn't leaving it up and running with Lily alone in the car. God only knew whom she'd contact. If things didn't go down well at the Sunrise, he knew SDF would figure it out fairly quickly, and SB303 could initiate any contact that needed initiating.

Putting Charlotte in first gear, he swung out from the curb and crossed into the Sunrise's parking lot.

"Wh-what are we doing here?" Lily asked.

"Getting the bracelet." He drove to the far end of the motel and parked Charlotte on the side of the building. He'd go the rest of the way on foot.

"Why? What's so important about the bracelet?" She sounded truly confused, and frustrated, and more than a little scared, as well she should be. "It's just macramé. It doesn't even have any beads."

She was right. There weren't any beads, just microdots. He reached into his gun bag in the backseat for a full magazine and a handful of flex cuffs. The cuffs went in his pocket. The magazine went in his Para. Switching it out, he glanced over at her.

"I won't be gone long," he said, dropping his other cell phone, the "bomb" one, into his pocket and checking to make sure his knife was still secure in its sheath on his belt. He couldn't be gone long. The cops would have IDed the corpse by now, noticed Paul Stark was from out of town, and immediately started searching the local hotels and motels. He had to get in, get the bracelet, and get the hell back out.

"You—you can't leave me here."

Yes, he could.

As a matter of fact, he could do a little worse than that. To his credit, he refrained from saying anything like "This is for your own good." Instead, he simply moved fast and clean, snapping the handcuff back on her, before she had a chance to see it coming.

"You—" She jerked on the cuff.

"Bastard." Yeah, yeah. He'd seen that coming—the same way he saw her other hand coming up, balled into a fist. He caught her wrist before she could connect her upper cut with his lower jaw, and he pulled her close. He did it hard.

Grit. She had it in spades.

"I am doing my best to keep you alive," he said, his voice deliberately harsh, his grip on her unrelenting, his face just inches from hers. "And my best is damn good, but you need to do *exactly* what I tell you to do, *every* single time I tell you."

Her gaze was narrowed on him, her body stiff, resisting—and he approved. He could work with tough. She was scared. He could see it in her eyes, hear it in the shortness of her breath, but she was going to fight. Good. Great. Just not with him.

"You can't stay here, in this town," he said, "not where you can be found, so think about what you want. If it's back to the Cross Double R in Montana, fine. I can make sure you get there. If it's somewhere else where you'll be safe, fine. I'll get you there. But you are not running loose anywhere in goddamn New Mexico. Not today." With that, he pulled her cuffed hand down low enough for him to snap the other cuff onto the seat post, the bar of metal holding the passenger seat to the floor of the chassis, and he locked her to the car.

She wasn't going anywhere, and she wasn't happy. It was written all over her face.

Bastard.

Yeah, he could read her mind, read her anger and the uncertainty in her eyes.

"H-how do you know about the Cross?" she asked, her voice a little shaky, her body still stiff with tension where he held her—so close, close enough to feel her breathe.

God, she was beautiful, drop-dead gorgeous even barely out of bed, her silky dark hair falling out of her braid and curling up over her ears, sliding down over her shoulders, her eyes with a slight exotic slant, so clear, such a pure, shattered blue and looking so intently into his, demanding an answer.

Under different circumstances, that could work for him. Under other circumstances, having her so close could work really, really well for him—very hot, very sweet.

Satiny skin promising a soft touch.

Artfully sculpted lips, carved in lush, full curves promising a soft kiss.

Three weeks, that's how long it had been since he'd dropped her off in Albuquerque, and he'd thought about her every goddamn day since. *Fuck*.

"I know everything about you, Lily." He told her the truth, then released her.

Opening the door, he got the hell out of the Shelby. He had a job to do, and only minutes to get it done.

Bullshit, Lily thought, watching him disappear around the corner of the motel. There was no damn way Alejandro Campos knew everything about her.

And if he didn't come back, what in the world was going to happen to her?

She brought her free hand up and held onto her other arm. She was shivering, even with the temperature warming with the sunrise.

He didn't know how truly frightened she was of him. Frightened beyond the violence of the morning, frightened beyond the handcuffs. He was a personal threat, a promise of annihilation. She didn't understand it, not at all. But she'd felt it when he'd held her so close, felt it running through her, deep in her core. He could destroy her. Or create her, and she wouldn't accept anyone having that kind of effect on her, that kind of power over her. She couldn't accept it.

Keep her safe? Yes, he could do that, too, if he so chose, but she wasn't at all sure that would be his choice, or if he'd live long enough to get the job done. The man in the hotel had been out to kill them both this morning.

Dammit. Goddammit. She pulled on the handcuff, and wondered, truly, if she had the strength to pull his damn car apart.

And what was with that damn bracelet? For the love of God, people were dying for it.

She started to shake again, almost uncontrollably. She'd killed a man, killed him dead in her house. She wouldn't change it, not for a moment. He'd been aiming straight at her, or Campos. She would never know for sure who had been in his sights, but it didn't matter. Given where she and Campos had been standing, the guy with the ponytail could easily have gotten them both with one bullet. A hollow-point bullet might not have had enough penetration, but one of her flat-point handloads would have cut through both of them like a hot knife through butter. Her dad made them for her, for his baby girl, living all alone in Albuquerque—and he'd made them for the exact situation she'd found herself in this morning.

Oh, God. Oh, God.

She brought her hand up over her mouth and squeezed her eyes shut. She'd done the right thing. The only thing. But who was the dead man? And this man at the motel—who was he? And were there other men out there, too? Men who wanted the bracelet?

Damn Campos—how dare he handcuff her again. It was the last time. She swore it.

Oh, God. She'd fallen asleep dreaming about him last night, wondering if she would ever see him again, longing for him. All because of what she'd felt three weeks ago in El Salvador. Some connection that shouldn't exist—but did.

He didn't know everything about her. He didn't know how easily, or how deeply, she got lost in his eyes. She'd never seen farther in anybody's eyes than she saw in his—and how could that be?

Goddamn him. If she wasn't safe in Albuquerque, why had he left her so helpless? Handcuffed. Unarmed. Exposed.

Zach—that's the name the girl on the PC had called him. It was his real name. She knew it. Not Alejandro Campos. The girl had known exactly who he was—*damn him.*

Denver—the girl had said that, too. Denver, Steele Street, SDF. Sister Julia had been going to Denver with her sister, Honey York, and the man who had been with Honey, Smith Rydell. Which all meant what?

Lily didn't have a clue. But Rydell was a good guy, right? Sister Julia was certainly no criminal, and Honoria York was practically famous.

And they all knew Campos. They'd all been at his villa. Sister Julia actually liked the man.

The sound of sirens in the distance sent a wash of fear down her spine. She'd killed a man and fled the scene. Self-defense aside, her actions were suspect, maybe even criminal.

She put her hand over her heart, just to feel the solid beat of it—and she breathed, watching the corner of the motel where he'd disappeared, watching and waiting.

He had to come back.

CHAPTER TEN

Saturday, 6:45 A.M.—Denver, Colorado

She ruled.

Cherie swirled her triple-shot latte around in her grande-sized commuter coffee mug before popping the top and taking another sip. Stretching her legs out, she rested her heels on the open windowsill of her personal double-hung window and relaxed back in her chair to enjoy the view.

Dylan had wanted fifteen minutes, and she'd given him exactly that: Charlotte's Bazo up and running, all signals go, in record time. Sometimes she amazed even herself—and now Dylan owed her. All she had to do was figure out what she wanted.

She could think of one thing right off the bat. Hell, she could think of two or three.

Swiveling a bit to her left, she glanced behind her into the rest of the office. The boss was back in his private lair with the door closed, and he was the only one with any rules.

So . . . so, maybe it was time for another cigarette.

She always thought better with a careful mix of caffeine and nicotine running through her, though truth be told, she already had a pretty good idea of what she was going to ask from Dylan.

She reached across her desk for her backpack and dragged it into her lap, then swiveled back to look out the window. One cigarette— what could it harm?

Your lungs, girl. Besides that, though, and she was quitting next week. She had it all mapped out on her calendar. Currently she was in the buildup stage, building up to the BQ, the Big Quit, the one that lasted for all time. At twenty-six, she was finally ready.

Damn. Twenty-six. When had that happened?

After lighting up, she exhaled a series of three perfect smoke rings and watched them dissolve against the window and a backdrop of the Front Range being revealed by the rising sun, slowly, steadily, inevitably, and brightly— very brightly.

And that was not a good thing.

She dug back in her pack for a pair of sunglasses, found the biggest ones she owned, and slipped them on her face. That was better, she thought. Sunlight was no friend to a girl who'd spent the night sipping champagne and hadn't been to bed.

Readjusting her feet on the windowsill, she settled back into her chair and went back to thinking about Dylan owing her and what she was going to get out of him, one way or the other.

A smile slowly curved her lips.

Inside job—*geez*, just the thought gave her chills. Dylan and one other unnamed person on the team knew something about 738 Steele Street she didn't. It wasn't Skeeter or Kid. The three of them were the Bitch Musketeers. She'd know if either of them had been holding anything back during their security reviews.

Her best guess would be Christian Hawkins.

Sure. It had to be Superman. But why would he take Charlotte? There were a hundred superfine cars in the garages, so why Charlotte the Harlot, instead of Charlene, the other Shelby Cobra Mustang? What set Charlotte apart from all the other iron in Steele Street?

She was one of the original Steele Street rides. Charlene had been bought about five years ago, but Charlotte had been with the boys since they'd been teenagers. Somehow that was the key, and Cherie was just about to slip that piece of the puzzle into place when her cell phone rang and startled her out of her whole damn train of thought. Surprised that anyone was calling her so early, that anyone she knew outside of the SDF office was even up at this ungodly hour, she gave the phone an annoyed glance.

Which lasted all of two seconds, just long enough to read the screen.

Sliding the phone open, she brought it to her ear. "Hey, Cooper."

"Congratulations, boss. Gallen Fund has contracted with Hacker International to design the IT system for their San Francisco office."

"You closed the deal?"

"Signed, sealed, and delivered last night," he said. Danny Cooper was her only employee, and between the two of them, Hacker International was grossing close to seven figures this year, enough that they were moving into new luxury quarters next week. For the last few months, they'd been housed at Steele Street's annex, the Commerce City Garage. The Gallen Fund deal wasn't a big one, but the venture-capital company was very high profile in Third World health clinics, and Cherie had wanted the deal.

"Super job, Danny." She was grinning a mile wide.

"Thanks. Sorry to call so early, but I was able to get a standby flight. I wanted you to know I'll be back in Denver by noon."

"Then we'll celebrate tonight. Bring your sweetie and all the Mini-Coopers, and we'll do something at the house." The house was Cherie's LoDo loft, about a stone's throw from Steele Street.

"No date, huh?"

Jerk.

"That's twenty Saturday nights in a row that you've been trying to hang out with my kids, and not a one of them over six years old. That's sad, Hacker, really sad."

"Jerk." She didn't keep it to herself this time.

"I can't imagine what that says about your sex life, all these dateless Saturday nights."

"And I can't imagine what all those Mini-Coopers are doing to your sex life." Danny had three kids.

"Lisa's pregnant again."

"Oh, for the love of God, Danny." She laughed. "Give the woman a break."

"What I'm going to give her is a foot massage, and if you don't need me today, I'll see you Monday morning in Commerce City and not a moment before."

"Monday."

"Ciao, boss."

"Ciao." She hung up and looked around for her soda can. The ash on her cigarette had gotten precariously long.

Geez. Where had the darn thing gone? And what did it take, really, to end up barefoot and pregnant, deliriously happy with three screaming-cute kids and some equally screaming-cute guy to massage your feet?

She was smart, *summa cum laude,* high school valedictorian, top kid in her kindergarten, could read when she was three, but she wasn't smart enough to figure out the whole "happily ever after" thing.

Well, actually, one time, a guy told her she was too smart. Actually, she'd been told that twice, maybe three . . . okay, maybe four times.

Maybe five.

So maybe the brainiac motif was working against her. She should still be smart enough to figure out a way around it, without having to resort to a lobotomy.

Lobotomies for love—she'd floated that by a guy once. He hadn't thought it was very funny, and as she recalled, she had not heard from him again.

She looked on the other side of a few stacks

of books and her half-dead plant, and then she remembered.

Oh, hell.

Very carefully, she slid off the end of her chair and got to her knees, then even more carefully, stretched out, reaching under the desk toward the soda can. She barely got her cigarette over the top of it before the ash fell— and landed perfectly inside.

Another grin curved her mouth.

It was official.

She ruled.

Gabriel Shore stepped out of the elevator with his older sister and took a moment to catalogue the scene before him. General Grant had briefed him extensively on what to expect at Steele Street: the cutting-edge professionalism of the SDF team, the top-notch skill levels of the operators, the higher-than-high-tech equipment—and what he saw were women. Everywhere. Just women. An office full of them.

The exceptionally hot blonde in combat boots and a bustier had to be Skeeter Bang-Hart, Dylan Hart's wife, and one of SDF's two women operators. The other was his sister, such as she was, Red Dog. He usually called her Gillian,

like he always had, whether she remembered
him as a kid or not—and the answer to that was
not. But in this environment, she truly was the
world-renowned sniper Red Dog, a very hard
act to follow.

The small blonde on the couch with the pixie
face was Honoria York, not an operator but
a journalist for *The Washington Post*, and a
celebrity of sorts in high-society circles. Grant
had told him she might be here, but Gabriel
hadn't expected her to be in the office. As politely as possible, he would suggest to Dylan
Hart that she be removed from the immediate
premises, at least while he was here. There
could be absolutely no leaks on the information
he'd brought with him from Washington.

And that left just one other woman, a mystery girl stretched out under her desk in a white
dress that billowed out above her knees and, in
her current position, barely covered her ass. A
faint cloud of smoke hovered over her section
of the office, with more coming out from under
the desk. She was smoking under there—*holy
cripes*—wearing what looked like a black leather
motorcycle jacket and what were definitely really
high heels, gold and shiny, with white pom-pom
things stuck on them.

She might have to be removed as well. He'd

make the call after he found out who she was and checked with Grant. His mission was top priority at his end of the Marsh Annex in Washington, D.C., where General Richard "Buck" Grant also had his office. Gabriel had been tracking an international businessman for his employer, the Commerce Department Security Division, CDSD, and two weeks ago he'd run across Grant's investigation of the same man, Sir Arthur Kendryk, Lord Weymouth.

Kendryk was showing up on a lot of people's radar lately, and normally, coming across another department's investigation would not have required Gabriel's intervention, let alone a cross-country trip, but in among the file requests made by Dylan Hart through General Grant's office had been the details of a large Uzbekistan drug deal, a ton of Afghan opium going from a man named Gul Rashid in Uzbekistan, to a buyer in Marseilles, with Tony Royce brokering the deal.

The name had hit him like a physical blow. Tony Royce was the man who had tortured his sister, and he was in a file Hart had put together on Kendryk. The whole thing had made his gut churn, and three days ago, his worst fears had been confirmed.

The connection between Rashid and Kendryk

had been vague and heavy on conjecture, like so many of the possible connections Gabriel had followed himself—up until Hart had tracked the deal backward from Marseilles to Weymouth and found the name Spencer Bayonne. For Hart, the trail had gone cold there, but for Gabriel, Bayonne was the key. He could directly connect Bayonne to half a dozen arms deals in western Africa, and now he could directly connect Bayonne to Kendryk.

That had been his glory moment, a solid success after a year's worth of work. Bayonne was the linchpin, the key to connecting Kendryk's legitimate international empire to the darker world of multimillion-dollar gunrunning, drug trafficking, and the illegal sales of highly complex, dual-use technology, but Gabriel had come to Denver because of another name he'd found in Hart's files—Gillian's. Buried deep, but there, a shadow player, a ghost in Uzbekistan, and through her interference what had begun as Tony Royce's deal had gone to Bayonne instead. Gabriel was betting it had also gone to Kendryk.

It was his fault. All of it. What had been done to her. What had happened to her since. And especially what she'd become.

He glanced at her, standing next to him, and felt a familiar tightness in his chest. She was so sleek and hard, and so wired for action. Her levels of alertness were almost eerie. All her switches were on, lit up, topped off. She lived at a heightened sense of readiness, and was always armed to the teeth—a .45 in her shoulder holster, two knives he could see, and whatever else he couldn't see. In the closed world of elite warriors, she had a reputation that crossed all borders, not only for the savage elegance of her skills, but also of her face, and of her heart. She took her orders from Dylan Hart and executed them with clean, efficient precision. She'd been tapped to guard heads of state, oil-rich sheiks, and fact-finding U.S. senators. Over the course of the last two years, she'd fulfilled dozens of missions in all corners of the globe, and he'd come to Denver for only one reason: to protect her.

Him.

The little brother.

"Gillian," he said, glancing through the office one more time, in case he'd missed the man whose name General Grant had given him. "I need to speak with Dylan Hart."

Sir Arthur Kendryk and Spencer Bayonne had both entered the country three days ago in New York, and whatever connection had existed between Kendryk and Gillian on the Uzbekistan deal, the English lord wanted more. He wanted her back.

The bounty he'd offered was two million dollars. The only condition was that she be brought to Kendryk alive.

CHAPTER ELEVEN

Given enough time, and it really didn't take all that much, Zach would put his negotiating skills up there with the very finest. He was good. He knew it. He understood that negotiating, by its very nature, required discourse.

He and Jason Schroder had shared a little discourse in room 276. As far as Zach could tell, he'd been "discoursed" once in the ribs and once on the damn shoulder that had already been "discoursed" on Somerset Street. And then they'd run out of time, or at least Jason Schroder had run out of time—Zach had made sure of it. But if Schroder kept his wits about him, he would definitely live to fuck up again.

Zach came around the corner of the Sunset Motel, holding his upper right arm with his left hand, damn glad Charlotte wasn't any farther away than the side of the building.

Coffee, that's what he needed; hot would be a nice bonus, sleep would be good, preferably with Lily Robbins stretched out next to him, and a couple of stitches probably wouldn't hurt.

But he had the bracelet, and the polymer strand was still securely woven into the macramé.

Mark up another win for the good guys.

Now all he needed was to get the hell out of Albuquerque. He couldn't say it hadn't been an interesting visit. A little short, but considering how things had been going, he was okay with short.

Sliding in behind Charlotte's steering wheel, he tossed Lily the handcuff key.

She caught it in midair, and despite his aches and pains, and the goddamn blood running down his arm, he almost grinned—almost, but not quite. The girl was quick, damn quick, and he was impressed, but he was also hurting like hell. He fished the Shelby's key out of his pocket, and giving it his best guess, hit the eject button on the eight-track.

Score.

The Bazo rolled out of the tape deck like R2-D2, tilted itself up, and came on, lighting up with a stream of pixels and data washing down its screen.

"SB303," he said, and the baby-faced blonde appeared.

"Ensign," she said, surprising the hell out of him.

Good God. The girl had dug deep to get "Ensign." Maybe Dylan needed to put a leash on her, or double-check the security access on his systems.

He pushed down on Charlotte's clutch and a sudden, painful twinge in his thigh reminded him of the last time he'd gotten shot, and yes, now that he thought about it, he might have had a little "discourse" in room 276 on that part of his anatomy as well. *Geezus.*

"I need the shortest route to Interstate 25, heading north," he said, turning the Harlot's key and just ignoring the girl's "Ensign."

Four hundred and twenty-eight cubic inches of displacement, impeccably timed, roared to life, then settled into the growling purr of impeccably tuned headers. Dylan had lied about the fifteen-second quarter miles. Someone was taking damn good care of Charlotte. She was running like a dream, and only Quinn could have done her headers. The chop-shop boy's signature touch reverberated in every decibel, and there was definitely something about having a 428 pulling 450 horses under him that made Zach feel better, safer, like he was going to get through the day.

Yeah, get through the day. *Geezus*. What were they teaching Vegas wiseguys now? Some kind of Way of the Warrior hand-to-hand combat technique? He'd come close to getting his ass kicked in room 276.

Killing the guy would have been easy.

Merely overpowering him had taken effort and, honest to God, breaking a chair on the guy's head. Admittedly, the Sunset was not buying quality furniture. The chair move had barely slowed Schroder down.

Fuck. A grappling match was not what he'd planned for his motel moment this morning. It had been brief and ugly, and convincing Schroder to give up the bracelet had taken even a bit more "discourse" and those negotiation skills he prized so highly.

"Roger," SB303 said, and the tracking map on the computer screen changed, instantly showing him where he needed to go.

"Thank you." He put Charlotte in gear. He could get used to having his own personal intelligence jockey onboard.

Next to him, Lily was huddled over her hand, getting the key in the cuffs' lock.

"Did you get it?" she asked. "The bracelet?"

He didn't answer. He never answered questions. It was just good SOP, good Standard Operating Procedure. Ask questions. Don't answer questions.

"You did," she said. "I can tell."

No, she couldn't. He never gave anything away. He heard the click of release, and the cuffs clattered to floor of the car, the one cuff still connected to the seat post.

"So you should let me go now. You have the bracelet, not me. Anybody who wants it will have to come after you."

She was almost half right, but not quite.

"Nobody knows I have it. Everybody out there looking still thinks you have it. Sorry, babe, but you're still number one on the hit parade." Literally on the hit parade. "And you need to decide what you want."

He knew what he wanted, and despite what it looked like so far, he hadn't hauled his ass into New Mexico for a kidnapping.

"I want to get out of this goddamn car," she said without a moment's hesitation, her voice very clear, her conviction ringing true, right along with a distinct edge of anger.

"Getting out of the car is not an option at this time." His voice was also very clear. He shifted up through second and into third, holding Charlotte in as they cruised out of the Sunset

Motel's parking lot and back onto Santa Ana Drive. "What I had in mind was some kind of cooperative arrangement."

"Arrangement?"

Yeah, he'd be a little skeptical, too. He usually was, just as a matter of course. But in this instance, a little cooperation could go a long way. She'd be safer, he'd be safer, and those parts of his brain that had been devoted to keeping her under his control could be put to better use—like keeping on top of the mission and staying one step ahead of whoever else was out there. Vegas wiseguys didn't dream up a position for themselves in international espionage. If Thomas Banning had sent them, it wouldn't take the mob boss long to figure out something had gone wrong. There would be a reaction, and the higher up the ladder this thing went, the swifter and harder the reaction would be.

Given the importance of the data on the bracelet, Zach figured there was a good chance Banning was taking orders, too. The trick was finding out who was giving them.

"SB303," he said, calling her back.

"Ensign," she replied.

He took the next left, simultaneously downshifting and spinning Charlotte's wheel.

"Can you pass all the information you've given me back to Scorpion Fire?"

"Roger that."

"Every scrap, including every mile you've tracked me in Charlotte, and tell him I've got the item we were after."

"Yes, sir."

He powered back up into fourth gear.

Alex knew who Kesselring's "other interested parties" would be; he could start tracking this disaster from the other end, find out who they were up against, find out who was connected to Banning—and the quicker he got started, the better.

Until then, an arrangement with Ms. Robbins would definitely be to both their advantages. Plus—and, yes, this was very unprofessional of him—he just needed something. He wasn't sure what, but he'd thought about her every day for three goddamn weeks, and he needed something, a concession of some sort.

"So you did get the bracelet?"

That wasn't it, not even close to a concession, and even though he'd just secured the fate of the free world for another day, maybe a day and half, her question sounded more like an accusation than an honest inquiry, let alone a moment's praise for his skills.

"Did you kill Jason Schroder?" she continued

in the same accusatory vein. "Is that how you got the bracelet?"

He was glad he never answered questions. It saved a lot of wear and tear on his moral ambiguity.

But he was going to make an exception.

"No. I didn't kill him." And then he changed the subject. "We're six hours out of Denver, and I can't guarantee your safety until we get there." If it hadn't been for the tracking device coming out of Steele Street, he might have chosen to take her someplace else.

In fact, he would have chosen someplace else. But they were hooked in to SDF now, which played into Alex's hand, which made it a great plan, despite the narrow abyss in his mind that he had carefully set apart with a demilitarized zone on each side. It was a place he didn't go, and the farther away from the streets of Denver he stayed, the less chance he had of accidentally stumbling into it.

But hell, he was skirting the edge now. Joya Molara Gualterio, Jewel, his ex-partner, ex-girlfriend, ex-lover, ex-everything, would love that. She'd been a big proponent of him going into the abyss and sorting through the pile of crap at the bottom of it, right up until the day she'd left him.

Hell, it was just his life. He didn't know why it had to be such a big goddamn deal.

"Working together would be a good idea," he continued, glancing over at Lily. "Team building. You're a teacher. You know the drill."

"You've got the bracelet," she said. "Why do you need me?"

"I don't need you. You need me. Don't doubt it, Lily, not for a second." That was the God's truth, and she had to know it. "So what do you say? You and me on the same side, backing each other up on the drive? Or do I put the cuffs back on you, and we do this the hard way?"

"To Denver?" she asked, wrapping her arms around herself and doing everything over there on her side of the car except relaxing. She looked ready to bolt, but at least she'd given up the hand-on-the-door-handle idea.

"Yes."

"Why Denver?" she asked. "Because the girl is there? SB303?"

"Yes." Precisely. Because the girl was there, and everything she represented—SDF, Steele Street, Dylan. It was all there, in Denver.

"She called you Zach."

Yes, SB303 had called him Zach.

"That's your name, isn't it. Your real name, not Alejandro Campos."

Yes, but he kept it to himself. Nothing she could know about him would do her any good.

"Did the pilot work for you?" she continued. "Have I ended up in the middle of ... of one of your drug deals?"

He slanted her a glance. That was her nightmare, he realized, being involved in one of the most sordid businesses on the planet, having those kinds of people be aware of her, be after her.

Well, he couldn't blame her for that. Those kinds of people were after him on a regular basis, and yeah, it was a sharply dangerous position to be in, very nightmare worthy.

"There's no cocaine involved in this situation. I promise." At least he could give her that.

"What is the bracelet, then? Why is it so damned important? What ... what's happening here?"

She was full of impossible questions. He didn't blame her, but neither would he answer her.

"Nothing I can't handle, if I have your cooperation." It was pure party line, and he couldn't remember, really, the last time he'd sounded so damn pompous.

Just as well. His pompous moments were best forgotten.

"Bullshit," she said, very clearly, even with

her arms wrapped around her and looking scared as a rabbit.

Great, they were in agreement. He hadn't thought his lousy answer would win him many friends, let alone her cooperation.

"The more you know, the more of a target you become." And that was another God's truth. "No matter how far you're willing to go into that arena, I have my limit, and you've already reached it."

"The less I know, the more likely I am to end up dead," she countered, and he couldn't argue with her, not and be honest. Information and intelligence were two staples in his survival kit.

But there was only so much information he could give her, and it all came down to "not much."

"I'm here working as an agent for the government."

"Whose government?" she shot back. "El Salvador's?"

Touché.

"Your government." *Our government. My government.* He'd spent most of his adult life working for his government and was damn proud of the fact.

The sound she made was one of pure disbelief.

He didn't blame her, but neither was he going to explain himself any further. In six hours, she'd be out of it, and despite what she thought, once this was over, the less she knew, the better off she'd be.

As long as she went back to the ranch in Montana and kept her pistol loaded.

Fuck. Devlin had done her no favor by giving her the bracelet. But Devlin had done exactly what Zach would have done under similar circumstances—deep-sixed the information with a civilian, rather than chance it falling into the wrong hands.

"Do what I tell you, and we'll get to Denver without anybody ending up dead." It was up to Alex to decide how much he thought Lily Robbins needed to know.

When he didn't get a reply, he silently admitted that ultimatums might not be his best tactic with her. Okay, so it was time for Plan LMNOP.

"There's another way to look at all this," he said. "You've got ten thousand in cash, and I've got a car. With even a little imagination, we've got a first-class road trip here. Six hours, that's all I ask." He threw another quick glance in her direction, hoping for a better reaction, but she was looking at him like he was crazy.

"Albuquerque to Denver in six hours isn't a road trip," she said. "It's a suicide mission. I've driven it dozens of times, and it's nine hours, bare minimum."

Nine hours?

Only if you did it in reverse.

"In your truck, sure," he conceded. Hell, in her truck it could take two days to get to Denver. "But we're driving Charlotte."

"Your car has a name," she said deadpan, one of her eyebrows lifting upward.

"Charlotte the Harlot."

And that almost got a smile out of her—almost.

She glanced out the passenger-side window. "I don't really have a choice here, do I?"

"No." Not really.

"And you'll let me go? Once we get to Denver?"

"Once I know you're safe," he clarified. "SB303 works for the Department of Defense. There's a good possibility that I'll be turning you over to her, while I continue on with the bracelet alone. There are ways to neutralize its importance, once it's in the right hands. When it's no longer important, then you're no longer important." It was the best he could offer her.

"I—I killed a man this morning." She sounded suddenly weary, and he realized he liked her better angry.

"*We* killed a man this morning," he said, clarifying the facts for her again. "Self-defense, and yes, we won the gunfight. Thank you." He spun Charlotte's wheel, downshifting for the turn onto the interstate's northbound ramp.

There was more traffic heading north than he would have expected so early on a Saturday morning, but it was bound to thin out once they got out of Albuquerque, and that's all he wanted right now—out of Albuquerque.

"Where did you learn to shoot?" he asked. There hadn't been any luck involved. There was no luck in shooting, not even at four yards, not with the split-second precision with which she'd done it.

"My dad's a sheriff's deputy in Chouteau County, and I was the Montana Girls' State Champion in pistols for five years running."

A shooting champion? He'd be damned. He'd known her father was a deputy. The information had been in the file Alex had gone over with him. But nothing in the file had mentioned her being a state champion shooter.

Hell, a pistol champion, sheriff deputy's daughter riding shotgun in the passenger seat was probably exactly what Charlotte had always wanted, probably what she'd always needed.

Maybe it's what he'd been needing, too.

He'd sure as hell been needing something, but unless his luck had changed dramatically in the last three weeks, a gorgeous, dark-haired, blue-eyed sheriff deputy's daughter probably wasn't what he was going to get.

Well, hell, and wasn't that always the way of it.

"So what have we got here this morning?" he asked, hoping for that damn concession, something that said she didn't think he was an out-and-out scum-of-the-earth kind of guy. "A kidnapping and hostage delivery to representatives of the United States Department of Defense? Or a road trip?"

"Road trip," she said after a slight hesitation.

Good, he thought, great. He could work with that. Now all they had to do was keep the cops off their ass.

"SB303, can you give me radar detection?"

"Coming up. Check your screen on the lower left side. The megaphone icon will blink and you'll get an audio cue when you're in range of getting clocked."

Very cool.

"I think I'm falling in love with you." The girl was great.

"She's married," a man's voice came over the PC. There was no visual of the guy, but Zach didn't need a visual. The voice was enough, even after more than eight years, and the proprietary tone said it all. Dylan was married to

Little Miss Jailbait with the tattoo and the bustier.

Geezus. There had to be one helluva story behind that amazing piece of news. Dylan and a tattooed street girl? Married?

"You got lucky," he said, smiling in spite of all his damn aches and pains.

"See you in six" was all Dylan said.

Yeah, six.

Charlotte slid through the traffic, and when they hit the edge of town, Zach opened her up and let her run.

CHAPTER **TWELVE**

Saturday, 7:00 A.M.—Albuquerque, New Mexico

This was a sad sight.

A bleached-blond, punk-ass, steroid-abusing jerk-off cuffed to a chair.

Spencer stood in the doorway of room 276 of the Sunrise Motel and shook his head. Someone had gotten to Jason Schroder first. Someone was moving very quickly through this day, and Spencer wasn't buying for a second that it was the Albuquerque schoolteacher.

No, this sad sight was the work of the shooter.

There had definitely been a fight. Shards of glass littered the carpet, and the other chair in the room had been broken. Drawers had been pulled out of the dresser, and the lamp was on the floor, busted into pieces. There was a hole in the wall—he looked again—make that two holes, and the paper copy of a cheap-ass reprint of three ears of corn was in shreds on the floor, its metal frame twisted like a pretzel.

Jason Schroder certainly looked like hell, and Spencer couldn't imagine that the other guy didn't, too.

He took out his phone, took a picture of Schroder, and sent it to Mallory. Not even his girl could have done a better job of tying him up, and she was the flex-cuff queen.

Reaching under his suit jacket, he pulled the Recon Tanto out of its sheath. A pair of wire cutters would have been better for Schroder, but Spencer wasn't all that concerned about what was better for an idiot who had let himself be bound and gagged, and cuffed to a motel room chair.

However the fight had gone down, Schroder had lost, and Kendryk didn't pay losers.

Not very carefully, Spencer slid the seven-inch blade up under one of the flex cuffs holding the gag in Schroder's mouth. He drew blood, but that was the price to be paid, and Schroder was bleeding anyway. After he cut the cuff, Spencer used the tip of the blade to remove the gag from the man's mouth, then stepped back while the guy hacked, and coughed, and generally got his bearings back.

Spencer didn't bother to remove the other

restraints, the ones holding Schroder's ankles to the legs of the chair and holding his hands to the back of the chair. It was too convenient to leave them in place.

"Where's the bracelet?" he asked.

"Fuck you," Schroder said. "You cut me, you asshole. Who the fuck are you?"

Of course, Spencer thought.

"Spencer Bayonne," he said. "We were supposed to meet this morning for breakfast. You were going to brief me on Lily Robbins."

"Oh. Oh, yeah. Sure, man." Schroder lifted his head and nodded. "Bayonne. That's right."

"So where's the bracelet, Jason?"

"I—I don't know," the younger guy said. "We never found it. We thought we'd get it this morning, make things easier for you, but . . . but there was a guy with her, at her house, and he took us by surprise, and . . . and Paul's dead."

Spencer considered himself a student of human nature, a graduate student working on his third doctoral degree, and Schroder was lying. He knew, because given the same set of circumstances, he would have lied, too.

Dead partner, cops raining down like shit on Shinola, the woman gone, and no bracelet—it all looked so bad, Schroder probably figured he didn't have anything left to lose.

He was almost right.

"Who was the guy at her house? Was it the same guy who did this to you?"

"I don't know, man. The guy who jumped me could have been the same guy as at the house. Yeah, it was probably him, but it was dark this morning, and it was crazy with Paul getting his fucking head blown off, with that guy killing him like that, and...and he's gonna pay for that, the sonuvabitch. He's gonna pay. Banning isn't going to let that slide. No way, man."

Spencer was a betting man, and he was betting Thomas Banning and Jason Schroder were the least of the shooter's concerns, especially if he had the bracelet. Schroder had already proven to be less than a worthy adversary. Banning was big in Las Vegas, but if Schroder couldn't give him a name, Banning didn't have the resources to come up with one out of thin air.

Kendryk did.

"What did this man look like? What color was his hair? Is he tall, short? What? Is he fat, skinny? Help me out here, Jason, and maybe I can help you."

"You should cut me loose, man. That would help."

"Give me some answers I can use, and I'll see about cutting you loose."

"Shit." Schroder's chin dropped to his chest. *"Shit."*

Not an answer, not helpful, but resignation was definitely a step in the right direction.

"Did you see him, Jason? Or did you just faint and roll over when he busted in here?"

"Fuck you." Schroder jerked on his cuffs. "Fuck you, man. I almost broke his fucking head, and he was bleeding when he left here, man. Wherever he is, he's bleeding."

And you're handcuffed to a goddamn chair.

"So what does he look like?"

"Dark hair. Not fat. He was fast. He moved really fast. So did the girl."

"The girl was in here with him?"

"No. Just him."

"So when were they moving fast?" Spencer asked, curious.

"When they ran out of the house. I was shooting at them like crazy, but I don't think I got 'em."

Spencer had known some very sharp operators to come out of Las Vegas. Jason Schroder was not one of them. Possibly Paul Stark had been the senior member of this less than dynamic duo.

"You must have seen something else. What was it, Jason? What else did you see? Think about it. Help me out here."

The guy shook his head again, muttering something under his breath.

"What?" Spencer asked. "What was that you said?"

"I said he was an asshole." Schroder's chin came up, his resignation turning to belligerence. "I could see that, an asshole with a big fucking scar down the side of his face."

Now they were getting somewhere. Even Schroder seemed surprised by his statement.

"Yeah. He had a scar," the guy continued. "I saw it at that bitch's house, too, when I came out of the stairwell. The light was shining on them, where they were standing in the bathroom, and then I blasted them, but I missed, and then they were running. But Paul, man. Paul was dead. There was nothing left of his head. So I kept blasting, and blasting, and blasting, chasing that asshole out of the house. I chased them all the way, until they got in their car, and then I ran back into the house to . . . uh, get the bracelet, but I couldn't find it."

His words had "lie" written all over them, so much so, even Schroder didn't seem to be buying it.

"Yeah. It's the same guy who jumped me. That asshole at the house this morning. Same asshole with a scarred face. Guaranteed. We were just doing the job, man. We'd been to her house before, looking, thinking we could find it early for you," he continued, and Spencer let him rattle on. Maybe something would come out of it. "But there wasn't any macramé anywhere, not in the whole damn house, and I looked, man, I looked hard."

Spencer wondered if perhaps Banning had given out a few directives of his own, above and beyond what Kendryk's office had requested. Las Vegas mob bosses certainly knew what to do with a top-secret piece of international espionage. Unfortunately for Banning, Arthur Kendryk knew what to do with people who didn't follow orders.

"When you chased them out of the house this morning, what kind of car did they get into?"

"The *Bullitt* car, man." The poor slob's face actually brightened. "A Shelby, a '68, red, with white racing stripes. Man, you should have heard that baby. She had a set of pipes on her."

A solid fact complete with description was exactly the kind of thing Spencer was looking for, and his opinion of Jason Schroder went up a couple of notches, just not enough to save the guy.

"That's great, Jason. Really great." He was looking for a dark-haired man with a scarred face who drove a red 1968 Shelby Cobra

Mustang with white stripes. There couldn't be too many of those running around. "Now I just have one more question, and I'm going to keep asking it until I get the right answer. Okay?"

Schroder's expression instantly turned suspicious, then wary, then went beyond wariness. Rightly so. He had every reason to be afraid.

"I'm not answering any more questions until you get me out of this goddamn chair."

"Where is the bracelet, Jason?"

The younger guy put his head down and gave it a shake, the muscles in his face and across his shoulders tightening.

He knew he was going to get hit.

"Where is the bracelet, Jason?"

"I told you I don't know. We never found it. The bitch Robbins has it. She's probably wearing it. Yeah, that's it."

Possibly. But Spencer thought Jason had something more concrete to offer than a "probably." To test his theory, he raised his hand in a tight fist, locked his wrist, and using the leverage of his whole arm and his shoulder, backhanded the guy nearly into next week and laid open the cut he'd already made with his knife.

Blood poured down the side of Schroder's face.

"Where is the bracelet, Jason?"

It took two more question-and-answer periods before the guy broke.

"I had it, man," he sobbed. "I found it myself. She had a suitcase packed in her bedroom, and I figured she'd be taking her jewelry, and I was right, man. I was right. It was there, in one of those little bags. I took it and ran, man. I took it and ran." His shoulders shook during a brief pause in his rambling, and when he spoke again, his voice was weaker. "I had it made, man. I was gonna be rich."

A curious idea, Spencer thought.

"Do you know why the bracelet is important?" he asked.

"No. No." Schroder shook his head, spluttering the word through blood, saliva, and broken teeth. "But Banning wouldn't have sent me and Paul if it wasn't worth a lot of money. He loved Paul, man. Paul was like a brother to him, and that asshole is going to pay . . . he's going to pay."

"And where is the bracelet now, Jason? Do you still have it?"

The guy shook his head. "No. No. The asshole took it."

"Took it from you?"

"Yeah, I had it, but he was, uh, was going to shoot my dick off, jammed his gun right down on me, man. He meant it, too. I swear he did. I never seen anybody more serious in my life as that asshole."

"So you gave him the bracelet?"

"Yeah. Yeah, I did. You would have, too, man, if he'd had that .45 jammed up against your dick."

Spencer didn't let anything get jammed up against his dick unless it purred, and he'd lay odds his kitten was a helluva lot more dangerous than the shooter.

"Thanks, Jason. That's what I needed to know." He moved around to the back of the chair, the Recon Tanto still in his hand.

His killing strike was clean and swift and silent, a Wingate maneuver, with the knife blade sliding up under Schroder's skull and severing his brain stem. The guy immediately went limp. Spencer withdrew the blade and wiped it clean on Jason's shirt.

On his way out the door, he speed-dialed Mallory on his cell phone.

"Hey, Kitten. Two things. One, scramble a nine-one-one call into the police, let them know there's a dead body in room two seven six of the Sunset Motel, and tell them you saw a 1968 red Shelby Cobra Mustang leaving the scene."

The Albuquerque police could track down the car faster than he could.

"And two, make sure we're monitoring the local police band and the state troopers. Rig your system to cue on the car, and—"

"That's going to be three things, baby," her voice came over the phone, soft, and silky, and sultry. No one had a voice like Mallory Rush.

"Three." He grinned. "Call the car in to Weymouth and have somebody there track down all the red 1968 Fastback Shelby Cobra Mustangs with white racing stripes they can find registered in the States. I want names, addresses, and photos."

"That's a pretty tall order, Spence."

"Not as tall as you might think. I bet there were less than a thousand of them made. Didn't one of Kendryk's tech guys break into the New Jersey Motor Vehicle Department's computer system last year and get away with a couple hundred driver's licenses?"

"Yes. Rick Connelly is very skilled."

"Then get him on it. Have him start in New Mexico and work out to the bordering states. Everyone in Weymouth knows this job is at the top of Kendryk's priority list."

"Second to the top," Mallory countered.

Spencer stopped for a second and almost let out a sigh. She meant the damn girl. Kendryk was not thinking clearly when it came to Gillian Pentycote. He needed to walk away. Sure, she

was a strange bird, and as word of the two-
million-dollar bounty got around, it was going
to whet a lot of appetites. But Spencer's money
was on the girl this time. No matter how much
money Lord Weymouth promised, Spencer
didn't think it was possible for anyone to take
her alive.

Kendryk needed to walk away, or all he was
going to get was one dead girl.

Spencer remembered when Kendryk had
captured her. It had been on a hit in Amster-
dam. Gillian Pentycote had been after the same
man as Kendryk's assassination team. She'd
been wounded when she'd been brought to the
estate in Weymouth, and over the course of the
next month, as she'd healed, Sir Arthur had
fallen in love. It had been a disturbing thing to
witness, the stone-cold Lord Weymouth form-
ing an attachment to the only woman Spencer
had ever met who was as cold and ruthless as
Kendryk was himself. Over the next year, the two
of them had cooperated on a number of deals,
including the sale of a ton of Afghan opium
between a man in Uzbekistan and a buyer in
Marseilles. Spencer had brokered the transac-
tion. Then the woman had disappeared, and the
longer she'd been gone, the more desperate
Kendryk had become to find her.

He wanted her back—back in his control,

back in his life, and back in his bed, and for two million dollars, Lord Weymouth thought he could get her.

Spencer didn't, but he kept his opinion to himself, sharing it only with Mallory.

"The woman is personal," he said into his phone. "This is business."

"Top-priority personal business, that's what she is," Mallory said. "Kendryk didn't come to the U.S. to hold your hand while you got the bracelet for him. He came for the girl. If that bracelet doesn't show up, he'll find something else to bargain with for the gas leases. The information on the bracelet is timely and expedient, that's all. The girl is not expedient."

They'd had this argument half a dozen times since Kendryk had announced the two-million-dollar bounty a week ago, and expedient or not, the bracelet was worth five times what Kendryk was paying for the girl.

"I'd feel safer if he was back in England," Mallory continued. "His being here can only be trouble."

Spencer agreed, but he was working for Kendryk on this deal, not himself.

"Are you ready to scramble that call?" He could hear her fingernails tapping across her keyboard.

"Yes, Spence."

"I'll be there in one minute," he said, coming down the outside stairs of the Sunset. "You remember meeting the girl, right?"

"Yes, a strange bird," Mallory said, echoing his own sentiments.

"So how would you do it, Kitten?" he asked. "How would you go after her, if you wanted the two million?"

"I wouldn't go after her, Spence."

He was about to tell her just to think theoretically, but her next words proved her ahead of the game.

"I'd go after somebody she cared about."

With anyone else, Spencer would have wholeheartedly agreed. There were few quicker ways to bring someone to heel than to threaten the life of someone they loved. The trouble in this situation, as everyone else who came up with a similar plan would find out, was that Gillian "Red Dog" Pentycote didn't care about anyone else on the face of the earth. Her memories and her emotions had been wiped clean off her brain by the drugs she'd been given. It was what made her such a superlative operator. There were rumors of a lover, sure, but Spencer couldn't begin to count the number of lovers he'd seen sacrificed by countless agents, handlers, Mafia bosses, operators, thugs, warlords, and spooks on every continent, and on and on and on.

Sex, in and of itself, was not a tie that bound.

No, he thought. There was no way to bring her in alive. Kendryk wasn't buying anything with his two-million-dollar bounty except a one-way ticket home in a box for anybody who tried to collect it.

In contrast, all Spencer had to do to get the bracelet was track down one guy in a hot car who by seven o'clock this morning had already killed a man, kidnapped a woman, been in one helluva fight, and all around had one helluva start to his day. One guy who thought he was home free. One guy who thought he'd seen his enemy and vanquished the bastard.

Spencer didn't know who he was, but he knew that guy hadn't seen anything yet.

CHAPTER THIRTEEN

Saturday, 7:15 A.M.—Denver, Colorado

Dylan looked at the young man in his office, then shifted his gaze to the woman standing next to him. There was no doubting the family connection. If it weren't for the age difference, Red Dog and her brother could have almost passed for twins. They both had dark auburn hair, though Gabriel's leaned more toward brown than Red Dog's red, and they had the same expression around the eyes. The underlying bone structure of their faces was undeniably genetically similar. Gabriel Shore's mouth was wider, his eyebrows thicker, his jaw more squared than Gillian's feminine curve. His nose was bigger, wider across the bridge, but the resemblance was unmistakable.

It was easy to see that underneath his severe

black suit, plain white shirt, and narrow black
tie, his general musculature was far larger than
Red Dog's. The kid was definitely a male version of his operator. Gabriel's neck was thicker,
and he definitely had the height advantage—
but he did not have a clue about his sister.

"You have been temporarily assigned to SDF
at General Grant's request to do what?" Dylan
couldn't possibly have heard the boy right the
first time.

"To provide personal security for my sister."

That's what Dylan had thought he'd heard,
and nothing could have made less sense.

"A PSD, a personal security detail, for
Gillian?" For Red Dog?

"Yes, sir."

Amazing. The kid was standing right next to
her and must have noticed a few things, like she
was ripped, armed, and had a natural low level
of threat constantly emanating from her, a
threat Dylan guaranteed she could deliver on.
As under the radar as SDF kept, he knew people in their business were aware of his top-notch,
first-class female sniper. Grant got enough requests for her services to keep her busy twenty-
four/seven. Dylan made sure that didn't happen.
Despite her superior skills and lightning-quick
mind, she had her weaknesses, and he took
them very seriously, and very personally. He de-

manded she take downtime between missions, even on the short rotation he allowed, or he'd lose her. It was as simple as that.

"And what makes you and General Grant think she needs a bodyguard?" He hadn't made his report to Grant yet, and there was no way in hell for some kid working at the Commerce Department to have heard the information Dylan had been given two days ago in Japan. And yet Gabriel Shore had come halfway across the country in the middle of the night. Dylan didn't know what could have spooked him, but he knew nothing spooked Buck Grant.

"That information is classified, sir," the kid said, "and you have a couple of women in the main office, one I don't know, and one who is a reporter for *The Washington Post*."

Dylan leaned to one side, to see past the guy, and sure enough, Honey was still on the couch, reading the morning papers.

"Honey," he called out, and the small blonde looked up. "We're open for business."

He didn't need to say more. She immediately rose from the couch and headed for the elevator. Dylan could have told the young Mr. Shore that Honoria York had very recently returned from a mission for the State Department in El Salvador, carrying highly classified material, but like most things, those facts only concerned the people who were involved.

"The woman at the communications console is one of SDF's operators," he said, referring to Skeeter. "She's clear."

"Yes, sir, I recognized her. It's the other one I don't know. The one in the white dress."

That was Cherie, but Dylan couldn't exactly see her anywhere.

"I'll vouch for her as well," he assured the guy. "So tell me what brought you here."

In answer, the younger guy's gaze shifted to his sister, his reluctance to speak almost palpable.

Again, Dylan was amazed.

"I don't keep anything from her, Mr. Shore, ever." It was another way he protected her.

"Yes, sir, I understand," the guy said, but he didn't take his eyes off Gillian. If he was intimidated, he should have been. After another long second, he dropped his gaze and reached up to loosen his tie.

Dylan watched, intrigued, as the guy unbuttoned his collar button and then pulled a lanyard out from under his shirt and slipped it off over the top of his head. A flash drive dangled from the other end, a very unusual-looking flash drive.

"General Grant assured me that you had the appropriate hardware to download the files on this drive."

If he did, it was news to him. *Shit*.

"Is there a reason Grant didn't call and tell me about any of this?"

"Given my connection to Gillian, and that I was the one who created the files, he thought it safer to send the information by courier under the guise of a family visit. No one will question my being here."

Except me, Dylan thought.

"I thought you worked for the Commerce Department, Mr. Shore." He didn't bother to hide the deeper question implied in the statement.

"Yes, sir, I do. But I'm in the Marsh Annex, where General Grant's offices are, as you know."

Apparently, Dylan didn't know jack.

"And you're here to protect Gillian?"

"Yes, sir."

"With that?" He pointed at the flash drive, a small, multiported polyhedron studded with half a dozen USB-style connectors in a configuration Dylan hadn't seen anywhere, let alone in his own damn offices.

"Yes, sir, and I . . . uh, I brought my gun."

"Gun?" Well, that unnerved Dylan a bit.

Pencil pushers with guns were dangerous things. "Where is it?"

In answer, Gabriel's gaze slid to his sister—and thank God for that.

"A .40 caliber Beretta," she said. "I put it in the safe."

"Good." Dylan was succinct. Visitors did not bring firearms into his building. "Now give me the short version of what's on that drive, and we'll see where we go from here."

The kid nodded. "A businessman under the scrutiny of the Commerce Department, Sir Arthur Kendryk, who is the head of Kendryk Worldwide Enterprises, has offered a two-million-dollar bounty to anyone who can bring him Gillian alive. I entered that piece of data into the files myself shortly after midnight last night."

Well, that was definitely to the point, and exactly what Dylan had been told in Tokyo two days ago, and exactly what he'd told Gillian. Apparently, word of the bounty was spreading fast.

He glanced at his operator to get her reaction, and got just about what he would have guessed—a slight tightening of her mouth, a narrowing of her gaze, and a glint in her eye that said "Bring it on."

Fuck.

He'd planned on talking to her today, obviously the sooner the better, and he was going to have to sit the Angel Boy down and read them both the riot act. The rest of the team was going to have to be alerted as well. A threat to one of them was a threat to all of them. They worked together. There were no Lone Rangers at SDF—except him. He was the boss. It set him apart.

"How did you come across this information?" he asked, turning his attention back to Gabriel.

"I've been investigating Kendryk for the last year, and have developed a few assets who specifically report to me on his actions. Combining their intelligence with the data I receive from my more general contacts at various places around the globe enables me to positively confirm certain facts." The kid paused for a moment, and Dylan could almost feel the utter sincerity of his next statement building up inside him. Whatever came out of Gabriel Shore's mouth next, he wanted to be believed.

It was enough to unnerve Dylan all over again. He had never, not even at fifteen, been as young and earnest as the twenty-seven-year-old man in front of him—and he was not at all sure, even at the ripe old age of thirty-six, that he had the kind of contacts this kid was talking about.

Multiple assets tracking Kendryk and reporting to him? Global contacts, again in the multiple numbers? Who was this guy? And how many pencils was he pushing just to keep up with all his informants?

"Mr. Hart." Here it came, the utterly sincere revelation. "I can one hundred percent guarantee the validity of my information on the bounty. He is after her. He is ruthless, and he will not stop until he gets her, whatever the cost."

He was right. Dylan's informants in Japan had said exactly the same thing. But like the informants, Dylan knew Gabriel Shore had misinterpreted Kendryk's intent. Lord Weymouth was ruthless, true, but it wasn't murder he had in mind when it came to Gillian—quite the opposite.

He swore silently to himself. Murder was exactly what Travis James, the Angel Boy, would have in mind when he heard about the bounty. In his mind, Kendryk had taken advantage of Gillian in a way no man who loved her could tolerate, and Travis loved her.

Well, hell, this was a fine fucking tangle.

"And you came to offer yourself as her bodyguard? To protect her from anyone out to collect the bounty?"

"Yes, sir. I believe I'm the only one who can."

"Explain yourself." The kid looked physically

tougher than Dylan had expected, but nobody could look at Red Dog and think she couldn't take care of herself. She did it on a daily basis in places a helluva lot more dangerous than 738 Steele Street.

"The only way to neutralize Kendryk is to kill him or isolate him," Gabriel said.

Those were terms Dylan understood.

"An assassination is unlikely to be authorized in this instance, not without Kendryk posing a bigger, more violent threat to our national security, which I can assure you he is capable of doing. If it comes to that," Gabriel continued, "if he allies himself more clearly with terrorist elements, if he sells nuclear technology to our enemies, which is the biggest threat he currently poses, the solution would, of course, come under your jurisdiction before it came under mine." And that was a very unexpectedly calm and cool-headed summation of potential assassination from a pencil pusher. "Isolation, on the other hand, is something I believe I can create with the information I brought with me on the flash drive."

"How?"

The younger guy cleared his throat. "Historically, there are three ways to isolate a despot, which for the sake of this argument is an appropriate description of Arthur Kendryk.

Politically, financially, and physically. Financially, Kendryk has about ten percent of his working capital tied up in arbitrage right now. The current climate in currency is edging toward the kind of volatility that lends itself to unexpected outside influences. If he were to lose big on his next trades, it would create an opportunity for—"

Dylan leaned back against his desk and just let the kid run. He understood the theory of manipulating the markets, but Gillian's brother was talking about actually doing it, on a very large scale. By the time the guy got through with the other two parts of his three-part lecture on how to dismantle a billion-dollar worldwide conglomerate and throw the head guy in jail, Dylan was convinced—of everything, whatever the kid was selling.

"Well, Mr. Shore," he said when Gabriel was finished. "I—"

"Actually, it's Dr. Shore."

Of course it was.

"Economics?" Dylan asked.

"Yes, sir. Cornell, and I did my computer work at MIT, also on the doctoral level."

It took a lot to impress Dylan.

And he was impressed. The kid had packed a helluva lot of stuff into twenty-seven years. Two doctorates? Dylan was definitely impressed.

"Well, Dr. Shore, my question to you is why now? Putting a bounty on a Defense Department operative isn't enough to get this ball rolling. Not on a target the size of Arthur Kendryk."

"No, sir, it isn't. But we've been after Kendryk for a long time. Me, personally, for a year. The guy before me for over five years, trying to build a case. I found the key to doing that in the Gul Rashid/Uzbekistan Afghan opium deal you requested the files on five months ago." He paused, and Dylan felt another very important revelation coming, and he could pretty much guess what it was if it had come out of the Uzbekistan file. "I also found Gillian's name in that file."

Dylan nodded, glad the kid had gotten that weighty piece of information out of his system. It was a good thing the guy worked in an office in an annex somewhere. He wouldn't last an hour on the street.

"She was working for me in Uzbekistan, in all capacities of her involvement," he said, and it would take a Senate subcommittee to get more out of him than that.

"Yes, sir." The guy was visibly relieved, and Dylan wondered briefly if he ever played poker. He hoped not.

"The work she did in Uzbekistan couldn't be the key to isolating Kendryk," Dylan said. "Kendryk's ties to that deal were thinner than smoke."

"No, sir. The key is a man named Spencer Bayonne. You connected him to Kendryk, and I can lay half a dozen illegal arms deals in western Africa directly at Bayonne's feet."

Sometimes, every now and then, things just went a person's way. This was one of those times. General Grant had sent Dylan to London five months ago to investigate Kendryk, especially to investigate his involvement in the global arms trade. Grant had wanted facts he could take to the undersecretary of defense.

Gabriel Shore had just supplied them.

"Gillian?" He turned to his operator. "What do you know about Spencer Bayonne?"

"I met him a few times; very professional, very cool-headed. He has a solid reputation, well deserved."

In other words, he was dangerous.

He returned his attention to Gabriel. "I don't recall coming across anything that would connect Kendryk to a sale of nuclear technology." Dr. Shore was right. If they could tie Kendryk to nuclear espionage, the undersecretary of defense would have what he needed to go straight to the top, the very top. Kendryk would become an enemy of the state.

"That's a very recent development," Gabriel said. "Dr. Mila Yanukovich, one of Russia's and the world's leading nuclear scientists, has been secretly going in and out of Iran for the last two years. We have documented—or rather we *had* documented proof of her involvement in the Iranians' successful conversion of yellowcake into uranium hexafluoride gas, and in the sale of a dozen centrifuges for their underground enrichment plant in Natanz, south of Tehran. Unfortunately, the data was compromised. It disappeared in transit, and even though it was recovered, we don't know who all else might have it now."

"Wasn't it encrypted?"

"Yes, but the encryption key was also lost in transit, which has started a feeding frenzy. All the sharks are in the water on this, everybody putting their resources into finding it, including our government, the Russians, the Iranians, of course, and every major player in the international black market, including the Russian mob. The code is worth millions of dollars, but its real value is as a political bargaining chip. Whoever comes up with it and decodes the documents has the potential to reshape foreign

policy in half a dozen countries. And that is unacceptable. Our government *will* authorize assassination before it lets some thug dominate
any kind of political arena within our sphere of
influence."

Dylan took a moment to breathe, because
the kid hadn't.

"And you work for the Commerce Department?" he asked. Gabriel Shore did not sound
like any Commerce guy he'd ever met.

"Yes, sir, their Security Division in the Marsh
Annex."

Well, that had to be one helluva division over
there at the Marsh Annex. He needed to ask
General Grant what the hell went on next to his
office on the other side of the boiler room.

"And Kendryk is one of the sharks?"

"A great white." The kid's glance strayed back
to his sister. "And he's here. He entered the
country three days ago with Spencer Bayonne.
There's been a lot of activity up and down the
Potomac and into Virginia over the last few
days, a lot of those major players slipping into
the country. We at Marsh think the code is going to surface, and I think Kendryk is here to
claim it when it does."

"And Bayonne? What does he do?" Dylan
didn't look at Gillian, but he'd felt her reaction,
felt her kick everything up a notch. He'd never

asked her doctors over at Walter Reed, but he'd been wondering for a while if the drugs they'd both been given had created some sort of synergy between them. He couldn't read her mind or anything, but he could read her to a far greater extent than he could any of the guys, and they'd all been together for a very long time.

"Given the importance of the code, my guess is that Kendryk hired Bayonne specifically to retrieve it. You have to understand, a man like Kendryk has an intelligence-gathering system that exceeds most Third World countries' abilities, and in some areas, his network can almost rival our own."

"And where are Kendryk and Bayonne now?"

"New York."

"I think we need to take a look at your files," Dylan said. "Unfortunately, I don't think we've got a piece of hardware that can accommodate your—"

"Yes, we do," Gillian said, and Dylan gave her a curious glance, a damned curious glance.

"Good." *Jesus.* He always thought he should spend more time at the office, but he never did, and things happened here. Important things, and they happened a lot faster since Skeeter had taken over the place. "Then we'll—" He gestured to the main office, but Gillian interrupted again.

"It's not here, sir. It's at the Commerce City Garage, one floor up from my place."

"Why?" he asked. Weapons, languages, tactics—those were Red Dog's areas of expertise, not computer systems.

"Hacker International took over the third floor a couple of months ago. I think you were in Singapore at the time. Cherie and Danny are working out of there, until they can get into their new office space," she said. "Hopefully, next week."

"And she's got what we need?"

"Yes, sir."

And that made perfect sense. Computers were the forte of the Bitch Musketeers, and anything advanced enough to hold Gabriel Shore's attention was guaranteed to hold Hacker's.

"You're storing a Marsh Annex DREAGAR 454 Subliminal Neuron Intel Interface in a garage?" Dr. Shore looked highly skeptical and more than a little appalled.

Kids these days, Dylan thought, and their damn Subliminal Neuron Intel Interfacers. *Jesus*. The flash drive was hanging back around Dr. Shore's neck and looked like something he could have gotten out of a cereal box.

"It's a very secure installation, Dr. Shore. The

Commerce City Garage is our version of an annex," he said, which seemed to appease the guy.

"Then we can download there and send the files over a secure line to you here at Steele Street."

Dylan liked people who could think on their feet. They only needed one more ingredient to make the plan work.

Walking over to his door, he yelled out into the office. "Hacker! Get your butt in here."

Cherie had drifted off.

She'd finished her cigarette under her desk, gotten back in her chair to think about the best way to approach Dylan—and she'd drifted into dreamland, where there was this guy who looked like Henry Stiner, surfing on the ocean, and her on the beach, waving at him, but he never got any closer. He just kept surfing, out on the ocean, and never came in to the shore, and then he yelled at her.

"Hacker!"

Her eyes came open, and for a moment, she was disorientated.

"Get your butt in here."

That was not Henry Stiner. That was Dylan Hart, and he wanted her butt in the lair. She was not in Cabo San Lucas, standing on a beach. She was at Steele Street.

She blinked behind her sunglasses and carefully lifted her feet off the windowsill and put them solidly on the floor.

"Have you been smoking in my office?" he yelled again.

"No, sir." She took a breath. Champagne, all-nighter, too many cigarettes, not much food, less sleep, about—she glanced at her desk clock. Oh, she'd nodded off for about fifteen minutes, just enough to really screw her up.

And the boss was yelling at her.

She took a breath, and then another, and gave herself a small shake to make sure she was awake, before she rose to her feet. She couldn't possibly be in trouble. She'd just saved everybody's ass by getting the Bazo up and running.

Yawning, she crossed the main office and headed into Dylan's private office. She was still yawning when she passed through the door. This was torture. Dylan only had one chair in his office, and it was his.

"Hey, Gill-ian," she said through her yawn, noticing her friend standing next to Dylan.

So this was going to be a meeting, she thought. Well, they were going to have to move it to the main office, because no way was she going to stand there, swaying on her feet, teetering on her heels, and hanging by a thread while Dylan went on about whatever. She started to tell him, but he spoke first.

"Hacker." He gestured to his left, and Cherie's gaze followed—and froze, her pulse taking a sudden leap, her attention riveted by an exquisitely delicate piece of electronic gear hanging by a black lanyard against a backdrop of starched white cotton.

"A Marsh Annex DREAGAR 454 Subliminal Neuron Intel Interface." She breathed the words, transfixed by its multifaceted shell and microscopically applied metallic fluoride coating. The small polyhedron caught the light with every breath its owner took, glinting purple and blue and yellow.

"Exactly."

Dylan sounded so far away.

"Cherie," Gillian said off to her left. "If you'll lift your gaze about eighteen inches, I'd like to introduce you to my brother Gabriel."

That's right. Gillian's brother was visiting this morning, the pencil-pushing geekazoid from Washington, D.C. She lifted her gaze the proscribed eighteen inches—and her pulse took another, much more erratic leap.

Gabriel, an auburn-haired Archangel with his very own DREAGAR 454, who dressed like the Men in Black. He looked like Red Dog, except bigger, with more angles than curves, higher cheekbones, a narrower gaze, and the hint of a dimple. His hair stood a little on end, as if he'd dragged his hands through it a few times on the flight to Denver. His tie was loose, one of his shirt buttons undone, and he was cute, very cute, startlingly so for a geek.

"Cherie," she said, holding her hand out. "Hacker."

"Gabriel," he replied, taking her hand. "Shore."

"That's a DREAGAR 454 flash drive." She shook his hand.

"Yes."

"From the Marsh Annex."

"Yes."

"I was there in April, a couple of months ago," she said.

"I didn't see you."

"Rhonda Blake showed me around, at General Grant's request." His grip on her was very solid, and warm, and they were still shaking hands.

"Oh, you're the . . . uh . . . the, uh—"

"The CEO of Hacker International. We're going to be supplying your 2Z8s for the DREAGAR."

"The, uh, girl with the shoes."

Cherie smiled, surprised and delighted by the designation. "Yes."

"Rhonda really liked your shoes." He was still shaking her hand.

"My Michel-Leon's."

"She said they were orange."

"Persimmon."

"High heels with shoestrings."

"Silver braided rope."

"And clunky heels."

"Patent leather stacks."

"And, uh, holes in the sides."

"Teardrop cut-outs."

"Yeah," he said, a shy smile curving his mouth. "That's what she said."

Cherie couldn't stop shaking his hand, and she couldn't stop smiling, and yet everything was shifting inside her, like psychic tectonic plates. She could see big chunks of her life sliding about, making room, and he was smiling, too, and still shaking her hand, and he was so incredibly damn cute, and he was Red Dog's little brother.

From where he stood next to the two of them, Dylan checked his watch, wanting to record for posterity the moment he'd first seen the opening moves of the genius-level computer geeks' mating ritual.

It was an awkward thing, with a lot of hand-shaking involved, and it explained why there weren't more genius-level computer geeks to go around. With an opener like the one he was observing, he couldn't imagine that they got to the reproductive stage of the game all that often.

He glanced at Gillian, who cocked an eyebrow in his direction. Yeah, she was thinking the same thing.

"Well," he said, "with the introductions out of the way, may we continue here."

Two people turned their heads to look at him, but curiously, they did not let go of each other's hands.

"Hacker, I need you to take Dr. Shore to Commerce City and give him complete access to whatever it is you've got in the garage as it pertains to the DREAGAR 454."

He didn't get any response, and for a moment he wondered if she'd been mesmerized by Dr. Shore, or if she'd fallen back asleep behind her sunglasses.

"You mean my DREAGAR 454 hard drive?" she finally said.

Yes, he supposed that was what he meant, unless she had a DREAGAR 454 ice-cream machine, or a DREAGAR 454 boom box she was keeping up in Commerce City.

"Yes," he said.

"Uh...yes, sir," she said. "I'll be...uh, happy to do that."

Good. He liked his people happy, even if they didn't have any more sense than to stay out all night. He shifted his attention to Gillian's brother.

"Dr. Shore, while you are in Denver, you are under my command. I want that clear before this goes any further." If he'd been assigned to SDF, however temporarily, then he belonged to Dylan for the duration.

"Yes, sir," Gabriel said—and he was still holding on to Cherie's hand.

Dylan liked the kid. He liked him a lot—just not as much as Hacker, who either didn't mind or hadn't noticed that she and Red Dog's little brother were doing some kind of hand meld.

This, Dylan decided, could easily turn out to be a very long day. He had the whole thing with Zach, and the CIA, and Albuquerque going, and no clue, really, what it was all about—a condition he wasn't going to allow to continue past the next few minutes. And now this whole Kendryk and the DREAGAR 454 situation had landed in his lap.

"Gillian, make sure he has his gun before he leaves."

Red Dog nodded. "Would you like me to go with them?"

"No," he said. "I need you here when the team calls. You helped plan the mission. They're going to want to talk to you."

"Yes, sir."

"Hacker, how long is it going to take you to set up a secure link and download the files off Dr. Shore's flash drive back to me?" he asked.

"Download?"

"Yes." Isn't that what she did all day long? Download stuff?

"An hour, maybe . . . uh, two, or longer, boss," she said. "I'll have a better idea once I get there. Maybe Dr. Shore should stay here with you, and I'll just run up to Commerce City with the DREAGAR flash drive myself."

An hour, or two, or longer? That seemed a little vague for someone who had just jerked the Bazo into shape in record time. But she really was the expert in the room—along with Dr. Shore, of course, who gave her a curious look, very curious considering that he was still holding her hand.

"The DREAGAR 454 Subliminal Neuron Intel Interfacer doesn't go anywhere without me," the young doctor said.

Yes. This was definitely going to be a long day.

"I agree," he said. "Dr. Shore keeps his flash drive, and maybe he can speed up the downloading process. Then as soon as you're back,

Dr. Shore and I will go over the information."
And figure out what in the hell to do with it.

"Yes, sir," Cherie said.

And where in the hell was Hawkins when he most needed his second in command?

Disneyland.

Unfuckingbelievable.

There wasn't going to be enough coffee to get him through this day.

"Uh, Dylan." Cherie spoke up again. "I got dropped off by limo this morning. We're going to need a car."

Oh, God.

"And I suppose you'll want—"

"Roxanne."

Roxanne, Superman's ride, a 1971 Dodge Challenger R/T in Sublime Green. Cherie loved the beast. She swore it brought out the highlights in her strawberry blond hair. Hawkins thought Roxanne was trying, so help her God, to bring out Cherie's inner NASCAR, so he'd taught her how to drive, but Dylan had ridden with her once, and once had been enough. He wondered how high Gabriel Shore's Thrill-O-Meter went, because he could guarantee Cherie was going to redline it.

"Roxanne," he agreed. "She's down on the third floor. Gillian"—he turned back to Red

Dog—"get them what they need and see them out."

He watched the three of them get on the elevator, and then turned back to his desk. He needed to call the general and find out how Grant wanted them to proceed on this. Gabriel Shore's three-point plan, brilliant as it was, was a year-long project, minimum. The bounty on Gillian was an immediate threat. Two million dollars took his shadow warrior and put her directly in the spotlight, the last place any of them wanted to be.

"Dylan," Skeeter called out to him from the main office. "This just came in. Listen. I'll run it back for you." She turned up the volume on her console, and a dispatcher's voice came over the speakers.

"All cars prepare to copy information on a BOLO out of Albuquerque. A 1968 Shelby Cobra Fastback Mustang, red with white racing stripes: Be advised this car has twice been seen leaving a crime scene this morning, a fatal shooting on Somerset Street and a knife killing at the Sunset Motel on Santa Ana Drive. Proceed with caution."

Fuck.

"Call him—"

"And tell him to get his butt off the interstate," Skeeter finished his sentence, her fingers already flying over her board.

"And call—"

"Alex Maier. Tell him what's happened. He's either got to let us in on this, or—"

"Run interference with the New Mexico cops."

Their eyes met across the length of the two offices.

"Are you sure about him, Dylan?" she asked. "Two bodies in a couple of hours. I don't know. If we're going to go out on a limb . . ." She let the question hang in the air.

"I'm sure." He hadn't seen Zach in over eight years, hadn't spoken to him, but he knew who he was dealing with, and not because they'd worked the chop shop together. Those years were far behind them. People changed.

But Rydell had been damned impressed with Alejandro Campos, with the operation he'd run down in El Salvador, with the way he'd dealt with the situation. Dylan had heard the same from others over the years, and he'd always been damned impressed with C. Smith Rydell. They were all on the same team, no matter how many years had passed between them.

If he was wrong, if Zach had cut himself loose and crossed the line, then he'd be dealt with like anyone else who went rogue. And if Dylan was tagged for the job, he wouldn't hesitate.

"Make the calls, Skeeter. Let's do everything we can to get him back to Denver."

CHAPTER FOURTEEN

Saturday, 8:00 A.M.—north of Albuquerque, New Mexico

Heat wave—Lily felt it building into the day, the wind blowing against her cheeks hot even at a hundred and twenty miles per hour.

Not Charlotte's top speed, Zach had said. The Shelby's top speed was over a hundred and thirty.

Zach, not Alejandro Campos. No last name had been forthcoming with the silent admission. So here she was, all but flying down two lanes of asphalt heading north, white stripes blurring, mirage beginning to rise on the horizon, sitting next to a stranger who oddly felt like so much more—and yet she felt so alone.

She tightened her arms around herself, taking little comfort in the Shelby's three-point seat belt system and the roll bar welded inside the car's frame. It wasn't a concourse car. The Cobra GT500KR was meant to be driven. It had been engineered, and designed, and built to be driven like a bat out of hell, and that's exactly what he was doing. But the fear of dying in a flaming ball of crashed Mustang metal wasn't what was eating at her. One thing Zach knew how to do was drive. Considering the sheer amount of pure American muscle under his control, he was amazingly smooth in all his actions. He'd coaxed the Cobra pony up through her gears, and done it in seconds. He didn't jam and jerk. He slid the shifter. He didn't stomp the pedals. He pressed them.

"Are you doing okay?" he asked, surprising her. At a hundred and twenty miles per hour, regardless of his skills, she thought it might be better if he kept his attention on the highway.

"Fine," she lied. "Just a little hot." Charlotte didn't have air-conditioning. What she had was horses and torque, pure power. Lily felt it in every square inch of her body, the roar in her ears, the rumble shimmying through the chassis and up into her veins.

"There's a bottle of water in my gun bag," he said. "You're welcome to it, and as soon as we can stop, we'll get a few supplies."

He was right. Water could only help. She had a little edge of panic working on her, and she really, really needed not to go there. She needed to take back some control, and she couldn't do it if she started crying.

So no tears, she told herself.

Take hold.

Buck up.

Drink water.

She unhooked her seat belt and leaned into the backseat. She found the bottle without any problem. It was shoved in an outside pocket.

"Lemon-flavored Perrier?" He had to be kidding. Lemon-flavored Perrier was his idea of a bottle of water?

"Yeah. We'll just have to make do, until we can stop."

"No Gatorade?"

"No," he said. "I'm not a big sports-drink aficionado."

She wouldn't admit it for the world, but she was a real connoisseur of sugared electrolytes. She knew them all by brand name and flavor. But sure, she could make do with his ritzy water.

His gun bag was unzipped, and while she was stretched out into the backseat, she went ahead and took a quick look inside. It didn't take more than that for her to find her pistol, for all the good it did her.

"Are you going to give me my magazine back?"

She'd watched him drop it into his pocket when he'd disarmed her. It was an eight-shot magazine, and she'd had her pistol loaded eight plus one. But she'd used the cartridge in the chamber.

And that's what was eating at her, that's what was making her skin hot, not the wind, not being thirsty or dehydrated, but killing the guy with the ponytail. His partner had a name now, Schroder, and somehow that made the dead man all that much more real, made what had happened all so much worse. She kept seeing him, the impact of her bullet into center mass, the explosion of Zach's bullet into his face.

"No," he said. "Not until we get everything sorted out in Denver."

"Sorted out?" she asked, easing herself back into the passenger seat, hating that her voice sounded so damn tremulous.

After buckling up, she clutched the water bottle to her chest and gave the lid a twist.

"What do you mean? What sorting out?" She really wanted to know, because she felt very shaky about all the things she didn't have sorted out this morning, which was everything.

"You'll be safe in Denver, but I'm not sure how long you'll be there. It could be we'll have to move you someplace else."

That sounded ominous, and with her fingers

still on the lid, she started to tremble above and beyond what the Shelby was making her do.

"What do you mean? Move me where, and why? Why can't I just go home?" Oh, God, was she whining? Whining was panic's kissing cousin.

"You've got a house full of cops right now, and that's not going to change for a while, and as it stands, we don't have a whole lot we can tell them."

"I meant *home*." Her real home, not the house where she'd been living alone for the last year, since she and Tom had split the sheets. "To the Cross, to my dad's ranch."

"Yeah," he said thoughtfully. "After you've been debriefed, that might work. It's a better idea than Albuquerque. I'll suggest it."

Suggest it? To who the hell whom?

"Someone else is in charge here that I don't know about?" If so, she wanted a name. Now. Who in the world was going to make the decision, if it wasn't him? Not the girl in the computer. They'd just met. Was it Scorpion Fire? And what the hell kind of name was that? Or was it the "see you in six" guy? Or were those two the same person? Hell, she'd be more than happy to make the decision, if she could manage to escape without getting herself killed— and if he wouldn't track her down.

The thought sent another chill through her body. She had a feeling he was very good at tracking people down.

"My boss," he said.

"Your government boss." She didn't really believe him about working for the government. Government guys didn't drive 1968 Shelby Cobra Mustangs. They didn't race around with guns breaking into houses in the nick of time. They didn't kidnap women and handcuff them to cars, and they didn't set themselves up as cocaine kingpins in El Salvador.

That last thought gave her pause, because, actually, she could think of one kind of government employee who would set himself up as a cocaine kingpin and have information sent to someone called Scorpion Fire.

She gave Zach another, more careful look. He'd cut his hair since she'd seen him last. He'd worn it tied back in a sleek ponytail in El Salvador, but now it was short, almost severe, still the same silky black, but cropped close. It made him look very dangerous, a promise echoed in his eyes. They were the color of a cold sea—pack ice in green. His face was exactly the same as she remembered, and she seemed to have it chiseled in her memory banks—the underlying elegance of his bone structure, straight dark eyebrows, and a narrow nose leading to a firm mouth. And then there was the scar, a long-healed line of white tracing his hairline down the left side of his face. The story behind it had to be ugly.

He went by a different name in the States, and of all the damn things in the world to get killed over, the guy with the gray ponytail had chosen a nondescript macramé bracelet, a bracelet Zach had come thousands of miles to get from her.

If she put her mind to it, she could think of a lot of things that could fit in a macramé bracelet, the most obvious being information. Maybe it was knotted in Morse code.

"I know how it looks, Lily," he said, "but I'm doing my best to get you out of the middle of this situation. The pilot put you here, not me, but in his place, I would have done the same thing."

She didn't doubt it. The problem was, up until this exact moment, she hadn't had a clue what "situation" she was in the middle of, or what situation the pilot had been in, other than they'd both proved extremely dangerous.

But she'd just gotten her first inkling. Zach was right. This was about the pilot, who had been dragged into the church by guerrilla soldiers of the *Cuerpo Nacional de Libertad*, a rebel group fighting the Salvadoran government in northern El Salvador. This wasn't about drugs. Zach had said as much. This was about information coded into a nondescript, therefore easily hidden, bracelet that the pilot had not wanted to fall into the guerrillas' hands—so he'd given it to her.

This was about politics.

And political players with multiple names, who lived well in foreign countries, running drugs, and who owned hot cars in the States with absolute cutting-edge technology sliding in and out of their eight-track tape decks, only brought one thing to mind.

He was a spy.

And, oh, God, she didn't exactly find that comforting either.

"So you . . . uh, did get the bracelet back from Schroder? Right? I mean, you did tell the girl—SB303—to tell Scorpion Fire you had it." She wanted to look at it again, see what she'd missed. She'd had it in her keeping for three weeks, but she hadn't had a reason to examine it, until now.

He shot her a curious look across the interior of the car.

"Don't get all excited," she said. "SB303 gave you Schroder's name, and trust me, I'm paying attention. In my situation, you'd do the same thing. There's a dead guy in my house, and God only knows what you did to convince Schroder to give up that damn piece of macramé, and now we're hauling ass to the border, trying to elude the police, who I have *always* thought of as the people to go find when there's trouble, and it's hot, and those two guys tried to kill me this morning, and...and..." She gave it up, her words trailing off into a pool of silence marked only by the white stripes slipping away under Charlotte's wheels.

Damn him. She was on the verge of an epiphany or a nervous breakdown, and she was going to hate him if the damn breakdown won out.

Six hours to Denver. He was crazy, and what was worse, he was right. At the speed they were going, they could get to Denver by lunchtime. She hoped to hell she made it, hoped to God her nerves lasted that long. They were unraveling one by one and simply letting go, bringing her closer to tears, and she wasn't sure how much longer she could—

"Let me tell you something about that dead guy," he said, drawing her attention back to him and away from her tears.

She took a steadying breath. Good. She was listening.

"But you need to drink your water first," he said, gesturing to the bottle she still had a death

grip on in her hand. "Before you faint or something, and then, after you've had something to
drink, I'll tell you about that guy."

"S-so you did know him?" She finished
screwing the lid off the bottle and brought it to
her lips. The water was warm, but drinking it
gave her something physical to concentrate on
besides her fraying nerves.

"No, not him in particular." He gave his head
a small shake. "But I've known hundreds of
guys like him, and they are all bad. They've got
bad histories, and bad presents, and bad fu-
tures, every one of them. Ninety-nine percent
have juvenile records. They graduate up into
felonies, working for some street boss somewhere, or they go straight to the mob. Murder is
part of their resume, along with extortion, kidnapping, assault of every kind you can imagine
and a few hundred you can't. If they're out of
Las Vegas, they're into prostitution. They're
mean. They have mean jobs, and they live mean
lives, and I can A-one guarantee you that if you
had not had the skills and the mind-set to pull
the trigger in the situation you found yourself
in this morning, you would be dead. If your father is the one who taught you to protect yourself, whatever it takes, and how to do it, then
you owe him a thank-you letter."

Even as shaky as she was feeling, she knew

all that, and her dad was going to hear about it, almost everything about it, and she could pretty much A-1 guarantee she'd be lucky to ever set foot off the ranch again for the rest of her life.

That had been another of Tom's big beefs with her father, that her dad had not wanted her to move to New Mexico. She was a Montana girl, Deputy Robbins had said, and Montana girls belonged in Montana, close to their dads, and not hell-and-gone to Albuquerque with some damn foreigner they'd met at a college fraternity party.

Her father had been right. She'd been a fool to marry Tomaso Bersani, with his exotic accent, and his exotic looks, and his exotic morals.

And here she was, getting ready to be a fool all over again.

She took another slow sip before lowering the bottle. "Why do you know so many bad guys like Schroder and his partner? Because of your drug business?"

He made a small, noncommittal movement with his hand. "I do all kinds of business, and part of any of my businesses is to know guys like them, and all over the world, those guys are the same, whether they're Asian, Latino, or straight out of Iowa. Honestly, I've known some pretty cruel bastards to come out of Iowa."

"Is it your business to be mysterious?"

He let out a short, humorless laugh. "Yeah, I guess you could say that." He laughed again and slowly shook his head. "Yes. You could definitely say that."

He reached out for the bottle, and she gave it to him, and after taking a long drink, he gave it back.

"I'm going to get you to Denver, Lily, take you to a place where you'll be safe. It shouldn't take more than a couple of weeks for word to get out that the bracelet is no longer of any value, that it's been neutralized. At that point, all the guys like Schroder and his dead partner, they all move on to the next big score, and the name Lily Robbins stops meaning anything."

"And what do you do, while I'm busy being safe in Denver, waiting to become blessedly anonymous again?" She really wanted to know.

"I do what I do best. Disappear."

"Back to El Salvador?"

"No." He shook his head again.

Lily took another slow swallow of water from the bottle, watching him. She'd seen how he lived in El Salvador, like a prince, with an elaborate villa, and dozens of servants and soldiers at his beck and call. He'd had a coffee factory, where he'd roasted and packaged his own special brand, AC-130. He'd brought her home on a private jet.

Nobody built themselves a life like that and walked away.

"You really aren't Alejandro Campos, are you?"

His answer was no answer. He just kept driving.

"So who's living in the villa now? And how did you get replaced? Bloodless coup?"

He shot a quick glance in her direction. "What makes you think I got replaced?"

"The setup down there is too sweet to let it go to waste. If it wasn't really yours, whoever it does belong to would replace you just to keep the whole place up and running—the villa, and the fields, and the coffee factory—not to mention that whatever you are today, three weeks ago you were the biggest drug dealer in Morazán Province. They wouldn't want to lose all that."

"Jesus." He swore under his breath, way under, but she heard him.

"You're thinking too hard over there, and you're going to get yourself in trouble," he said after a while.

"We already had that conversation, and honestly, do you really think I can be in more trouble than I already am?"

"Oh, hell, yeah," he said, keeping his attention on the road. "We aren't out of this yet, babe. Not by a long shot."

She almost smiled. She almost felt better,

even though she didn't know what disturbed her more, that they weren't "out of it yet," even at a hundred and twenty miles an hour on their way to Denver with the bracelet in hand, or how much she liked having him call her babe.

"DEA?" she asked after a few minutes of silence.

"Excuse me?" he asked, giving her a quick glance.

"DEA," she repeated. "The Drug Enforcement Agency." That's what made the most sense to her. The DEA probably had agents set up all over Central and South America, monitoring the drug trade, even facilitating it in undercover operations in order to take out the bigger dealers. His profile would fit the DEA.

But he neither confirmed nor denied her assertion.

"FBI?" That one seemed like a longer shot to her. Her dad, though, had once been assigned to an international case originating in Canada, and he was just a Chouteau County sheriff's deputy.

She took Zach's silence as a denial.

All right. There were a dozen more U.S. government agencies with reasons to be involved in Central American drugs and politics, but there was only one with a rich and checkered history running the length of the whole isthmus, one whose undercover, nonuniformed pilots could conceivably be carrying the fate of the free world in a piece of hemp macramé.

"CIA?"

He shifted slightly in his seat, and she figured she had a done deal.

How awful. The CIA. Everybody knew those guys were barely human. They lived shadowy lives, full of secrets they only revealed to each other, and only rarely were the details of their deeds exposed to a larger world.

She knew about one small but vital deed of his, though. She knew how close her life had come to being a nightmare in El Salvador, and she knew he was the only thing that had stood between her and the very real threat of degradation and death she'd faced. The morning the rebel soldiers had shown up at the villa, their captain had demanded that she be turned over, released into his custody so that she could be brought to justice, his justice.

She'd seen the captain's justice, in the church's chapel where he'd shot and killed one of his own soldiers, and she'd seen it when he'd stripped and beaten one of the nuns and chopped off her hair.

Alejandro Campos—Zach—had said no to the demand, flatly, succinctly. The deal he was negotiating with the rebel leader would be done without her involved, or it would not be done at all. Her life was not for sale.

It was one of his finer moments, she'd been told by his cook Isidora, who'd heard it straight from his manservant Max, who had beamed with pride to tell the tale. Isidora had been beaming as well, so proud of her *patrón*.

And because of that one fine moment, he'd created the opportunity for another this morning, and now he'd saved her life twice.

CHAPTER FIFTEEN

CIA?

Now where had she gotten the idea he was with the CIA? Zach wondered. Nobody outside of a very tightly monitored and controlled group of people knew he existed, let alone was with the CIA, and most of them worked for the CIA.

She did not.

At least he didn't think she did. Was it possible she could be somebody's deep-cover asset? Somebody buried on some other agent's payola roll? Somebody who maybe had been planted in El Salvador to watch him? Or it could be some kind of double-agent asset scheme, where Kesselring's other interested parties had planted her with the nuns to watch the rebels and make sure Devlin's plane went down and the information he'd been carrying—okay, that was getting a little complicated even for him, especially since she'd actually gotten the damn information Devlin had been carrying and apparently hadn't had a clue of what to do with it.

Or so it seemed.

Fuck. Blood loss was always mildly paranoia-inducing for him, and even though he'd finally stopped bleeding, his shoulder was messed up from his little run-ins this morning. But paranoia didn't explain away the very real fact of the ten thousand dollars in her suitcase, or the damn plane ticket to Tahiti, which all led him to the question—"Who was out to get his ass this week?"

Well, hell. That list went on forever, every week, and every week it changed.

Geezus. Was he getting taken for a ride here?

CIA. CIA. Maybe the question he should be asking himself was—"Who was out to get Alex's ass this week?"

He'd read Le Carré. Hell, he lived Le Carré. Everybody in his business did, and people got set up and whacked every day.

"You're thinking too hard over there," she said. "And you're going to get yourself in trouble."

Oh, she was sweet, all right, throwing his words back at him, and he couldn't help it—he grinned. The CIA—at least she had him on the side of the good guys.

"Here," she said, handing him the bottle of Perrier. "Have a drink, before you faint or something."

And at that, he laughed out loud.

"You have a smart mouth, Ms. Robbins." Smart and probably sweeter than hell, which was a whole other problem he had with her— she smelled good. He'd gotten close enough to her a few times this morning to know it for a fact.

Jewel had told him something a long time ago, something she'd read about men thinking about sex once a minute, and he figured he was right on track, or maybe even a little ahead of the game when it came to Lily Robbins. He'd been thinking about having sex with her since the night she'd shown up soaking wet and scared at his villa in El Salvador. She didn't even need to be in the same country for him to be thinking about her naked and willing and wanting him, and here she was in the same car, giving him attitude and making him want her all that much more.

If it was a test, he was planning on failing.

He took the bottle from her, and the computer rolled out of the tape deck.

More good news, he hoped. The girl had done great so far.

"Ensign." Her face washed onto the screen in a stream of pixels.

"SB303."

"You've come up on a statewide BOLO out of Albuquerque. New Mexico police and state troopers are looking for you in connection with two incidents that happened this morning. One at Lily Robbins's house on Somerset Street, a fatal shooting. The other a knife killing at the Sunset Motel. We're recommending that you get off the interstate, unless you want to answer a lot of questions."

A knife? Zach thought. He hadn't used a knife on Schroder.

"You're two miles from Exit 392, which we are highly recommending," SB303 continued. "Take it and head northeast. There are a few small towns and a lot of empty spaces in that direction where you could hole up for the day. I'm mapping routes out of the area and into Colorado for a suggested midnight run."

Yeah, making the run to Denver after dark off the beaten track was by far the better option under the current circumstances.

"Do you have a name for the vic at the Sunset Motel?" Jason Schroder had been very much alive and in reasonably good shape when he'd left him. It was a long shot, but maybe SB303 was referring to someone besides Schroder, to another incident entirely.

One could only hope.

It would make his life so much easier.

"Jason Schroder," SB303 said, and his heart sank a bit in his chest. *Fuck*. What in the hell had happened after he'd left the jerk tied to a chair?

"He was alive when I left him. He should have lived for another forty years."

"Then we have a bigger problem."

No shit.

"Have you contacted Scorpion Fire?" he asked.

"Yes, and for unnamed reasons, he prefers for the primary operation to remain clandestine."

Alex didn't have to name any reasons, and SB303 knew it as well as he did. Alex didn't explain his actions to anyone who wasn't in his direct reporting chain, and he sure as hell didn't expect to be put in a position where he had to explain the actions of one of his agents to a local police department. The CIA was involved in a lot of operations inside and outside of the United States, and they seldom invited peripheral involvement in any of them. Very seldom.

Alex wanted the bracelet, and he expected Zach to get it without anyone who hadn't been in that morgue in Langley knowing what he was doing. It was a compartmented operation. His case officer would expect it to stay that way.

Well, with two dead bodies and a description of his car floating through the New Mexican airwaves, Zach would say it was getting a little late for clandestine—but he got the drift of the message, and he wasn't surprised. Alex had made the Company's priorities clear. Zach was on a salvage mission as much as an information retrieval mission. His primary mission order had been very specific—keep our ass out of a sling and get the bracelet.

He had the bracelet part of the mission accomplished, but the ass-in-the-sling thing wasn't looking too good. He didn't think there was any way to lay two dead bodies on the State Department, despite how much Alex would love it, and he was disinclined to lay them at SDF's feet, despite Alex's directive—and he sure as hell wasn't going to take the fall for them alone against a bunch of New Mexico cops. Luckily, with the bracelet in his possession, Alex shouldn't have any trouble throwing federal weight around in New Mexico and clearing up any problems the Albuquerque law enforcement community had with two dead bodies of known criminals trying to sell the nation's top-secret data to foreign interests. But that job would definitely be easier if Zach remained a complete unknown. Give the cops a murder and a suspect, and they inevitably got damned possessive. An anonymous agent of the federal government who nobody had seen was a helluva lot easier to let go.

"Contact him again, and tell him I need to know who on his end is connected to Banning, Schroder, and Stark. I need to know who sicced them on Lily Robbins. They're the ones who killed Schroder, not me." And they'd killed him for fucking up.

"Who do you think sicced the cops on Charlotte?" she asked.

It was a damn good question, with all sorts of repercussions.

"She could have been seen at the Robbins house this morning." If anybody on the block had been up and looking, which was very likely.

"What about at the Sunset?"

That was more of a mystery.

"Less likely. I parked on a different side of the building from where Schroder's room was located."

"Could Schroder have identified Charlotte for whoever killed him?"

Aye, and there was the rub.

"Possibly, even probably."

"Then your bigger problem just got bigger and more personal, and if they're listening to the cops this morning like the rest of us, you're going to wish you had more ammo."

She was right. She couldn't possibly know how much ammunition he had, but there was no such thing as too much.

"We're almost to the exit, and we will be taking your recommendation and disappearing into the wilds of New Mexico." Truthfully, he couldn't get his ass off the interstate quick enough at this point.

"We'll be watching everything from our end," she said. "Tracking you and listening to the police. If you're spotted, I'll contact you immediately."

"Thank you, SB303."

"Roger."

On his screen, Zach saw the girl swivel around on her chair and get up to walk away—and then he saw her walking away.

Geezus. Combat boots, pink bustier, all that platinum blond hair in a ponytail, a waist-length skein half twisted up and half falling down, and a pair of skintight black-and-white-striped leggings hugging the most perfect ass he'd ever seen.

Geezus. This was Dylan's wife?

A guy's face suddenly loomed into view, obscuring the whole screen.

It was Dylan, and the odd sensation he'd felt in his chest when he'd first seen SB303 slammed into him again, only more intense.

"Come home, *pendejo,* and I'll introduce you," Dylan said.

Home. Yeah, Steele Street had been his first home, the first place he'd ever been safe, and it had probably been the last place he'd ever been safe. He sure as hell hadn't lived anyplace safe during the Asian years, and in El Salvador, his life had been on the line every day. His budget for that job had included a big line item for hiring and maintaining a security force, his own small army, because the job required a small army—and even that wasn't enough to guarantee safety. No one in the drug trade lasted long without a paramilitary force backing them up.

Hell, no one in the drug trade lasted long, period.

"I'd like to meet her," he said, his voice uncomfortably gruff with an emotion he would prefer to keep to himself.

"She wants to know how you got in the building last night," Dylan said, and Zach let out a short laugh.

"You didn't tell her?"

Dylan shook his head.

"Then she isn't getting it out of me." The steel grate in the street led down a rabbit hole.

"Just watch yourself," Dylan said. "That's all I'm saying. The girl can read minds." The look on his face said he was serious, and Zach was instantly intrigued.

"You know what it's like down there. Tell her the route is dark, dirty, and dangerous." No one who looked like SB303 wanted to be crawling around under the streets of Denver.

"Dangerous and dark doesn't scare her. She's worked with Creed for too long."

Well, the day was getting jam-packed with surprises. Cesar Raoul Eduardo Rivera, Creed, had always been a night hunter, even at the ripe old age of thirteen, when Zach had first met him under the steering wheel of a 1968 Mercury Cyclone GT that had been "Fast-backed, 4-stacked, and Radial-tracked." Dylan had been watching the car for months, and when an order had come in, he'd sent the new boy, Creed, and one of the older, more experienced thieves then working for the chop shop, a street rat named Kenny, to go pick her up.

The two kids had found the Cyclone in a warehouse complex up in Commerce City, on a moonless night so still, the city had been under a pall, steaming from the day's record-breaking heat and smelling of grime. By the time Zach had gone looking for the pair, Creed had been on his own . . .

"Hey, kid," he said, hunkering down next to the Cyclone's open driver's side door. "Where's Kenny?"

"Spooked," the scrawny boy with a mop of blond hair said. He was stretched out under the steering wheel, skinny legs poking out of the car, his T-shirt torn and greasy, with a penlight stuck behind his ear, shining on the steering column.

"That asshole ran off and left you?" Kenny's ass was grass.

"He got scared."

"I thought he was 'sposed to be teaching you the ropes." Whatever the kid was doing under the steering wheel, he wasn't being very effective, and honestly, stealing cars was a very, very time-sensitive career.

Zach rose up a little on his feet and looked over his shoulder, checking out the parking lot. Except for the Cyclone, it was deserted, and more than a little creepy. If the car was here, where in the hell was the driver? There weren't any lights on in any of the warehouses. They were all just looming up into the night, their outlines visible *only because of the bright lights of Denver to the south.*

But this was the address on Dylan's sheet, all right, and they had found the car.

Now they needed to get it the hell out of there.

But first, a word of warning to the kid.

"You need to pay better attention to what's going on around you. If you don't have a lookout, then you need to do it yourself. I could have been anybody sneaking up on you."

"No, you couldn't," the kid said, still working under the steering wheel, his little penlight a weak-ass tiny glow above his ear, which couldn't be doing a damn bit of good. "You could only be you."

Whatever the hell that meant.

"Pay attention, or you're going to get hurt." Dylan had dragged this one in too young, and Zach was going to tell him.

"Fuck you, pendejo. I knew it was you, 'cuz I heard you coming a mile away." Pale green eyes cut toward him from under that tiny light. "You got those deep-tread boots, and something's stuck in the left one, a rock or something, and every time you take a step, I hear a snick. So snick, step, snick, step—that's nobody sneaking anywhere, asshole. That's you."

Zach just stared at the kid. Sonuvabitch. That was good. That was damn good.

But whatever he was trying to do under the steering wheel was getting him nowhere. That asshole Kenny was out. This was the last job he screwed up.

And leaving the kid out here alone. That sucked. That was unacceptable.

"Come on, Creed, get out from under there." Dylan had balked at the kid's name, which had gone on forfuckingever, and started calling him Creed almost from the get-go. And Zach didn't care that his last name was Rivera; the kid was no Chicano. He wasn't going to mention it to the boy, but he must have noticed that he was a green-eyed blond and didn't look a damn thing like his brothers and sisters, of which he had so many, the kid didn't get enough to eat. Dylan had actually found him outside Mama Guadaloupe's, a restaurant on the west side, waiting for kitchen scraps, of which Mama made sure she had plenty for the younger kids in the neighborhood. The older ones were on their own.

But no, Zach wasn't going to mention that Creed's Anglo mama must have gotten it on with the mailman or some other white dude. He was in no shape to be dishing dirt on other guys' mothers, not with the mother he had.

"And pay attention," he said to the kid after he'd squirmed out from under the steering wheel. "You got wire on you?"

"No."

"Well, you need wire. You're always gonna need wire, so you might as well get some and keep a roll of it in your pocket. You can use it for a hundred different things on a car." He walked toward the front of the Cyclone and popped the hood. A timer in his head went off at the sound. That was the other thing the kid was going to need, a timer in his head that he was always going to be trying to beat. "And Dylan sent you after a Mercury, so somebody should have brought a screwdriver."

"Kenny had a screwdriver."

"Yeah, well, me too. Shine that light on the solenoid," Zach said, leaning under the hood and getting to work. "Now look. We're going to use the wire to connect the coil to the ignition post on the solenoid." It took him ten seconds to pull off the circuit wires and rig the connection. "And we're going to use the screwdriver to feed power to the starter." He laid the screwdriver on the starter post and the positive battery cable simultaneously, and a flurry of sparks shot out from the connection. The engine also turned over, just as if he'd used the key. He pocketed the screwdriver and slammed the hood.

With the Cyclone softly rumbling and ready to go, Zach took one more look around at the dark buildings and the empty spaces in between them, *and for a split second, he thought he saw something flit across one of the alleys.*

The hair instantly rose on the back of his neck. Effen-ee-fuck.

"So . . . uh . . . what spooked Kenny?" he asked the kid.

In answer, Creed turned off his penlight and stuck it in his back pocket.

"Well," he said, turning his back to the Cyclone and looking out over the deserted parking lot and the warehouses. "There's a couple of things running wild around here tonight. He got scared."

Fair enough.

"And you didn't?"

The boy shrugged. "Ain't nothing out here wilder than me."

Zach hadn't admitted it then, and he wouldn't admit it now, but listening to that skinny kid's offhand dismissal of whatever in the hell had been prowling through a Commerce City compound that night had sent the hair on the back of his neck rising all over again.

And the blonde in the bustier worked with Creed, SDF's jungle boy?

"She's an operator?" he asked Dylan, not quite believing it, not really.

"I'll put you in the gym with her for five minutes, and you tell me."

He'd be damned. Steele Street had obviously improved considerably over the years.

"Is she going to kick my ass?" he asked, and this time it was Dylan who grinned.

"If she couldn't, I wouldn't let you anywhere near her."

Fair enough.

CHAPTER SIXTEEN

Saturday, 8:00 A.M.—Commerce City, Colorado

Cherie pulled Roxanne to a stop in the alley next to Steele Street's Commerce City Garage, turned off the key, and took a breath. Driving relaxed her, especially driving Hawkins's Challenger, and she'd definitely needed a little relaxation after the meeting in Dylan's office, and a little more relaxation in order to face the third floor of the Commerce City Garage with Gabriel Shore at her side.

She took another easy breath, and let it flow through her. Roxanne had power and looks, and handled like a dream since Skeeter and Superman had redone her suspension.

Cherie was no mechanic. She never worked on the cars, but she could drive with the best of the big boys, and Skeeter, of course. Red Dog drove the way she did everything else, as close to the edge as she could get, which sometimes gave the impression that she was out of control.

She wasn't. Ever.

Neither was Cherie. Ever. But sometimes she got a little un-relaxed, this morning being a case in point. So thank goodness for Roxanne. She'd been taught to drive the Challenger by Christian Hawkins, a.k.a. Superman, and he'd given her supreme confidence in her skills.

Not to say that riding in any of Steele Street's muscle cars was for the faint of heart. She'd had to build up to it herself.

She slanted a glance at her passenger to see how he was holding up, and was pleased to see him relaxed back in his seat, his hands in his lap.

"Gillian's apartment is—" she started.

Without so much as a flicker of emotion, or in any other way acknowledging her presence, Gabriel held up two fingers, like a benediction. She instinctively understood he was asking for silence, she supposed because he was dreaming up a brilliantly insightful plan for interfacing the DREAGAR 454 with a secure link to Steele Street and downloading the mysterious files that had Dylan all wound up—for all the good that was going to do him.

She took another breath and just relaxed into

it. Good Lord, the man worked in the Marsh Annex, and in about five minutes or less, he was going to enter her shop. She didn't think Dylan appreciated what an incredible place the Annex was, or the kind of beyond-the-cutting-edge technology the people there produced. Ostensibly, the Marsh Annex was part of the Department of Commerce. At least it had started out that way, an offshoot of the department's security division, specifically in charge of keeping the U.S. government's latest and greatest gizmos out of the hands of the opposition. In today's climate, sometimes keeping them out of the marketplace and off eBay was an even greater challenge. It hadn't been too much of a stretch from protecting the technology to improving upon it. Some of the best minds in the country went through the Marsh Annex.

Cherie's security clearance hadn't granted her total access when she'd been there, but when General Grant had put her name in the hat for the DREAGAR 454 2Z8s contract, the Marsh people had been very pleased to meet her. She had a reputation, all good, especially with government folks dealing with classified information—and she would like very much for everything to stay that way.

"I—" she started.

The two fingers came up again, cutting her off, and she saw him visibly take a breath.

"I'll be driving back to Steele Street," he said.

She didn't think so.

"No, you won't. Superman doesn't let just anybody drive his car."

"You weren't driving his car," he said. "His car was driving you. There's a difference, and by Superman, you mean Christian Hawkins, correct?"

"Yes, but—"

"There aren't any 'buts' about it. You drive like my grandmother, and from here on out, I will be taking over the transportation duties. I am sure Mr. Hart will clear me on the car."

Cherie blinked at him.

"Your grandmother?" He had a lot of gall. She knew what he meant, and he was wrong. She was careful, that was all. "I bet a hundred dollars your grandmother has never driven a 1971 Dodge Hemi Challenger R/T." Actually, she'd bet a thousand. There just weren't that many 1971 Hemis out there to be driven.

"Neither have you," he said, sliding a glance in her direction. "Do you even know about fourth gear?"

Of course she did.

"Fourth gear is a highway gear, and we never got on the highway." Keeping to the back roads and staying off the interstate, where people drove like maniacs, was no crime. It was just good sense.

He shook his head. "I can't believe Christian Hawkins lets you drive his car. How many clutches has he had to put in this thing?"

"A few," she admitted, not quite seeing his point, "but that's what they do at Steele Street, fix cars, put in clutches, do valve jobs, time things. The cars require constant maintenance, and—"

"Is he in love with you?" The young guy's gaze narrowed on her, which she found somewhat discomforting. "I mean, are you with him, like his girlfriend?"

Well, that startled the hell out of her. "No," she said, then said it again for good measure. "No. He's married."

Her and Superman? That was actually an alarming thought. Christian Hawkins was so . . . so much. Too much.

No, no, no. When she went for a guy, and she'd had any number of boyfriends over the years, she went for guys like Henry Stiner, the Seventeenth Street lawyer, and there was no denying that she thought Gabriel Shore was exceptionally cute. She had a penchant for computer geeks, tech guys, brainy guys with the skills to hotwire DREAGAR 454s rather than

1970 Chevelles, even if the brainy guys never quite seemed to be brainy enough. Truly brainy guys were proving hard to come by.

Still, she would never, had not, did not go for guys like the SDF operators. Oh, God, no.

"Then why does he let you destroy his car?" Red Dog's little brother looked confused, and he was definitely cute, but he was also a little insulting, and starting to sound a little bossy.

"Well, in the first place, I'm not *destroying* his car."

"Yes, you are," he interrupted, sounding very sure of himself—which, when she thought about it, wasn't a trait she found particularly appealing in men on a personal level.

"I have never so much as gotten a fingerprint on it, let alone any kind of a dent." He couldn't know that, of course, which was why she was telling him, which put her on comfortable ground. She liked telling men what they didn't know, and she usually had plenty to say.

"I'm not talking dents," he muttered.

She ignored him.

"And second of all, Superman believes that Roxanne and I are soul sisters of a sort, that she wants to bring out what he calls my 'inner NASCAR.' So he lets me drive her, and if any little problems occur, they get fixed."

"Inner NASCAR?" He looked incredulous at

that, which was also probably an insult. "Ms. Hacker, you don't even have an 'inner Soap Box Derby,' let alone an 'inner NASCAR,' so maybe you should go back to driving whatever it is you usually drive, like a . . . a . . ."

He seemed to be having trouble coming up with something, so she helped him out, which also put her on comfortable ground—telling men what they were trying to say.

"A Prius."

"Yes," he said. "A Prius." Amazingly, he made that sound like an insult, too—and to think she'd almost been interested in him.

Well, she wasn't now, that was for damn sure.

"And I suppose you drive a—"

"Viper."

Oh.

Well, everyone knew the Marsh Annex people were overpaid and probably underchallenged, so they needed constant infusions of "newer, better, faster," and she supposed a Dodge Viper gave him plenty of that.

Still, she was surprised. He'd seemed so nice at first, with his lanyard and his DREAGAR 454 Subliminal Neuron Intel Interface.

Gabriel took another breath and wondered what in the world he'd been thinking in Hart's office, but he didn't wonder long. He'd been thinking she was beautiful in an odd, angular, stunning way. She had very pretty strawberry blond hair, long and sleek, stick-straight to her shoulders with bangs and very sophisticated, like her dress and those shoes with the pom-poms on them.

He knew her by reputation, Cherie Hacker of Hacker International. Everybody in his field had heard of her, but no one had ever said she was so gorgeous.

Maybe because they'd ridden with her in a car, and their brain cells had been so shook up from being lurched and jerked around they hadn't been able to think straight. Or maybe the smell of a burning clutch had ob-scured their reason. Or maybe they'd gotten so exhausted watching her trying to find a gear—and she only used three—that their eyes had crossed.

Because she was gorgeous. Or she had been up until she'd gotten so bossy.

Or maybe other guys thought she was too skinny. Rhonda had used the word "elegant." Either way, Gabriel didn't know what was hold-ing her dress up. Maybe she had it pinned to the inside of the motorcycle jacket—a fashion statement that was obviously no statement whatsoever on her risk-taking abilities. She not only stopped for the yellow lights, she slowed down for the green ones in case they turned yellow.

He'd never seen anybody slow down for a green light. It was incredibly disconcerting.

Stylish, Rhonda had also called her.

After half an hour in the car with her, Gabriel was going to stick with bossy, and he still wished she would take off her sunglasses so he could see her eyes.

"Yes, well, Vipers are very nice cars," she said, opening the Challenger's door.

Nice was a ridiculous understatement, but he let it pass. His V-10 Viper kicked ass, and if she'd known anything at all about cars, like how to use fourth gear, for instance, she would have known that.

"There's one at Steele Street," she continued. "Maybe you'll have time to look at it when we're finished downloading the DREAGAR files."

He doubted it. Once they got back to Steele Street, he and Dylan and Gillian needed to get to work, and Ms. Hacker could go back to grinding gears and endangering someone else's life at twenty-five miles an hour. He honestly hadn't known he could get an adrenaline rush at twenty-five miles an hour—not until he'd lurched across an intersection with her, praying to God they made it before the light turned red.

"Please don't touch anything while I'm disarming the security system." She kept talking, and he just let her. He knew what he was going to do, and it didn't have anything to do with what she had to say. "And please don't touch anything once we get inside, not until after you've checked with me. My setup here will... uh, undoubtedly be different from what you're used to dealing with, so it's best if you let me take the lead."

Very bossy.

But sure, if she wanted to do the work, he was fine with watching. It wasn't as if he hadn't designed the whole DREAGAR 454 system and knew it inside out, upside down, and backward better than anybody on the planet. He had, and he did.

But if she wanted to stumble around with it and show off her setup, he'd stand back and watch—up to a point, and then he was taking over. The DREAGAR was his. The only reason she even had one was because she'd won the contracts on the 2Z8s.

She got out of the Challenger, and he followed suit, keeping a step behind as she climbed the stairs up the outside of the garage. His mom and dad had been to Gillian's place on the second floor a couple of times, but this was his first visit. No matter how much his sister

CUTTING LOOSE ✳ 251

was a part of his memories, she didn't know him from Adam.

Passing a dull gray, iron door on the second landing, with the name "Red Dog" spray-painted across it in red paint, Gabriel's mood took another dip. A couple of years ago, when General Grant had mentioned he needed a new secretary, Gabriel's first thought had gone to his sister. Recently divorced and back in Washington, D.C., she'd just gotten an apartment and was looking for a job. He'd thought it would be great to have her in the Marsh Annex, but she hadn't been in the job very long before she'd fallen into the middle of one of Grant's black operations and been irreparably harmed.

She was never going to be what she'd been, and now she lived above a garage with graffiti on the door.

It was her choice. He knew that. Dylan Hart had offered her one of the lofts at Steele Street, but she preferred being out here in the urban jungle.

When they reached the third landing and a heavy steel door, he glanced around the area. It was bleak, very industrial, and looked like a crime spree could happen any minute, even at midmorning. A dry riverbed filled with junk and trash bordered the building to the south.

Smokestacks from a factory a few blocks over jutted up into the sky.

His gaze went back to Cherie Hacker in her expensive high heels and flouncy dress, trying to cover up a yawn and key in a code on the alarm system, and suddenly, he wished she would hurry the hell up.

Two million dollars was going to bring every world-class cutthroat and gunslinger on the planet down on Gillian's head, and more than a few of them would figure out to come looking for her here.

And why, oh, why, hadn't he thought of that while he'd been standing in Dylan Hart's office? He could have gotten the security codes from Ms. Hacker and left her well enough out of it. Despite what she or Hart might think, there wasn't anything she could have done to her DREAGAR that he couldn't figure out.

"Can you get back to Steele Street on your own?" he asked, as she finally, thank God, entered the last number into the system.

"I get around Denver on my own all the time," she said, watching a stream of equations scroll across a small screen at the top of the digital keypad.

"Then as soon as you get the door open, I think you ought to go back. I'll take care of everything on this end."

She mumbled something under her breath he didn't quite catch.

"Excuse me?" he said.

"I'm not going anywhere, until we're done here. If that's what you were thinking, that I was going to let you into my shop and then you were just going to pack me up and send me home, you are mistaken."

"I don't think being stubborn about this is in your best interest," he said plainly.

"Gee," she said, still watching the equations roll by. "I was thinking the same thing about you."

He gave her a very perturbed look, which she failed to notice. They'd gotten off on the right foot, but it had all gone to hell pretty quickly. Maybe he'd been a little too blunt about her driving.

"Can you speed this up a little?" He'd be happier once they were inside. He knew what his sister could do with an exposed target, and he and Cherie Hacker were sitting ducks on this landing.

She pushed an alpha key twice on the eighth equation, and he heard the lock release. A second later, another lock released, and then another, and so on down the line through a series of seven, one after the other, until the door swung open—into Wonderland, a hacker's paradise, a room so full of equipment, he felt instantly at home. There were walls of drives, and screens, and peripherals, rows of them, everything on, lit up, running code, and in the middle of it all was the DREAGAR 454 hard drive—in a couple hundred separate pieces, strewn from one end of a worktable to the other.

CHAPTER SEVENTEEN

Saturday, 9:00 A.M.—Paysen, New Mexico

They'd found it.

Zach had looked for years, and more than once had thought he'd stumbled upon it.

He'd been wrong.

This was the real deal, right here: the middle of nowhere, Paysen, New Mexico, population 28, or so the sign said. If the number was true and correct, then the town was bigger than it looked. He'd counted population 5, and that was if he included the four coonhounds lounging in the dirt in front of the convenience store.

He stepped over the one stretched across the entrance and wound his way through the rest of the dusty pack, carrying two bags of food and supplies.

SB303 had said get off the interstate. Zach

was pretty sure they'd gotten off more than that. Nothing but scrub, yucca, and a single narrow ribbon of asphalt stretched to the horizon in either direction. At the Road Runner Motel, Gas Station, and Grocery, they'd landed in the hub of Paysen's commercial activity. There were two trailers baking in the heat on the other side of the road, both of them sporting canopies held up by lodge poles. One had a small pen with a few goats close by. The other had two picnic tables pushed together in front, in the shade. Neither had so much as a square inch of paint on it anywhere. The sun had cooked it all off a long time ago.

He crossed the hard-pack parking lot, heading toward the end unit, number eight. He'd filled Charlotte's tank before he'd gone in to pay for the room, then parked her behind the building, on the other side of a rusted-out tractor. Once he went inside number eight, the Road Runner would look as deserted as it had before he and Lily had arrived.

Lily. Yeah, the beautiful woman he'd snatched out of her bathroom and her life this morning. Better not to think too much about her, not the way he liked to think about her. He'd paid for a double with all the amenities, which included a small fridge, microwave, and coffeepot. After

he got patched up, and they'd both had something to eat, it would be best to get some rest.

Best for everyone.

Right.

Once the sun went down, they'd be back on
the road and heading for Denver in a straight-
through drive. Alex could advise him then how
he wanted to handle Lily Robbins.

Possibly Alex would let her go to Montana,
after she was debriefed, and then debriefed
again, and probably again. For reasons outside
her control, she'd become a major player in an
international incident—but she wouldn't be for
much longer.

Possibly he would put in a request to be the
one to take her to the Cross Double R. He'd
never been to Montana. He'd like to meet her
dad, thank the man himself for what he'd
taught his daughter.

He knocked on the door to the room before
he used the key to let himself in, just to let her
know he'd returned. Inside, he set the grocery
bags on a small table. She was at the back of the
room, standing over the sink, splashing water
on her face.

"They had a couple different kinds of sport
drink," he said. "I got you both."

She turned, using a towel to dry her face, and
she was perfect, standing there in her cowboy

boots and low-slung jeans, with her water-splashed tank top and her midnight-dark hair damp and curling in tendrils around her face. Her skin was pale and creamy, with a light dusting of freckles across the bridge of her nose and onto her cheeks. Robbins—she looked black Irish. Lines of strain marred the easy beauty of her face, and he felt a pang of guilt just for the general hell of it.

He hadn't done anything since he'd met her except try to keep her safe, and somehow, he wasn't quite getting the job done. Instead of being at home or headed to her family and the ranch, going about her days, she was here with him in this two-bit, run-down, flea-bitten dive of a motel, waiting for nightfall and a run for the border.

"Thanks," she said, finishing with the towel and setting it aside.

She crossed the room, and his fascination with her increased with every slim-hipped, long-legged stride she took. It was ridiculous, and inappropriate, and absolutely impossible to ignore. She was so exquisite.

He might have to go sleep in the car, and that was even more ridiculous. Plus, it would probably kill him. The temperature was well on its way to the hundred mark. Inside Charlotte, it would be another ten to fifteen degrees.

And inside Lily, it would be so fucking sweet.

"We've got soup, crackers, canned fruit, cheese, and the best candy bars money can buy in Paysen, New Mexico," he said, so cool, so steady, so in control.

Yeah. Right.

He unloaded the groceries onto the table, including the paper bowls and plastic silverware he'd bought—the whole point being to get out of Paysen and the Road Runner without getting ptomaine.

"What kind of soup?"

"Chicken noodle, and uh . . ." He reached out and turned the second can around. "And chicken noodle. There were some sandwiches in a deli section of the cooler, but they looked like death in plastic wrap to me."

"You're spoiled," she said, opening up one of the cans of soup and pouring it into the bowls.

He grinned.

"Too spoiled to eat mystery meat on white bread," he agreed. "You had Isidora's croissants."

"Don't remind me." She let out a short laugh. "And don't tell me you want this heated in the microwave."

She pushed one of the bowls in his direction and started to sit down at the table, but then paused for a couple of seconds and changed her mind, instead walking toward the back of the room and the bathroom. He watched her disappear inside, and didn't think too much about it, going ahead and eating without her, downing a couple bowls of soup and half a sleeve's worth of crackers with cheese. Partway through one of the cans of peaches, he glanced toward the bathroom and wondered if she was okay.

There was plenty of food left. He wasn't worried about her going hungry. He'd get her to eat something when she came out.

Chewing another mouthful of peaches, he glanced at the bathroom again and swallowed. The air conditioner in the room rattled and whined and whirred in the window, throwing out a pitiful stream of barely chilled air, proving itself more of a noisemaker than a cooling device.

Alejandro Campos had always stayed at five-star hotels. It had been one of the nicer perks of being a cocaine drug lord. But Zach had a feeling that was all in his past. Alex had been right to pull him out. He'd gotten in so deep in the last eight years, had so many suppliers, so many buyers, so many deals in the works, he might never have seen the end coming, the underhanded double cross, the unexpected turf war in a place he thought he had under control, the disgruntled cartel partner. The drug business was dirty and dangerous, and supremely violent.

Yeah, it was good he was out.

Without taking his eyes off the bathroom door, he picked up the peach can and drank some of the juice.

Something wasn't right, and under the rattle and whir of the air conditioner, he thought he heard what.

Fuck.

Setting the peaches down, he pushed away from the table and headed to the back of the room—and the closer he got, the worse he felt.

Shit.

He should have been paying closer attention. She was in there crying. Sobbing her heart out, from the sounds of it, and *dammit,* he couldn't just stand out here and hope for the best, that she'd pull herself together, wipe off her face, and come out to sit down and eat with a smart-ass smile on her lips.

That was Jewel, not Lily.

Actually, it wasn't Jewel. Jewel baby didn't cry. Ever. She sure as hell hadn't been crying when she'd walked out on him.

He hadn't been either, not really, no matter what it had looked like. He'd just felt like doing it for about five months. Okay, more like twelve. Scotch had helped get him through it, and if he'd been any less of a man than he was, he would have left the room and headed back to the Road Runner's convenience store to see if he could get a pint of whatever rotgut kept people from shooting themselves in Paysen, New Mexico.

Then he would have had a couple of shots before he came back, still hoping she'd pull herself together all on her own.

He wasn't a heartless bastard, not really. It was just the whole helpless thing with the tears and all. There wasn't much a guy had to offer in these situations—and yeah, he kind of remembered Jewel telling him that was one reason she never cried in front of him, the futility of it.

As he recalled, that was the day he'd starting winning points for his Asshole of the Year badge, one Jewel had been happy to award, though in his defense, it had taken her a while. He'd had to work at it to get her to walk out on him. She hadn't left willingly.

And maybe, just maybe, that was the first time he'd ever admitted that to himself.

Well, great, a fucking epiphany in the Land of Enchantment. He was so glad he'd made the trip.

Sure he was.

And Lily was still in there, sobbing.

Fuck. Sobbing was so much worse than crying.

He took a deep breath, lifted his hand to knock on the bathroom door, then swore again under his breath.

Looking down at his shoes, he knocked twice. Yeah. He committed. Acknowledging emotional distress in a woman was the first step off the cliff—and a guy only got one. He'd always thought sex was the first step, but Jewel had dissuaded him from that convenient conceit. He'd never had any trouble committing to sex.

In response to his knock, there was a pause in the sobbing, and he used it.

"Lily. Come on out and have something to eat. It'll make you feel better." It always made him feel better; not as good as Scotch, but better. "We'll talk."

He paused with his knuckles just a couple of inches from the door again, wondering where in the hell that had come from. He hadn't meant to say that, at least not and leave it quite so open-ended.

"Lily?" He reached for the knob and gave it a turn, and it opened.

He didn't see her at first, not until he peeked around the door. She was sitting on the edge of the bathtub, leaning against the wall with her face in her hands. She looked up when he opened the door, and something unexpected happened. He didn't get the urge to run. Quite the opposite.

"Hey," he said, stepping inside and gently taking hold of her arm. "Come on. You're tired, and you need to eat something."

He pulled her to her feet and got her back out by the sink, thinking he'd get her a wet washcloth, so she could wipe the tears off her face. But once he got the cloth wrung out, he decided to just go ahead and do it himself.

That was the smart move.

Sure it was, because it got him something he wanted—closer.

Closer to all her soft, warm skin. Closer to her body. Closer to her mouth.

Carefully, he smoothed the cloth down one of her cheeks and over her bottom lip.

Sweet thing, her gaze lifted to his, and he thought, *Nobody falls this fast. Not like this. Without even a kiss.*

Yeah, a guy at least needed a kiss.

So he took his .45 out of his shoulder holster and set it on the counter, pointing away from them. Then he shrugged out of the holster and moved closer to her.

Slowly, he slid his nose down the side of hers and softly kissed the corner of her mouth. Her hand came up and closed on his waist, and he kissed her again, gently moving his lips over hers, breathing her in—and she sighed in his mouth.

Yeah. That was it. He cupped the side of her face with his hand and tilted her face up while opening his mouth over hers and pressing her back against the wall.

Contact. Her breasts cushioned against his chest, her hips cradling his, her other hand sliding up the back of his neck, pulling him closer. He loved the hot sweetness of it, the way she softened against him.

He slid his tongue in her mouth and felt the sharp need of desire take hold, the taste of her, the delicacy of her tongue sliding against his, teasing him. Yeah, this was going to work. Her hand slid under his T-shirt, her palm soft and hot against him, sliding over him and pulling him closer.

Closer and closer. He felt the edge of her desperation, could taste her tears, the salty dampness of them where they'd pooled in the corner of her mouth, and for a moment wondered if he should stop. But then she bit him, so softly, so gently, closed her teeth on his jaw and licked his skin, then moved to his neck and did it again, and all the while her hand was traveling across his lower back, her fingers sliding below the waistband of his pants.

No, she wanted this. If nothing else, she wanted the mindlessness of it, to just feel. She needed a break. He knew, because he needed a break, too. A reprieve from thinking, from running.

He brought his hand up to caress her breasts, loving the weight and softness of them. Then he moved under her tank top, and further, under her bra, and yeah, that was when his own breath caught a little. Touching her was such an instantly erotic sensation, an instant addiction to intimacy and heated, satiny skin.

"Zach." She whispered his name, and he started unbuttoning her jeans, one slow button at a time. He wanted this to happen, felt the inevitability of it taking over. If she wanted to stop, now was the perfect time to let him know—but she lifted her hips and kept kissing him, her tongue sliding deeper into his mouth, again and again, until he pushed her jeans and panties partway off her hips and slipped his hand between her legs. He cupped her, held her—and he found her with his fingers and rubbed her, very gently at first, exploring her and just letting the soft wonder of her get him hard.

Geezus. Everything about her felt so good, and then he must have done something really right. She twisted against him, a small cry breaking free of her mouth, and he grinned.

And he did the right thing again, teasing her just so and taking her mouth with his. She melted, she sighed, she pushed herself against his hand, and he kissed her, letting her take her time and her pleasure. It was such a luxury, a rich gift to have her naked and moaning with just the touch of his hand. He sucked on her neck, then licked her before moving lower. With his other hand, he pushed her tank top and sports bra up over her breasts, and with his hand between her legs and his mouth teasing her tits, she started to come.

Sweet, sweet geezus—she rose to her tiptoes, both her hands burying themselves in his hair and holding him closer, her breath getting short.

His cock pulsed with the need to push up inside her, to thrust into her, but what he wanted even more was what she gave him next—a long moment of rigidity, her body stretched taut, her breath caught, and then the long hot slide into ultimate pleasure.

She came apart for him, her hips jerking against him where he held her so firmly against the wall, her hands clutching him, a soft groan sighing from her lips. He kept sucking on her, playing with her, until she pulled his mouth back up to hers and slid her hands down and began unbuckling his belt.

"Please," she whispered so breathlessly, so sweetly, her fingers fumbling with his zipper. "Please."

He took over the job, helping her out, helping himself, and hearing every one of her unspoken words. *Please . . . please fuck me. Please, I want to feel you inside me.*

He toed out of his shoes and shucked out of his pants, and then he was there, filling her. Her hips came forward, and her head went back on a groan. *Geezus.* He pushed deeper. *Geezus.* She was tighter and shallower than other women he'd had, and every time he thrust, she tightened around him, a sweet clenching of her inner muscles that made his head spin. She felt so good—like sex, warm and vital in his arms, her body moving with his. She smelled so good—like sex, exotic and erotic, female in every subtle shade of scent.

He looked down to where they were joined and felt a new surge of urgency. She was so pretty, the curve of her hip, her breasts so full, the long silky length of her legs—and her face. She was holding on to the counter with one hand and a towel bar with the other, riding him, and she looked transported, her mouth partly open, a damp sheen of sweat making her shimmer in the cheap light, her hair gone wild.

He wanted to tell her she was so fucking

beautiful that he'd fallen in love, that she felt so good, he wanted to do this forever. But she hit a new rhythm and it was all over. He came up against her hard, thrusting again, going deep, and again, going deeper, and again—and he came, his climax jerking through him, his muscles tensing, his body shaking. His left arm went around her like a vise and he braced himself against the wall with his right. *Geezus*. His head came down, and he opened his mouth on her neck, grazing her with his teeth, filling himself with the taste and scent and softness of her.

He thrust into her one more time near the end, and when it was over, all he wanted to do was hold her and fall asleep, just pass out while he felt so damn good.

CHAPTER EIGHTEEN

Saturday, 10:15 A.M.—Paysen, New Mexico

Lily was limp in his arms.

It had been so long since she'd had anything like what he'd just given her. She hadn't forgotten about sex since her divorce; she just hadn't been able to find anyone, and certainly, she hadn't ever found anyone like him. Not even Tom, who had considered himself one of God's and nature's gifts to women.

God, her body was pulsing with pleasure. She felt suffused with it, her skin warm, the tensions and fears of the day forgotten for a moment, and all she wanted was to forget about them for a moment more. He must have felt the same.

The room was small, and one of the beds was less than an arm's length away. He stepped over, and with one hand pulled everything off the mattress except for the bottom sheet. After she stretched out and claimed her pillows, he reached back for his pistol and moved to sit on the edge of the bed.

Like her, he kept his pistol cocked, locked, and loaded, and like her, he checked to make sure he had a cartridge in the chamber, ready at an instant's notice. Then he set the pistol on the nightstand and lay down next to her.

Pulling her close, he smoothed her hair back off her face.

"Hey," he said, leaning down and giving her a kiss.

"Hey." She kissed him back, and the next thing she knew, he was asleep, just like that, with his leg over the top of hers, and his arm wrapped around her waist, his hand on the small of her back, and his mouth still touching hers in a kiss.

Gone. In an instant.

She wasn't offended. She was charmed senseless.

He hadn't admitted to anything, but she knew what he was, even if she didn't know what acronym claimed him. DEA, FBI, CIA, DIA, NSA, DOD—or any of dozens more she didn't even know. It didn't matter. He wasn't a man who trusted anyone or anything, and he'd just fallen asleep in her arms.

Come home, pendejo, *and I'll introduce you.* That's what the dark-haired man on the screen had said to him, meaning he'd introduce Zach to SB303. The girl was classy, smart, and beautifully, exquisitely dressed, so incredibly stylish. Everything about the two of them was professional, from the girl's expertise to the man's demeanor—and he had a history with Zach. That much was clear. The two of them shared a secret about the building in Denver where Zach was taking her, and the man and Zach both knew someone named Creed.

Yes, there was definitely a history between the two of them—and affection, too. That had been obvious in all their exchanges.

Next to her, he let out a soft snore, his body softening deeper into the bed, his arm going slack on her waist, his leg sliding off hers.

Very carefully, she inched away from him. He needed sleep. She needed to eat, and with him asleep, it was time to reclaim her pistol and take another look at the bracelet.

She didn't hesitate to go through his pockets until she found her magazine, but the bracelet was nowhere to be found, and she actually turned his pockets inside out. Giving up on the bracelet, at least for now, she walked over to where he'd put his gun bag on the motel desk. Her pistol was still inside, and once she had it in her hand, she felt better, more secure. After checking the chamber, she released the trigger, slammed the magazine home, and racked the slide. Then she flipped on the safety and stepped over to the table, taking the gun with her.

The air conditioner in the room was nothing short of a travesty, and while she ate, curled up naked on one of the chairs, she did her best to ignore all its banging and rattling, and concentrated instead on him.

He'd rolled partway onto his stomach, with one of his legs drawn up, and he was so beautiful that even though she was hungry, she found herself forgetting to eat—and that was with him being only half naked. He hadn't taken off his T-shirt. Looking at his shoulder, it was easy to see why.

She'd known he was hurt, but it was hard to gauge the extent of his wound with the shirt on. Maybe when he woke up, he'd let her take a look. Of all the odd things, she'd noticed he had a couple of suture kits in his gun bag.

Or maybe that wasn't so odd.

Bringing an open can of peaches to her mouth, she took a small swallow of juice—but she didn't take her eyes off him, and when he rolled onto his back, still sound asleep, she took another small sip and licked the juice off her lips.

She loved men. She'd almost forgotten how much, and he was particularly gorgeous, more powerfully built under his clothes than she would have guessed. He carried himself with such elegance, with such fluid grace. His shirt had ridden up, revealing the dark hair covering his chest and arrowing down to his groin, and a sigh lifted her chest.

Damn. He was beautiful. Watching him, a wave of heat built inside her, lovely and erotic, and compelling—very compelling.

She pushed out of her chair and walked back to the bed. For now, he was hers. Unbelievably, three weeks of wondering and longing had brought them both here, naked in bed with the rest of the day to while away. She stretched out beside him, then slid lower and simply indulged herself, taking him in her mouth.

Holy Mary, sweet Mother of God—Zach woke up on a wave of pleasure so intense, he almost came. Fortunately, a shred of reason kicked in. A smart guy would ride this out as long as he could. Yeah, that was the plan, just let her have

her way with him for as long as she wanted.
Yeah, Plan X, Plan SEX, Plan YES.

Plan—*sweet geezus*. He looked down, riveted
by the sight of what she was doing to him, of
her wrapped around him. She ran her tongue
over the top of him again, then closed her mouth
and sucked, and his hips came off the bed—
okay, maybe he wasn't as smart as he thought,
because too much more of that, and it was going to be over.

And yet he most definitely wanted more of
that.

Reaching down, he tunneled his fingers
through her hair, holding her, and he moved
with her—just gave himself up to the soft, wet
heat of her mouth and the firm but gentle
stroking of her hand. *Oh, yeah*, she was sweet.
He spread his legs a little wider for her, and she
slid her hand farther down to massage his
balls—and yeah, it was a short trip from there
into never-never land, where he never, never
wanted her to stop.

The temperature in the room was hovering
somewhere between swelter and melt, despite
the air conditioner, and his body was hovering
in just about the same area. Sweltering was
good, she had him so hot, her mouth working
him over, her hands doing the same—*geezus*, he
probably was in love, or maybe it was just that

he always felt like he was in love when a woman was going down on him. Except he remembered he'd felt like he was in love just a little while ago, when he'd had her up against the bathroom counter.

Of course, that was also a very emotionally vulnerable time for a guy, when he had a naked woman up against a counter, any kind of a counter.

So great. He was building a track record here. Sometimes that "You're going down on me and I'm in love" feeling disappeared as quickly as the woman's mouth, and sometimes it had been known to linger for a while, sometimes days, sometimes months.

He was three weeks into Lily Robbins already, and he could guarantee he wasn't giving her up after this, not for a long time, not until they'd had a chance to do this a whole lot more times, or at least until he had a chance to figure it all out.

And he sure as hell wasn't giving her up when she did that—a soft groan escaped him, and he felt himself straining into her mouth, pushing deeper.

"Sweetheart." He called her, wondering what she really wanted here—because he knew what she was going to get. "Lily."

In answer, she lifted her head, and the look on her face just about did him completely in. Her gaze was languorous, her hair damp, her mouth wet, and suddenly, it wasn't about what she wanted. It was about what he had to have— her, giving it up for him.

But he wasn't the one in charge. He started to pull her up so he could kiss her, so he could get between her legs, and she let out a soft laugh and pushed him back onto the bed, and when her mouth slid down the length of him again, he didn't fight it—oh, hell, no.

She played him until he didn't have a stray thought left in his head. He was focused, with a capital F, every breath, every impulse, every synapse on only one thing—the next touch of her tongue, the next stroke of her hand, the next pull of her mouth, and the next, and the next, and the next, until she took him exactly where she'd wanted him to go, straight over the edge, free fall all the way.

His body was tight, his cock rock hard—and his release one endless stream of hot pleasure coursing through him.

At the end, he pulled free from her mouth and dragged her up into his arms. *Geezus.* Holding her close, he slid his hand around the back of her neck and buried his face in her hair.

Geezus. And he held her, feeling the softness of her breasts against his chest, feeling her breath blowing warm against his neck, and feeling like he'd crossed a line he'd drawn in the sand a long time ago.

Sex was sex, he told himself. It always felt great. There was no reason to read anything more into it, no matter how good she smelled, and how good she felt, and how much she turned him inside out.

Yeah, sex was sex, and love was love, and the last time those two had slammed together in his life, he'd gotten his heart cut out. So a guy had to be careful. A guy had to be smart about things like this.

She sighed, and softened, her body relaxing against his, and as he held her, he felt her drift off to sleep in his arms.

Yeah, he was being careful all right.

Hell, he was the one who needed to fall asleep, but here he was, wide awake all of a sudden, and thinking way too hard.

Dammit. He hated it when this happened.

He kissed her shoulder, just because it was there, then arranged himself so he could stare at the ceiling and think about the mission, and the bracelet, and the thousand other things he needed to stay on top of to get them out of here, but it was so damn hot in the room, all he could think about was the heat.

Hell, it had been hot the first time he'd been in New Mexico, too. He'd been fifteen. July had been the month, and he and J.T. had been on a mission to rescue Hawkins from the evil clutches of a *bruja*, a west side sorceress named Alazne Morello who had spirited Christian out of Denver in the middle of the night and was holding him captive at some ranch in northern New Mexico.

God, talk about a road trip. He and J.T. had left the chop shop at noon, driving one of Sparky Klimaszewski's Cadillacs, a turquoise El Dorado with white leather interior, a convertible, and they'd driven it with the top down all the way, wearing sunglasses with the radio blaring. By the time J.T. had pulled the Caddy to a stop on a short rise overlooking a flat stretch of the plains, the sun had been going down . . .

"I don't think we're going to have any trouble busting him out of there," Zach said, looking at the small adobe cabin shimmering in the heat below. The place wasn't exactly what he'd been expecting. To hear Dylan and J.T. talk, it was damn near impossible to escape, taking superhuman acts of fortitude, strength, and will, like a fortress or something, and what Zach was looking at was more of an oasis, and honestly, not much

of a ranch, unless keeping a few goats and chickens counted as ranching.

The small house was very tidy, the outside walls painted a faded rose, the wooden door a sun-bleached robin's egg blue to match the shutters on the windows. A short rock wall with a big wooden gate enclosed a courtyard at the front of the cabin, and he could see flowers everywhere, fruit trees shading a table, and a water fountain bubbling in the middle of a stone patio, splashing water on the stones.

"More trouble than you think, Ensign," J.T. said, slouched back in the driver's seat, one arm stretched out over the steering wheel. His arms were burned brown by the sun, his white T-shirt coated with a fine layer of dust.

J.T. worked out, and his muscles were huge, even at seventeen. Zach had been doing the protein drink thing, trying to build a little bulk of his own.

He glanced at his arm where he'd rested it on the Caddy's door frame and very casually made a fist. Yeah, he was getting there. Nothing like J.T., not yet, but he was getting there.

"So what's the plan?" he asked, looking back over to the other side of the car. "We swoop down, snatch him, and swoop back out?" He hadn't wanted to admit it to J.T., but the whole idea of going up against a sorceress pretty much scared

*the crap out of him. He'd given it a lot of thought
on the drive down, and he thought clean and fast
was the only way to go. Get in. Get Hawkins. And
get out.*

"No," J.T. said, *his gaze not wavering from the
small, colorful house sitting down below, bathed
in New Mexican sunlight.* "She's going to want
to have wine."

Wine?

He had to be kidding?

"Uh, I don't think drinking with her is a very
good idea." *Didn't J.T. know anything about sorceresses? Geez, Zach did, and they could all be
summed up in one word—dangerous, especially
to men. The sorceresses didn't go after the women
so much. It was the men they wanted. Hell, they
were here to rescue Hawkins, weren't they? A
guy. And weren't they just a couple more guys?*

*Morgan Le Fay, he wanted to say, but some-
how, he didn't think J.T. spent a lot of his time
reading about King Arthur.*

*Zach did. A lot. And Morgan Le Fay had been
that guy's freaking doom.*

*But J.T. didn't seem to be listening. He was
watching the house, and being very still, or maybe
he was watching the water splashing out of the
fountain, or the wind drifting through the flower
beds.*

"You see that table over there under the trees?" he finally said.

"Yes."

"That's where she'll bring us food. It's a nice evening, going into dusk, and she'll want to eat outside."

How in the hell would J.T. know that? And "going into dusk"? What was up with that? It was almost poetic, and coming out of J.T., the biggest and baddest of them all, it didn't do a damn thing to reassure Zach that they knew what they were doing here. But it did a couple of damn things to make him wonder if the sorceress knew they were sitting up on the road, staring at her place, and she was sending some kind of spell up the hill to confuse them.

Confusion was a great trick of enchantresses, and they seemed to have a powerful knack for confusing men.

Dusk. J.T. didn't use words like dusk. Zach did, but he sure as hell didn't use them down at the shop.

He was beginning to think that maybe this was one scrape Hawkins should get out of on his own, or that maybe he and J.T. should have brought a couple more guys with them.

The place was a trap, and when J.T. reached down and turned the key in the ignition, starting the Caddy back up, Zach didn't know what *alarmed him more, that they were actually going down there, or the huge grin on J.T.'s face.*

Alazne . . . her name alone was enough to bring a grin to Zach's face, even after all these years. She'd been twenty-eight the summer she'd cast her spell over him, the summer he'd been seventeen. Dylan had been the first chop-shop boy she'd spirited away, and of them all, Zach thought the boss had come away the least scathed, the least changed. Alazne had met her match in Dylan Hart, and Zach figured that's how the whole connection between the west side *bruja* and the Steele Street boys had begun.

J.T., she'd cut, literally, with a sacred knife over a fire of mesquite and sage, three lines deeply incised in his upper left arm. He was a warrior, she'd said, and he'd needed a warrior's mark.

Hawkins, she'd given wings, literally, tattooed them in a great sweep up one of his arms and across his back and down the other arm to past his wrist. He was the dark angel, a savior. She'd kept him longer than all the other boys, over twice as long. Too long, Dylan had said the morning he'd sent J.T. and Zach down to New Mexico to bring him back.

She'd waited longer for Quinn, until he was almost eighteen, and it wasn't what she'd given him so much as what she'd taken, some of his anger. He'd had a lot as a kid.

Then she'd taken Zach, "spirited" him away one night in her old green pickup, making the moonlight ride from Denver to her place in New Mexico for a month of lazy days and long nights, and during those long days, and especially during those long hot nights, she'd given him something he'd had damn little of in life—trust, a hundred reasons and a thousand ways to trust a woman. He'd never forgotten the lesson.

Last, she'd taken Creed, and she'd taken him young, and of that encounter, all Zach had been able to surmise was that it had been Alazne who had been changed. Or maybe she'd run out of time for saving lost boys. No one knew, they only knew she'd never taken another, not from Steele Street.

None of the guys ever talked about their time with Alazne. They all knew what happened in New Mexico. That it was magical, and sexual, and profound. For a month each, or two months with Hawkins, she let boys be men, and there wasn't a one of them who hadn't thought he'd been up to the task. The experience changed them for life.

He looked down at Lily sleeping in his arms.

Life-changing experiences, yeah, he'd had a few. He avoided them for the most part— he bent his head down and kissed her on the forehead—but he sure as hell hadn't avoided this one.

CHAPTER NINETEEN

Saturday, 12:30 P.M. —Albuquerque, New Mexico

"Spence, I think we've got something," Mallory said from the balcony of their suite at La Paloma, The Dove. The hotel was exclusive, not listed in a phone book anywhere, and, of course, almost prohibitively expensive. Tucked away on forty acres of what had once been a much larger estate, the mansion epitomized the grace and elegance of southwestern architecture. Few concessions had been made to its transformation into a hotel, other than state-of-the-art business amenities and world-class communications in every room.

Mallory had been using all of them since they'd checked in for what he hoped would be a very short stay.

"What, Kitten?" he asked, walking out onto

the balcony. He'd taken a shower, washing off the day's dark deed, and had wrapped a towel around his waist.

At forty-five, he knew he was in his prime, steel-bellied, muscled, at the top of his game with years of experience behind him. He'd been told more than once that he looked like Bruce Willis, and he always thought that Bruce should look so good.

"It's a stray conversation on a police band out of Mora County. I set up my audio recognition to cue on the car, just like you suggested, and the word red gave me a hit, some squad complaining about a red car 'going over a hunnert' coming off the interstate."

She was a genius, and exceptionally beautiful, with chestnut-colored hair and exotic green eyes. She had pale skin, perfectly arched brows, and lush, generous curves, and she'd been solely and exclusively his for the last ten years.

"Where's Mora County?" he asked.

"North of Santa Fe."

"A lot of red cars can go over a hundred miles an hour." It was a lead, but not a good lead, and he didn't want to find himself north of Santa Fe and then discover he needed to be west of Albuquerque, heading to Las Vegas, and he had a feeling they were going to end up in Vegas.

Things happened there. Nothing happened north of Albuquerque, because there wasn't anything north of Albuquerque. Denver, Colorado, was up there somewhere, he supposed, but what in the hell ever happened in Denver?

He no sooner asked the question than a couple of answers hit him hard. There'd been a bloodbath in Denver five months ago. Lots of big names getting whacked, Zane Lowe for one, and Tony Royce for another, and a whole team of Royce's men—and they'd all been killed by Gillian Pentycote, Red Dog. Everybody knew the girl had been gunning for Royce since the day she'd come out of rehab. It was how she'd gotten hooked up with Kendryk. She'd gotten blown on a hit, and then she'd wanted favors.

Jesus.

He needed to think.

"Pull up the intel files Kendryk gave us on the bracelet," he said. "Especially the information Kendryk got from Irena Polchenko." Now there was a world-class criminal mind, utterly ruthless; ran her organization with an iron fist and a half-Greek, half-Guatemalan henchman named Ari Poulos and a very scary guy named Hans Klechner, a former East German intelligence officer.

Over the last year, Irena had coordinated and

executed a couple of very lucrative deals for Kendryk in South America. She'd also been the one to give him the heads-up on the CIA plane shot down in El Salvador three weeks ago. When it came to the people with the money, the clout, and the brains to truly run a criminal organization on an international level, the company got pretty rarified. Kendryk ruled the top level of black marketeering, partly because of the legitimate base of his operations, and Polchenko was a definite up-and-comer into the trade at those higher levels.

In comparison, he and Mallory were very small-time, more errand boys than movers and shakers, which was exactly the way Spencer had planned his career, but which in no way meant he could afford to be careless or sloppy.

"Got them," Mallory said, pulling the files up on her computer screen.

"Give me the names attached to this deal."

"Dr. Mila Yanukovich."

The Russian scientist, the Nobel laureate, who had sold out her country and the West by colluding with the Iranians on nuclear technology—she was the one who'd gotten this all going.

"Skip the Eastern Europe data, and go straight to what happened in El Salvador three weeks ago." That's where Irena had come into the deal, and her information was the closest they had to the last known location of the bracelet—until he'd gotten more recent intel out of Jason Schroder this morning.

"Alejandro Campos."

Spencer knew of him, but he was strictly small-time. He played well in Central America and northern South America, but he didn't get much beyond that.

"Diego Garcia."

Dead. Even alive he'd been very small-time on the world stage, but he had been the one tasked with downing the plane, Spencer was now guessing by Ivan Nikolevna, who had plenty of Ukrainian-gas-lease reasons to want the information encoded on the CIA's macramé bracelet. As low tech as the transportation device was, it was proving very effective. In three weeks, no one had seen hide nor hair of it, and all anybody seemed to have was a name, Lily Robbins, and nobody was having any luck finding her either, even with a goddamn personal address—except for the unknown shooter with the Shelby Cobra Mustang.

Spencer was going to end up hating that guy. He could already tell.

"Honoria York-Lytton."

She had been one of Irena's nearly priceless

pieces of intelligence. Whatever York-Lytton's connection to the bracelet happened to be or not be, she was next on Spencer's list. She was American, a Washington, D.C. socialite, and the bracelet had ended up in America, a fact confirmed by the hapless Jason Schroder mere hours ago.

From the looks of her, she'd probably take about ten seconds to break. Come to think of it, she was probably the perfect size for Mallory to sharpen her claws on.

"Miguel Carranza."

Big-time on the world stage, very big-time, head of the Cali cartel out of Colombia, business associate of Polchenko's. He was the one who'd contracted with Polchenko for the hit on Garcia. Spencer wasn't going to get within a thousand miles of the guy, no matter what Kendryk offered. If Carranza wanted the bracelet, he could have it.

"C. Smith Rydell."

Honoria York-Lytton's bodyguard, formerly with the DEA; he and Polchenko had worked together in Afghanistan. Polchenko had confirmed his connection to Joint Ops Central in Lima, doing counter-drug operations with the DEA, and that he'd been assigned to York-Lytton through the U.S. State Department.

And after that, nothing. He'd shown up in El Salvador, and disappeared from same.

"We've got two usable names," he said.

"Campos and York-Lytton," Mallory agreed.

"York-Lytton is closer." And the woman's life was an open book. Every move she made was splashed in a newspaper somewhere. If he and Mallory headed to the airport now, they could probably have York-Lytton tied up, literally, by nightfall. Even if she didn't know anything about the bracelet, she'd know something about her bodyguard. Any small thing would help.

"Give me five minutes to get us a flight out of here," Mallory said, reaching for her keyboard. Then she stopped and looked up at him. "We know from Irena's report that Rydell and York-Lytton flew into Ilopango when they arrived in El Salvador. She even had the load manifest for the cargo on the C-130 they arrived on. But she doesn't say how they left."

"Chances are it was out of Ilopango. Who do we know there?"

She laughed. "The only person we need to know is Kendryk. Let me put a call through. Irena has good contacts all over El Salvador, and especially good contacts at Ilopango. Someone in Weymouth can have her give us a call. It shouldn't take more than an hour or two."

"So what are we going to do until then?" he

asked, already coming up with a couple of ideas.

"Well, my love," she said, a very catlike smile curving her lips, "for starters, you could give me your towel."

CHAPTER TWENTY

Saturday, 2:30 P.M.—Denver, Colorado

Four hours.

That's how long it had taken Cherie and Dr. Shore to put the DREAGAR 454 hard drive back together. Four hours of almost nonstop lecturing on Marsh Annex protocols, and what was and was not allowed when doing contract work for the Marsh Annex, and how he was going to have to write her up for destroying an invaluable piece of Marsh Annex equipment of which there were only twelve in the whole world.

Bull, she'd thought. If he'd gotten his hands on a supercalifragilistic piece of hardware, he would have done the same thing, she'd told him, and then she'd very politely pointed out to him that the DREAGAR 454 had not been destroyed. That lo and behold, once they put all the pieces back together and tweaked them a bit, the darn thing worked perfectly.

Probably even better than the one he had in his office at the Marsh Annex—but he hadn't wanted to hear any of that.

And he'd driven Roxanne back to Steele Street—the jerk. She couldn't believe she'd thought he was cute, even for a minute.

He wasn't. He was obnoxious, and overbearing, and rather condescending, and she didn't like him at all, and he and Dylan were in Dylan's office—with an extra chair, no less—having their very important meeting, with Skeeter and Gillian going in and out, and Cherie being the only one specifically not going in, which left her specifically out.

She hated him for that, too, just for the hell of it.

Whatever was going on with the DREAGAR 454 was top secret, and she knew better than to be curious, but it just added to the whole damn day.

Setting her computer in her lap, she swiveled back around so she could see out her window, and she took another long drag off her cigarette. Her soda can was in plain sight on top of her desk, and they could all just lump it.

Dammit. If she lost the 2Z8 contract for the

DREAGAR 454 Subliminal Neuron Intel Interfacers, she'd never forgive herself. Danny wouldn't forgive her, either—and to think the day had started out with such promise. She should have just gone to damn Cabo San Lucas.

Smoking, and bitching quietly to herself, she scrolled down on her computer screen to the next schematic drawing of Steele Street. The building was old, built way back in the 1940s, but the original blueprints had still been around when she'd first started with Dylan and the boys, and she'd had everything converted to digital. New drawings had been done when Dylan had reinforced the building with steel, and there had been another set done sometime in between those two.

She was comparing all of the drawings, floor by floor, trying to spot something she'd never seen before—a weakness, a place her security system did not reach. After two hours of looking, she hadn't found it yet.

She scrolled to the next page, took another draw off her cigarette, and dropped the old ash in her soda can.

Everybody in the office was on edge, including Skeeter. Honey had left to go back to Washington, D.C., and Cherie had been sitting in the main office all alone since she and Dr.

Shore had gotten back. Normally, she would have gone home, but Dylan had very specifically told her to stay put at Steele Street.

He'd been a little upset about having to wait four hours to get the download off the DREAGAR. To his credit, Gabriel Shore had not blamed her for the problem. In fact, he'd taken all the heat himself, not even telling Dylan that she'd taken the hard drive apart.

She didn't regret it, not for a minute, and everything she'd learned taking it apart, she'd learned twice as well when she and Shore had put it back together. There were still three pieces that she'd kept intact, recognizing them for what they were—the heart and soul of the DREAGAR 454, the "subliminal" part of the subliminal neuron intel interfacer. She hadn't infringed on his copyright, and she'd been careful to point that out to him as well.

At least he'd taken the heat.

She probably owed him for that, though God only knew what someone as uppity and overbearing as Gabriel Shore would want in payment.

The next set of pages she scrolled to was the basement. She'd been over them half a dozen times, but logically, the basement was the most likely place for a breach, and this time when she looked, going over the damn thing millimeter by millimeter, she saw it, a small break in the line on the north side of the building.

It was either a breach, or it was a small widget in the drawings where someone had merely forgotten to connect the dots, and there was only one way to find out which it was—breach or widget.

Go look.

Fortunately, technically, wherever the widget break was would still be in the building. So fortunately, technically, even if she went looking for it, she'd still be staying put at Steele Street, and fortunately, she had a pair of cargo pants in her carry-on.

It took her all of two minutes to shimmy into the pants under her dress, another minute to get her Dior off over the top of her head, all behind the relative privacy of her big swivel chair, and about fifteen seconds to drag a T-shirt on. Her gold Blahniks went on the floor, next to her chair. One pair of socks and her desert tan tactical boots later, and all she needed was her backpack and her very own personal palm-sized Bazo VJX-UZ468 700 series PC.

She downloaded the drawings onto her Bazo, tightened the laces on her boots, slung her pack over the shoulder, and followed orders. She

stayed put at Steele Street. She didn't go anywhere—except down.

Spencer woke to the distinctive ringing of
Mallory's cell phone—the opening riffs of B.B.
King and Lucille doing "The Thrill Is Gone."

The thrill was never gone with Mallory. Smiling, he watched the sheet slide off her body as
she leaned over the side of the bed, reaching for
her phone. Pretty kitty, she was all curves, and
she was all his.

"Yes," she said, answering the phone, and a
moment later, she said it again. "Yes."

He slid his hand over her hip, loving the silky
feel of her skin. He pampered her, and it was
his pleasure.

"Thanks, Rick," she said, and he knew she
was talking with Rick Connelly, the head of
Kendryk's intel and information network in
Weymouth, England. "Let Kendryk know how
helpful Irena Polchenko has been. She's saved
us hours on this job, and go ahead and narrow
your Shelby Cobra Mustang search down to
Denver. The more quickly you could get us
those names and addresses, the better. Photos
would be helpful, but I know that's a lot to ask."

She laughed then, a throaty, sexy sound, and Spencer leaned over and gently bit her on the butt. She worked men with her voice, and Rick Connelly wasn't immune.

"That would be great, Rick," she said. "I won't forget."

She set the phone down and rolled back over to face him. "Three weeks ago, Alejandro Campos ordered up a private jet in Ilopango. The first stop was Albuquerque."

Which was no surprise.

"After Albuquerque, there was a change in the flight plan from Washington, D.C., to Denver, Colorado."

"So we head north," he said, and she smiled.

"We head north."

Saturday, 3:30 P.M.—Denver, Colorado

The damn CIA.

There was a reason Dylan and the damn CIA had been at loggerheads for the last fourteen years, and it wasn't only because they'd caught him unofficially "couriering" a few of their documents out of Moscow back when he'd been too green to stay out of their clutches. They'd used the word "stealing" back then, but as with most things concerning the CIA, it was a murky designation and had more to do with point of view than a viable prosecution.

They hadn't changed. Murky was still their calling card.

"What do you mean, he doesn't want to play?" he asked Skeeter, who was standing next to his desk with a very unhappy look on her face. Gabriel Shore had stepped out of Dylan's office to take a phone call, but Gillian was present, and she didn't look happy either.

"Alex Maier says his boy is good and can handle himself," Skeeter said. "That he's not running interference with the New Mexico cops, and that he's not letting us in on the deal, and he thanked us for hooking Zach up with the tracking device, but this was under his jurisdiction, and we were to stay out of it."

"Have you done a background check on Lily Robbins?"

"She's clean, Dylan. One hundred percent schoolteacher, born and raised in Montana, divorced for a year, went to El Salvador to film a documentary on nuns, just like Honey said."

"At the church where the CIA pilot died," he said. "They could have had contact."

"Which opens up a can of worms big enough to pull a deep-cover agent out of Central America and send him to Albuquerque to talk with the woman."

"Only to run into two guys with mob connections from Las Vegas already there ahead of him," Dylan filled in the next blank.

"Those guys both end up dead, real quick," Skeeter finished. "And whoever killed the second one is looking for the deep-cover agent, has his car identified, and isn't too far behind."

Yes, Zach was definitely taking care of himself.

"Dylan," she said. "We figured this all out hours ago. If we're really going to help him, if we're going to get ahead of this instead of just chase our tails, we need to know why he went after Lily Robbins, why the Vegas guys went after Lily Robbins. And the only thing that makes sense is that the CIA's pilot gave her something, either something physical, or some kind of code, which she may or may not even know she has."

"General Grant is working on it." And Grant had come up with the same damn idea: There had been contact between the schoolteacher from Albuquerque and the CIA pilot. It was the only plausible connection.

"We need more than Grant working on this, or we're going to end up with a dead chop-shop boy and wish we'd tried harder."

Dylan, apparently, had a little more faith in Zach than Skeeter did.

"He survived four years in Asia and eight in El Salvador without us," he said.

"And now he's knocking on our back door with a pack of wolves on his ass."

She was right.

He looked at Gillian, and she said the one thing they were all thinking.

"White Rook. Tell him to get on Alex Maier and get us what we need."

And then she said something nobody else was thinking. "Until then, I'll fire up Corinna and head to Paysen, New Mexico. That's where you've got the Bazo holding, isn't it, Skeet?"

"Uh, yes, but no, I—"

"No," Dylan echoed the sentiment. "You're not going anywhere."

"I could go," Skeeter said.

He gave her a look that very clearly said no, she wasn't going anywhere either, thank you very much—and again, for the record, what in the hell was Hawkins doing in Disneyland?

"Nobody's going anywhere," he said. "Skeeter, you stay on the police bands. If he's spotted, he needs to know immediately. I'll contact Grant again, see if he's been able to rattle any cages on his end."

"Tell him to rattle Alex Maier," Gillian said.

Gunners, he thought. He was surrounded by gunners on estrogen.

"We've got a problem," Gabriel Shore said, rushing back into the office.

They had more than one, Dylan could have told him.

"One of my contacts who covers Kendryk just called to confirm that Spencer Bayonne left New York late last night on a flight heading to Albuquerque, New Mexico." The young man looked distressed—whereas a quick look around the office showed everyone else looking pretty much flabbergasted. "I don't know what would make Bayonne think Gillian is in Albuquerque, but that's too damn close to discount it as a co-incidence. He has no connections anywhere in New Mexico. Albuquerque has never shown up anywhere in his files. I think he's going for the two million, not the encryption code. He's closing in on her."

Bayonne was closing in on somebody, all right.

"That's it," Skeeter said.

"We've got him," Gillian added, a wicked smile curving her lips. "Now we can get ahead of the game."

Gunners, Dylan thought, looking at his two female operators, and suddenly, the day didn't look quite so goddamn long.

CHAPTER TWENTY-ONE

Saturday, 4:00 P.M.—Paysen, New Mexico

Zach was inside her again, moving slow, staying half asleep, so lazy and sweet. She slid her tongue into his mouth, again and again, and he angled his head for a better fit.

Her body was hot against his, her skin hot. They were both damp with sweat, and he figured if they ever decided to get out of bed—and that was a long shot—they could hit the shower and do the same damn thing, over and over again, except with soap.

Yeah. That sounded like a great idea.

She lifted her hips against him, rocking into him, and he slid his hand down to cup her ass and hold her close. He was probably in love.

About an hour ago, she'd sutured his shoulder with one of his kits, five stitches across the top. He'd thought he'd only needed three, given the complete lack of anesthetic, but she'd gone the extra mile. Of course, she'd done it naked, so there had been some compensation for the pain. She was so stacked.

He thrust into her again, drawing her leg up over his hip, getting closer.

"You feel so good," she whispered against his mouth, and yeah, that pretty much summed up all of his thoughts, too—*You feel so good. Better than good.* His brain was melting.

What a perfect day.

Murder, mayhem, a hot car, a hotter woman, a killer on the loose, and the cops on his ass—he could give it up. Sure he could, all of it except the woman, and the car. He needed those. He didn't mind mayhem either, if he was the one instigating it on some lowlife. Murder never bothered him, though he preferred the less litigious and more accurate word "killing." Sometimes that's what the job took, and he'd never lost any sleep over doing his job. Not that aspect of it anyway.

"*Mmmm, Zach.*" She tightened around him, her breath sighing in his ear.

He loved it, the way she whispered his name, the silky wet heat of her.

Bearing her back down onto the pillows, he

moved into her faster and harder, until it was all over one more time.

He lay there for a few moments, just breathing in the lovely way she smelled, and trying to get his head back on straight. A smile curved his lips. It was hopeless. She was amazing, and he wasn't going to get his head on straight any time soon. Rolling off of her, he collapsed back on the bed and wondered, honest to God, could they really do this all day long?

Another grin curved his mouth as he settled in next to her and pulled her close. Yeah, he thought, they probably could.

The ringing of his phone told him it probably didn't matter what he wondered.

He reached over and picked his cell up off the nightstand.

"Yes," he said.

"Ensign, this is SB303 with all the late-breaking news."

"Go on," he said, checking his watch. Four o'clock—still midday. They had a few hours to go until dark.

"We think we know who killed Jason Schroder and that he is after the encryption key we believe you are carrying."

Fuck. He thought it, but he didn't say it— and he was now, officially, one hundred percent awake.

"Go on." He wasn't admitting to anything, not without direct orders from Alex.

"According to our source, a lot of sharks are in the water on this, and they're all going to be looking for you, or whoever they think has the encryption key."

Nothing new there, but how in the hell had SB303 found out about the encryption key? Then again, it was SDF, and Dylan Hart.

"Schroder's killer, we believe, is a man named Spencer Bayonne. He runs with a woman, Mallory Rush. Both of them are contract players, and they specifically do a lot of contract work for a man named Sir Arthur Kendryk."

"Never heard of any of them." Which didn't mean much.

"We're hoping they haven't heard of you, either," SB303 said. "But we can guarantee that they've heard of Lily Robbins."

He was beginning to wonder who *hadn't* heard about Lily Robbins and her ratty little macramé bracelet with the fate of the free world woven into its knots.

"Who's your source?"

"Family, sent to us by Grant."

Christ. It didn't get any better than that, and Zach wondered if Alex knew his case was leaking like an antique sieve. *Shit.*

His case officer had said a lot of people were

in on this, a lot of people trying to retrieve the bracelet, and a lot of people trying to cover their asses for the loss of top-secret, foreign-policy-shaking intelligence. Alex had been more worried about the State Department on the "covering their ass" end, but it seemed to Zach that the Department of Defense had a leg up on all of them. SDF sure as hell did.

"What are you recommending?"

"Stick with the plan. You come here. We secure the data, get it to your boss, and once he knows he's won, he can come in and clean up the mess. With everybody at the top happy, nobody is going to care too much about what we had to do at the bottom to make it so."

Make it so. Zach couldn't help but grin. How many times had he gotten a set of orders with the unspoken but strongly implied directive of "Make it so."

"Are you sure you don't want to claim this victory for yourself?" It was possible. It happened all the time, at all levels of the playing field.

"You're the one with your ass on the line and with some very bad people out to kick it. The boss says come home and you can have all the glory."

Glory. Zach did laugh at that. There was no glory. That was the point.

"And that's all the good news," she said.

If that was the good news, he went ahead and braced himself for the bad.

"Go on."

"Lily Robbins is officially a murder suspect in the killing of Paul Stark at her house this morning. Given the crime scene and that she fled, nobody in Albuquerque is particularly thinking self-defense anymore."

"They couldn't possibly have the coroner's report yet." Good God, it hadn't even been twelve hours since Paul Stark had come out of the stairwell.

"Their change of heart, from Ms. Robbins being taken hostage by whoever killed Stark to Ms. Robbins killing Stark, is based on a spent casing they found in her bathroom that matches the casings on a couple of boxes of hand-loaded cartridges they discovered in her gun safe."

"So we're all fugitives from justice."

"All three of you," she agreed, and he knew exactly who she meant—him, Lily, and Charlotte. The cops were looking for all of them.

Suddenly the border seemed a very long way away.

"What coroner's report? Who's a fugitive from justice?" The voice came from behind him, and he could have kicked himself. "Is that SB303?"

He turned to look at Lily, and gave her a short

nod. He'd tell her in a minute. He just wasn't going to tell her the truth. She didn't need any more bad news, especially when it was something he could get cleared up.

No, he decided. He wasn't going to tell her she was wanted for murder.

"What can you tell me about Bayonne?" he asked.

"Quite a bit, actually. He's got verified history of international arms sales. He's especially popular in West Africa. He's also moved a lot of heroin out of Asia, usually at Kendryk's bidding. He has an unsavory habit of cutting people up with his knife, which, as far as I've been able to glean from the scuttlebutt on the airwaves this morning, is what happened to Schroder, a clean Wingate. He apparently has a passing resemblance to Bruce Willis, likes the high life, expensive hotels, luxury cars, good food, rare wine, and his woman, Mallory Rush, not necessarily in that order. The woman is important to him. They've been together a long time, over ten years."

Zach was impressed, and also demoralized. He hadn't been able to keep a woman for ten years, and this scumbag Bayonne had?

There was no justice. Of course, Zach would be the first to admit that he didn't have a passing anything to Bruce Willis, let alone a resemblance.

"We have also verified that he was on a flight from New York to Albuquerque late last night, and no reason to be there except for the same reason you're there."

Didn't anybody have any secrets anymore?

"I'll watch out for him." Watch out for Bruce Willis with a knife.

"Good, Ensign, and I can guarantee we'll be watching out for you."

Yeah, Zach thought, hitting the disconnect and then just looking at the phone in his hand. Yeah, he believed her. For the first time in a long time, he really did believe someone was looking out for him.

CHAPTER TWENTY-TWO

Saturday, 4:30 P.M.—Denver, Colorado

Two hours, this time, Cherie thought. It had only taken her two hours to go from bad to worse, much worse. She'd found the breach. It had been a blind opening, where from even a short distance, no more than five feet, the brick wall on the north side of Steele Street's basement looked solid. It was only upon closer inspection that she'd noticed the wall was actually split, with one part of the wall about two feet farther back than the other part, and considering that whoever had come up with the amazingly simple access had put it close to a corner, it truly was almost invisible. The rats knew it was there, and whoever had stolen Charlotte knew it was there, and Dylan knew, and now she knew, too.

"Lucky, lucky girl," she muttered under her

breath, lifting her flashlight a little higher in hopes of seeing something, anything, she recognized.

She did not.

She was lost in a labyrinth of brick walls, and old tunnels, and abandoned utility access ways. For the most part, the tunnels were dry, but in some parts, she'd been slogging through standing water, and in a couple of places, she'd been slogging through running water, which she'd found particularly intriguing. Running from where to where? she'd wondered.

For a moment, she'd also considered following the running water to see where it went. Actually, she'd considered that course of action for quite a few moments, which is how she'd ended up wherever she'd ended up, somewhere in the dark with the rats and a few other things she wasn't going to think about too much.

This is what happened to girls who drank champagne, and stayed out all night, and didn't get enough sleep. They made bad decisions in tight places.

She could die down here, which seemed a particularly cruel fate, to wander aimlessly until she collapsed from exhaustion and starvation, nothing but a skinny pile of bones for the rats to gnaw on.

Her mother was never going to forgive her.

Crap.

She'd turned on a tracking device Skeeter had given her a few weeks ago that she'd stuffed in her backpack, but she had serious doubts about the signal going any farther than the next tunnel. Her GPS wasn't working, which didn't really surprise her. She had thirteen floors of steel-reinforced building on top of her, and no one "could hear her now" on her cell phone, either. She was in dead space.

Another lovely thought—*dammit*.

Stopping for a minute, she took a swallow of water out of the bottle she always kept in her pack. She also had two granola bars, but she was saving them for later. She needed something to look forward to, besides wandering aimlessly until she died.

What a freaking lousy day.

Pushing on, she decided to go left for a change instead of right. There was a way out, because there was a way in. She just had to find one of those things, the out or the in, and she wasn't too damn particular about which one she ended up with.

Saturday, 4:30 P.M.—north of Albuquerque, New Mexico

"Pull over, Spence," Mallory said, sliding her cursor across her computer screen. "Up on that rise. I've got something coming in."

Spencer pulled onto the shoulder of the interstate and waited to see what she came up with. He was hoping for something from Rick Connelly. He wanted the hot-rodder driving the Shelby Cobra. He wanted Lily Robbins, and he wanted the goddamn bracelet, and then he wanted the hell out of New Mexico.

There was nothing here. Absolutely nothing. He'd never seen so much flat, rolling nothing.

He didn't want to end up spending the night in Denver, Colorado, either. What he wanted was to be back in New York, where he and Mallory could enjoy themselves for a few days at Arthur Kendryk's expense.

He'd changed his mind about upping the price on the bracelet. With anyone else, he would come out ahead by pushing a little harder—but not with Kendryk. Gazprom gas leases in the Ukraine would bring Lord Weymouth millions of dollars, but there was more to that deal than just having the bracelet. Kendryk would know Ivan Nikolevna had sent someone after Lily Robbins, and when Spencer handed the bracelet over, with all its incriminating evidence against a Russian scientist colluding with the Iranians on weapons-grade plutonium, it would make a helluva impression on everyone.

Kendryk could get whatever he wanted with that kind of damaging intelligence. Hell, he could not only get Gazprom gas leases out of the Russians, he could get concessions out of the damn Iranians. That would be sweet, to make the Iranians pony up for a change. Kendryk would love it.

Spencer never had any trouble coming up with a contract for a job, but coming out ahead with this piece of work was going to make him the top "go-to" guy in the world.

"What is it, Kitten?"

She was busy over on her side of the car and didn't answer at first, and then she upped the volume.

"We have a sighting in Mora County, in the town of Paysen, on the BOLO out of Albuquerque," a dispatcher said. "The owner of the Road Runner Motel on Highway 92 heard our bulletin on his police band radio and reported a red Shelby Cobra Mustang to the Mora County Sheriff's Department. The car is parked behind the motel. Be advised, the two people with the car are armed and dangerous. Both are wanted in connection with a pair of murders in Albuquerque this morning."

"Where's Paysen?" he asked.

"I'm checking, Spence," she said, her fingers running over her keyboard. "Okay, it's not that far. We've got an exit about ten miles ahead of us."

He pulled back onto the interstate and gunned the Town Car's motor. Grigori Petrov was out there somewhere, and Spencer could guarantee that The Chechen would have heard the rumor on Somerset Street this morning about the *Bullitt* car, and Spencer could guarantee *Bullitt* played very well in Russia. Petrov would know exactly what he was looking for, and wherever he was, he would definitely be doing what Spencer and Mallory had been doing, listening to the police and waiting for them to find the car.

Mallory reached over and switched on their radar detector. The last thing the two of them needed was to get pulled over. Mallory's record was clean, but Spencer had been walking on the wild side since before he'd turned sixteen, and it had only been in his late twenties that he'd figured out how to play a more lucrative game by contracting his services out to much bigger players.

"Can you give me an ETA?" he asked her.

She looked at his speedometer and keyed the figure into an equation she'd pulled up on top of the map showing their location and the town of Paysen.

She really was amazing, and her computer skills were the least of her attributes. She finished running the numbers and smiled over at him.

"If you can give me another ten miles per hour, Spence, I think we'll be in Paysen in about half an hour."

That close, he thought, and that was perfect.

"Okay, Kitten, hold on." He pressed down on the gas, and the Town Car responded beautifully, with all the sleek, silent power he expected, and at a hundred and twenty miles per hour, New Mexico didn't look so bad.

Saturday, 4:30 P.M.—Denver, Colorado

"Okay, Dylan, this is it," Skeeter said from in front of her communications console. "The cops have tagged him."

Dammit.

"What have they got?" he asked.

"They're not on him yet. The guy who owns the Road Runner Motel in Paysen called in Charlotte, and they've just dispatched the report. Give him a call, tell him to get out of there ASAP, and I'll see who responds."

"It's only four-thirty. Still broad daylight."

"Yeah," she said. "I'm awfully glad I tuned that girl up last week. He's going to have to run Charlotte hard to get out of New Mexico."

Dylan was already on the secure line, making

the call. He didn't need to say it, but they both knew that in a flat-out run to the border, the police had all the odds on their side, not in speed, but in communication. Charlotte could outrun a POS, a Police Officer Special, any day of the week, but she couldn't outrun a Motorola. Alex Maier's secret op was going to be all over the front page—and that was the good news.

With the call going out on the police band, everybody else who was listening and wanted that damn code now knew exactly where it was: Paysen, New Mexico, at the Road Runner Motel.

CHAPTER TWENTY-THREE

Saturday, 4:30 P.M.—Paysen, New Mexico

"Come on, babe. We've got to move. We've been made." Zach swung up off the bed, hanging up his phone and pulling Lily with him. "The cops are going to be here in about ten minutes. Let's go."

He didn't need to say it twice. She was grabbing clothes and shucking into them, almost before her feet hit the floor.

"Ten minutes?" she said.

"Nine, now."

She tossed him his shoulder holster from next to the sink. He caught it and returned the favor with her jeans. It was commando all the way. Nobody bothered with underwear.

"Get the gun bag," he said, since it was closer

to her. He did a quick mental check for his pistol, holster, phone, wallet, and then he was heading out the door and grabbing one of the grocery bags as he went. He hadn't brought her suitcase in with them, or his duffel.

She was right next to him, with a shirt and her jeans on, her feet in her boots, and the gun bag over her shoulder. He also noted that she had her pistol in her hand.

Good girl, he thought, right along with *Zach, you better watch your ass.*

Two minutes later, he was firing Charlotte up, and for a moment, it looked like a clean getaway. Then it went to hell.

The old guy who ran the motel came running out the back of the damn store, toting a damn shotgun.

Shit! He jammed Charlotte into reverse and slammed on the gas. *Goddammit.* If that old fart shot his car, he was going to come back and run over him twice. *Goddammit.*

Ka-boom!

That old sonuvabitch. So help him God, Zach was going to—*Ka-boom!*

Dust was flying. Tires were squealing. Charlotte's engine was roaring—and that old sonuvabitch had just hit a goddamn Shelby. Right front quarter panel, *goddammit*. Zach had felt the hit as he'd spun the wheel to get around the goddamn building. He slammed on the brakes, spinning the wheel the other direction, and when Charlotte came around a hundred and eighty degrees, he slid her up into first and started power-shifting them the hell out of the god-damn Road Runner Motel.

They hit pavement in third gear.

Ka-boom!

But by then the old fart was shooting at air, and Charlotte was streaking toward the horizon at a hundred and twenty miles an hour in less than fifteen seconds.

A mile later, he slowed her down and hit the eject button on the tape deck. The Bazo computer came sliding out.

"SB303, I need a road." They had to get off Highway 92. Any deputy who was answering the call at Paysen would be coming one way or the other down Highway 92.

"You're on it," SB303 said.

"Ninety-two is it?" There had to be another road.

"For the next twenty miles."

Shit.

"I'm seeing a few going here and there," he said.

"Paved?"

"No." It might be a shit-for-brains idea to get

off on an unpaved road, but right now anything looked better than the highway.

"It's a bad idea, but it's the only idea," she said. "I'll do what I can on this end to keep you from getting rimrocked."

Rimrocked, corraled, ambushed—whatever, it was all bad. The old sonuvabitch at the Road Runner could tell the cops they'd gone north, and it wasn't going to take a rocket scientist to realize they'd gotten off the highway on one of these goddamn gravel roads throwing up a rooster tail of dust. All the authorities needed was one freaking helicopter, and it was all going to be over.

Getting caught by the cops in New Mexico wasn't going to look very good on his resume. As a matter of fact, it could be a career-ender. He didn't have any illusions about that. One deep-cover agent showing up on the radar was an easy sacrifice, if it helped smooth ruffled Potomac feathers.

But it wasn't really the cops he was worried about. It was the guy who'd killed Jason Schroder. He was out there, this Spencer Bayonne, and from everything SB303 had told him, Bayonne was a professional. The cops wouldn't shoot him or Lily on sight, not without provocation, which they weren't going to get. But somebody like Bayonne was a different story. If killing them was the quickest way to stop them, then he was going to go for it, or at least do his best. All Bayonne wanted was the CIA intelligence on the Russian scientist and the Iranian nuclear program, and if he'd gotten this far, he knew exactly what he was looking for, that damn piece of macramé that had been knotted into a bracelet.

He glanced over at Lily.

"Are you okay?" he asked her. She had the gun bag at her feet and a strong, two-handed grip on her pistol, finger off the trigger, straight along the slide. She was so ready—and for a second, she reminded him of Jewel.

"Yes," she said. "But I think we lost Charlotte's right headlight."

Yeah, he thought so, too.

"What do you want? On or off the highway?" he asked her, open to another opinion.

"Off," she said, and he realized she probably felt like him, like a sitting duck on this strip of pavement.

Hell. His instincts were screaming at him to get off the damn highway.

So he did, taking the next left onto a dirt road that, after a hundred meters, slid off behind a low-rising bluff.

Saturday, 5:00 P.M.—Paysen, New Mexico

There were three Sheriff's Department cars, one unmarked car, five deputies, and one old man with a shotgun standing in the parking lot of the Road Runner Motel when Spencer and Mallory cruised by at five miles an hour under the speed limit. A man in a suit was coming out of the room on the end of the motel, and there was a deputy and another guy in a suit on the other side of the highway, talking to two people who were sitting at a picnic table in the shade of a canopy hanging off the side of a trailer.

"Well, there's the motel," Mallory said. "Where's the town? Up ahead, do you think?"

"No, Kitten. This is it, the whole kit and caboodle, Paysen, New Mexico."

"There's no red 1968 Mustang."

"No." There sure wasn't.

A car crested the rise on the horizon, a silver Mercedes, coming from the other direction and heading down Highway 92 toward the motel. Spencer kept his speed even at five below the limit.

"Oh, my god," Mallory said when the car was almost upon them. "Do you see who that is?"

Yes, he did. *Dammit*.

"Grigori Petrov." The Chechen. Ivan Nikolevna's man.

The Mercedes passed on by, but not before Spencer felt laser-raked by the driver's gaze.

Two miles farther on, there was a blue Buick parked by the side of the road. One man was inside the car. Another was standing by the rear bumper with a cell phone, talking. The car was nondescript, but the men were anything but average. They looked like a couple of hoods in bad suits. Spencer could actually see the bulge of a shoulder holster under the jacket of the guy standing outside.

"I know that car," Mallory said. "It was parked a block down from Lily Robbins's house this morning."

"A blue Buick?" Spencer asked. "How do you know it was that one?"

"It has a University of Texas bumper sticker on the rear windshield and a broken antenna."

It sure did. He was impressed.

"Texas license plate number LV-3971," she said aloud as they passed by. "I'll send it to Rick Connelly and see what he gets."

His girl was the best, but not even the best was going to find a red Shelby Mustang in this huge expanse of empty landscape, not without some help. And the only help Spencer could think of that had a chance in hell of spotting the car was a helicopter, which he wasn't going to be able to get his hands on. If the cops managed it, he and Mallory, and Grigori, and the Texas hoods would all keep doing what they'd been doing—following the cops and coming up empty-handed.

Dammit.

"Remind him we still need names and addresses in Denver for the red '68s." He was beginning to feel like he was in the middle of a pack of vultures, and there was only one piece of meat on the ground, the damn Shelby Mustang. He didn't know where all these guys were getting their information, but for the first time today, he didn't feel like he was ahead of the game.

He needed to switch that around.

Mallory had her phone out and was keying in a number. "What are we going to do here, Spencer?"

"Keep heading north." These guys could hang around New Mexico all day and half the night, but whoever was driving that damn Shelby was getting the hell out of New Mexico and heading north, and that's exactly what Spencer was going to do.

Saturday, 5:00 P.M.—Denver, Colorado

Gabriel stood in the main office of Steele Street, staring at Cherie Hacker's desk and wondering where she was for about the thousandth time. Her shoes were on the floor in front of her chair, as if she'd just slipped out of them. Her dress was a big white pile in the seat of her chair, as if she'd just slipped out of it, and her motorcycle jacket was draped over the back of the chair—exactly as if she'd just slipped out of it.

So where in the world had she slipped to?

Dylan Hart had told her to stay put after the almost disaster with the DREAGAR 454, and Gabriel couldn't imagine that she would disobey a direct order, not from Hart. But she wasn't in the break room/kitchen area, and she wasn't in any of the bedroom suites he'd discovered farther back on the seventh floor, and she wasn't in the office.

He supposed she could be down in the garages somewhere.

That's what made the most sense.

He supposed.

Or actually, he didn't. What made the most sense was her staying in the office, which he was certain was what Hart had meant. This operation they had going with Bayonne, and the encryption code, and the bounty on Gillian, not to mention the whole thing with trying to bring an agent in from New Mexico, was the type of mission where everybody needed to be ready to do their part. Going off somewhere in the building to pout was unacceptable.

And he was positive that's what she'd done. He knew girls like her. Bossy girls who acted like they knew everything, because compared to most people, they did know everything. Brilliant girls who had gone to college before they'd gone out on a date.

Brilliant, bossy girls had been the bane of his existence. He'd been trapped in countless school-rooms, budding genius camps, and innumerable hopeless social situations with them, because they were his peers. They were the world's biggest pains in the butt, and the most fascinating creatures on earth. He had a real love/hate thing going with brilliant, bossy girls.

They were a personal weakness, but one he usually didn't have too much trouble keeping at a distance, because it was so seldom that he met one he thought was beautiful.

Cherie Hacker was beautiful.

And she should be at her desk.

But she wasn't.

"What's he doing out there, staring at Cherie's desk?" Dylan asked, leaning on his own desk and looking out his office door.

Skeeter tilted her head sideways to look him in the eye, and said, "I think he's got a little *thing* going for Cherie."

Dylan fought a grin and almost kissed his wife. He had a little *thing* going for her.

"He needs to get over it and get back in here."

Gabriel Shore was the expert in residence on Spencer Bayonne, the guy who'd killed Jason Schroder and the one who was after Zach. Dylan would like for him to concentrate on the job at hand, which was helping SDF know its enemy.

As far as what had brought Gabriel Shore to Steele Street, the bounty on his sister, well, that wasn't quite the crisis the boy thought. Dylan understood the kid's guilt, and his sense of responsibility, but if anyone could take care of herself, it was Red Dog, no matter what kind of money was on the table. That said, Dylan wasn't going to take any chances. He'd learned enough about Kendryk to be very wary of the guy. Two million dollars was nothing to Lord Weymouth, but it was more than enough to complicate Gillian's life. More than enough reason for Dylan to want to take him down—and for that, he could use a little help from Gabriel Shore.

"Dr. Shore," he called out. "If you don't mind,

I'd like to go over Kendryk's intelligence network files again."

"Yes . . . uh, sir," the guy said, and with a last look at Cherie's desk, he turned around and headed back to Dylan's office.

CHAPTER TWENTY-FOUR

Saturday, 6:00 P.M.—northern New Mexico

Zach had been wrong.

Paysen had not been the middle of nowhere.

This was the middle of nowhere, wherever this was.

An hour and a half of driving along dry, rutted tracks and washed-out roads had brought them to someplace he'd never been before: lost. Twice, he and Lily had found themselves creeping down the side of a canyon on a road so narrow, he'd been afraid Charlotte was going to completely balk.

Before, he'd always been of the mind that as long as there was a road, a person was not lost.

Well, he'd been wrong about that, too. He and Lily were on a road, they'd been on half a dozen in the last hour, and he was clueless, although he did have a growing suspicion that they were going around in circles.

He couldn't confirm the circle theory, because he'd lost SB303, and that was a hardship. He'd gotten attached to the girl and spoiled rotten by her intel. The road, and he used the term loosely, kept bottoming out in dry creekbeds and arroyos and killing their reception.

Where in the hell were they, he wondered, and why couldn't they get the hell out of here?

"You must have something to say," he said, throwing Lily a glance. She was yawning, just waking up.

No woman could possibly have nothing to say in this situation.

"We're lost," she said after finishing her yawn. "I'm hot, and I'm tired, and I'm hungry for something besides crackers, and this place kind of reminds me of home, all the wide open space. And you never have told me why we're running our asses off and why people keep shooting at us. You haven't told me what's on or in the bracelet that's worth dying for, or who in the hell you really work for."

Well, that was more than she'd been saying. She'd actually drifted off after the first half hour of driving, just slipped into sleep over on her side of the car, and he'd let her.

"I'm not sure we're heading north anymore," he said, making the only appropriate comment.

"We're not," she confirmed, and pointed straight out the windshield. "That's west."

Smart-aleck Montana ranch girl, he thought. "Uh . . . thanks," he said.

"So why are we getting shot at all over the place?" she asked.

"I think the better question is how do we get out of here and back to a paved road?"

To her credit, she didn't harp on the shooting, and she accepted his question at face value. She evaluated it, taking another look around at the road, and the scrub, and the dirt, and the low rolling hills that just seemed to keep rolling no matter how long he drove.

"Well, for starters," she said, "we could stop going around in circles. We have definitely been in this exact spot before. I think just before I fell asleep."

Finally, he'd gotten something right. *Dammit.* He should have been a Ranger. U.S. Army Rangers never got lost. Well, almost never.

"Got any ideas on how to get out of this spot?"

"Higher ground. We need to get the big picture," she said, and pointed to the left, yawning again. "Pull over up ahead, about a hundred yards on the left, at the top of that rise."

"I tried the higher-ground theory while you were snoring."

"I *don't* snore."

"Dream on, babe."

He drove the hundred yards or so and pulled over anyway, parking them on the rise in the same place he'd parked earlier, and then the two of them got out of the car and moved to the front. They both leaned back on the hood and took in the view. If it wasn't for the bracelet hidden in the heel of his shoe, a real tradecraft touch, Zach might have been able to relax and enjoy the view a lot more, because there was something familiar about it. Maybe it was just that so much of this part of northern New Mexico looked the same—exactly the same. Quiet, and still, with not much moving besides the wind and the mirage. Heat shimmered off everything, blurring the distinction between land and sky. A lizard darted from one rock to the next, the only sign of life.

And he meant *only*. There was nothing else out there moving, not in the heat of the day. The road they were on snaked across the landscape below, intersecting with two other dirt tracks before they all meandered over the horizon or disappeared behind a bluff. He'd turned right at the first intersection the last time they'd been down there, and they'd ended up here again, after five long, hot, dusty miles. He mentally checked it off the list of choices.

"This is nice," she said, leaning into him and taking his hand.

Nice because of her, he thought, and he was crazy—leaning back against Charlotte, looking at New Mexico, and feeling fairly content. What the hell was up with that? And what in the hell was he doing slipping his fingers between hers? Sleeping with her? There were no tactical advantages in the acts. They were personal, and he wasn't in any place to be getting personal.

He usually had better sense.

Correction: He *always* had better sense.

And yet he didn't let go of her hand.

"We're running because people are shooting at us," he said, watching the wind kick up dust devils on the scrubby terrain. "But you already knew that."

She turned her head and looked up at him, and he continued.

"They're shooting for one of two reasons: either to stop us, like the manager at the Road Runner, or to kill us, like the men in your house, which is just another way of stopping us." He looked down and caught her gaze. "You already knew that, too."

"Go on." A small smirk of a smile touched the

corner of her lips, and he was tempted to just kiss it off her.

"You know they want to stop us so they can get the bracelet, and you know why the bracelet is worth dying for."

"I do?" A slight breeze ruffled her hair, and she reached up to tuck it back behind her ear.

He held up two fingers. "Power and money. They're what makes the world go round, and the bracelet is loaded with both."

"And that's it? The answers to my questions?"

He nodded. "That's it."

"What about love?" she said, her gaze holding his. "I thought love was what made the world go round."

Yeah, love.

Love was a good question. Confusing as hell, but a good question. Love didn't make sense. He hardly knew her, but he had this damned compelling urge to find out everything he could about her. Not the dossier stuff Alex had given him, all the facts of her life. No, he wanted the good stuff. He wanted the inside stuff.

"Your mom died when you were eight," he said. "That must have been tough."

She gave a small shrug. "Sure it was. I still miss her sometimes. But I have an older sister who filled in pretty well, taking care of me, and

I've got three older brothers, and my dad, and a place where I always belong."

"The Cross Double R," he said.

"Yes, and that's a lot more than some people have. Maybe even more than most people."

She was right.

"So you're the baby of the family?"

She let out a soft laugh. "So to speak. I do have seven nieces and nephews now. But over-all, I think I still own the 'most likely to get into trouble when you least expect it' spot in the family."

"Like running off to El Salvador?"

She shook her head. "I *planned* that trip. There was no running off."

"There was plenty of getting into trouble."

She couldn't deny it, and she didn't.

"Bad timing on my part," she admitted. "I picked the week St. Joseph's self-destructed. Believe me, if I'd seen Diego Garcia coming, I would definitely have gone the other way."

"What about Tom Bersani? You must have seen him coming." It had been part of her file—the divorce, the marriage. It had only lasted six years, not very long in the scheme of things.

"What I saw was tall, dark, handsome, and exotic, someone from someplace besides Trace, Montana. Somebody who didn't talk about horses and cattle, and who didn't wear slant-heeled boots."

"He's Italian."

"Very Italian, complete with an Italian mama who thinks he can do no wrong—but how do you know about Tom? And where in the world did you find out about my mom dying when I was eight? Or do I already know the answer to those questions, too?"

He didn't say anything.

She let out a heavy sigh. "I bet one of the first things they teach you is how to answer questions without telling anybody anything they don't already know."

He almost smiled, then leaned down and kissed her instead.

"So why the divorce?" he asked after a moment of sweet, brief contact with her mouth.

"Donna," she said, and he gave her a quizzical glance. "Donna, and Debra, and Karen, and Tina. To my credit, I didn't know about Debra and Karen and Tina until after we'd already filed for divorce. I thought I was leaving him because of Donna, one of the secretaries at the law firm where he was an up-and-coming star. It was only after we filed that I realized it wasn't just one secretary, but the whole damn secretarial pool he was fooling around with."

How awful.

"I've been cheated on—twice, as far as I know. It made me crazy both times." Somehow, he'd never really blamed Jewel for leaving him. But he'd never had any confirmation that she'd been sleeping with the poet she'd ended up marrying within weeks of walking out on him. Consequently, there'd never been any confrontation.

And he'd been bad for her. In his heart, he'd been almost glad she'd gotten away. Not so with Sonja, a Swedish aid worker he'd lived with in Laos. He'd been hard in love with the blond beauty and could have killed her for screwing around on him. He'd left Laos instead.

"Have you ever been married?" Lily asked.

Finally, a question he could answer straight out.

"No."

"Girlfriends? Besides the two who cheated?"

"A few." He grinned. "How about you? How many hearts did you break before you married Bersani?"

"A few."

His grin broadened. "You're a quick learner."

"I have lots of other things I couldn't tell you."

"Like?"

"Like Shelby Cobra Mustangs are my favorite car. I could keep that to myself."

"Do you want to drive again?"

"Without the handcuffs?"

He at least had the decency to look sheepish. "I didn't have time to talk you into anything this morning."

"The cell-phone bomb thing really sucked."

"But it worked," he said. "It got you out of the line of fire and kept you exactly where I needed you to be."

She didn't say anything, only rolled in closer to him, bringing her body up against his, her head resting in the curve of his neck and shoulder. He felt a sigh leave her, felt her relax against him.

"I don't even know you," she said after another long moment of silence. "And I don't really understand what we're up against, no matter how much I can figure out or guess at."

And he'd probably already said too much.

"There are lots of things I can tell you, Lily, just not about the job. When we're out of this, maybe we can—"

"*Hola, pendejo.*" The Bazo came to life inside the Shelby. "If you're there, come in."

That was *not* SB303, he thought. He kissed Lily on the top of the head, then quickly walked back to the driver's door and leaned down through the window. SB303 had way too much class to be calling him an asshole.

"*Jefe,*" he said. *Boss.*

"Where have you been?" Dylan asked.

"You tell me," he said, hoping to hell Dylan actually could tell him where he'd been.

"We found a place for you to wait out the day, not too far from where you're at," Dylan said, looking ridiculously pleased with himself. "It's on a route we're mapping to bring you in the back door to Denver, keep you off the interstate as much as possible. It'll take longer, but it will be safer. As long as the cops know where you are, Bayonne knows where you are, and anybody else out there."

"Sounds good," Zach said. "But we haven't seen anything out here, and we've been looking." For almost two hours, he could have told him.

"This place is hard to find, which has always been the point of it, but you won't have any trouble."

Okay, he was hooked.

"What have you got in mind?" he asked.

"An oasis," Dylan said, a grin spreading across his face. "Sanctuary. Alazne's."

Alazne's?

"You're kidding." No wonder everything looked so damn familiar.

"Not at all." Dylan let out a short laugh. "Two miles north, on the road you're on. We'll put the map up on your Bazo. You can't miss it, and Zach?"

"Yeah?"

"Stay out of trouble."

"Sure, *jefe*." He could stay out of trouble at Alazne's. It's what they'd all done.

Half an hour later, Lily was no longer anywhere close to being tired. She was enchanted, delighted, and wide awake. Rose-colored adobe walls, robin's egg blue shutters and doors, a stone courtyard with a bubbling fountain and flowers everywhere—she'd never seen a prettier place than where the people in Denver had directed them.

"You know the woman who lives here?" she asked, even though he'd already said as much. It was just that the little house and the perfect gardens were so...so female, everything so lush and delicate. Even the barn where he'd hidden the car had been sweet-smelling, full of drying flowers and herbs. It was hard to imagine a man being here, being invited in...except in one way.

"Yes." He opened a wooden gate, and they entered the courtyard.

"How well do you know her?" She slid him a curious glance, and he laughed.

"Very well, and then some, and then even better than that." He grinned.

"You jerk." He didn't have to say it like that, even though she'd figured as much.

"I was seventeen. She was twenty-eight, and she kept me for a month," he said, closing the gate behind them, still grinning.

"Oh."

Oh, my.

"That must have been . . . uh, educational," she said, at a bit of a loss. She'd never heard of anybody who'd, well, who'd done anything quite like that.

"Very," he said, "and at the end of a month, she shooed me back home."

Walking over to a small table in the shade, she stretched up on her tiptoes to smell the flowers on the trees. They were irresistible, the branches heavy with blooms, filling the court-yard with scent.

He came up behind her and slid his arm around her waist, then bent his head and kissed the side of her neck. "But we keep in touch. We all keep in touch with Alazne."

"We?"

"The guys I grew up with."

"And did they come and spend a month with her, too?"

"Some did. The ones she chose." He kissed her cheek.

"Sounds like a racket to me." Honestly, what kind of woman did that?

"It was." He let out a soft laugh and kissed her again. "A lovely racket."

"Did she teach you this?" His mouth was warm on her skin, his body a hard wall of muscle at her back.

"She taught me everything." He kissed her one more time and took her by the hand, leading her toward the blue door. "Come on."

"And I have to meet this woman?" God, she'd barely met him.

"No," he said. "She's not home. If she was home, the door would be open."

Lily looked around at the goats in the pen, and the fountain bubbling, at the open windows and the curtains fluttering in the soft breeze. "The place seems pretty open to me, like somebody could steal everything without breaking a sweat."

"Nobody is going to steal from Alazne. She's a *bruja*, a sorceress."

Oh, great.

"Don't worry. She won't mind us being here, and when the sun goes down, we'll leave."

"For Denver," she said.

"Yeah. This will all be over in Denver, Lily. I promise."

She believed him, but somehow, instead of being a relief, the idea of it all being over depressed the hell out of her. She wanted the danger to be over, the damn bracelet, the getting shot at, the violence, but not him. She didn't want him to ever be over, and that hardly made any more sense now than it had last night, when she'd thought she'd never see him again.

Damn. She hoped this wasn't love. She wasn't ready for love.

But she was ready for Alazne's, for preparing a meal with him and finding out he could cook, for taking a shower with him and finding out how easily making love three times in one day could turn into four, and for sitting in the shade of the trees and listening to the fountain splash.

"So about those things you can tell me," she prompted, scooping up a bit of their freshly made *pico de gallo* on a small tortilla chip. "Does that include where you grew up?"

"Denver."

"And what kind of kid you were?"

"Wild."

A fleeting smile crossed her mouth. "This is hard for you, isn't it? Talking about yourself?"

He let out a short laugh. "Damn near impossible," he admitted.

She picked up another chip and scooped more of the *pico* onto it. "I knew everything about Tomaso," she said. "We went to Italy on our honeymoon, and he showed me every place he'd lived, and I met everyone in his family. We went to the schools he'd gone to as a child, and visited all his friends. He came to the States when he was fifteen to live with one of his older brothers in Chicago, and he got his law degree from the University of Denver. I could show you the apartment where he lived while he was in law school, and if you like, I probably still have a picture of his dog, the one he had as an undergraduate in Chicago." She popped the chip in her mouth and chewed slowly, until it was gone. "By the time we got back from our honeymoon and he started at the firm in Albuquerque, I thought I knew everything about him—and I did, everything except that he was going to make a complete and utter fool out of me."

"None of us ever sees that coming," he said, taking her hand and brushing his thumb across her knuckles. He had strong hands.

"So do you disappear once we get to Denver?" She could see that coming.

"I'm not a lawyer, or an accountant, Lily. I go where the job is, and when it's over, I go on to the next job."

Well, this sucked. Her heart was starting to break a little, just around the edges, and she wasn't sure how it had happened. Why in the world did she care so much, so deeply, for a man she didn't know, and didn't know anything about? She couldn't possibly have fallen in love.

No, absolutely not. Love was unacceptable. Besides, after Tom, she honestly didn't know what love was anymore. Lust was the closest she could concede, and that was no damn comfort at all.

CHAPTER TWENTY-FIVE

Saturday, 6:30 P.M.—Denver, Colorado

Gabriel had come all this way for nothing. He realized it now. After spending a day with his sister in Steele Street with the SDF team, he had a much better understanding of who and what she was, and a little less guilt about what she wasn't. Not a lot less guilt, but enough for him to give up his quixotic quest to save her from Sir Arthur Kendryk. She could do better by herself and with her team than with him getting in the way.

His other mission had been more successful, to deliver the DREAGAR files and the reports he'd written for his superiors in the Marsh Annex to General Grant's team, at least the ones they'd authorized him to share. The technology data stayed with the Commerce Department Security Division, the CDSD. That's what they were over there in Marsh, a think tank and a brain trust, not policy implementers, even if, because of their security designation, they were authorized to carry firearms.

Most of the guys didn't, but Gabriel did, and had put considerable effort into learning how to use his pistol and honing his skills, the same as he did with any tool.

None of which explained why he found himself standing in front of Cherie Hacker's desk again. He'd come over to refill his coffee, but he hadn't gotten past her desk and the clothes she'd left strewn on her chair.

In a slight breach of protocol, he reached over and tapped a universal access code into her keyboard so he could see what she'd been working on after they'd come back from Commerce City.

Blueprints came up, a whole series of them, with the subbasement of Steele Street being the last one up on her screen. From what he could see, there wasn't much down there. He scrolled back through her history and wondered why, with not much down there, she'd brought it up on her screen five more times than the other floors.

"Gillian," he said, walking back over to where she, Skeeter, and Dylan were working at a bank of computers. Their agent in New Mexico was secure until nightfall, so they'd gone back to studying the DREAGAR files and Kendryk. "Where do you think Ms. Hacker has gotten off to?"

Three pairs of eyes glanced up at him.

"This is her building," his sister said. "Her first big installation. It's how she got her company up and running, and it's still a signature Hacker piece, so she tends to spend a lot of time looking it over, checking connections, running software, doubling up on her checks and balances. She can't show it off, or tell anybody about it, but she can show off what she learned doing it. She's like a little spook in here. You can stumble across her anywhere."

"Even in the subbasement?"

Gillian glanced at Dylan. "Does Steele Street have an accessible subbasement?"

"Slightly accessible," he said.

"Very slightly," Skeeter concurred. "It's creepy down there."

She went back to her computer screen, apparently unaware that her husband's gaze had swung around and was riveted to her.

"When were you in the subbasement?" Dylan asked, his voice very cold.

"Three years ago," she said, continuing on

with her file search. "And once was enough, so you can get that tone out of your voice."

She tapped along for another couple of seconds, then stopped and whirled around to face her husband.

"Holy crap," she said, her eyes wide. "It's the breach. She's gone looking for the breach."

Dylan's gaze snapped up to Gabriel, and he could definitely feel the coldness in those icy gray eyes. "What makes you think Cherie is in the subbasement?"

"She's accessed the blueprints for that floor six times since we got back from Commerce City, and she hasn't been at her desk for the last four hours."

"Skeeter," Dylan said, "try calling her first. Let's make sure she isn't just up on the eighth floor or lounging on The Beach."

"Yes, sir."

Hart's attention shifted to Gillian. "If you have to go after her, get a tactical vest. The opening is in the absolute northeast corner of the building. It's cold and dark and empties out into every subterranean byway in the city. If she's lost, she's going to be damn hard to find."

Gillian nodded once, very clearly, very succinctly. "Yes, sir."

"I'll go, too," Gabriel said, quickly stepping forward. "In . . . uh, case Gillian needs help."

He knew how ridiculous that sounded, Gillian needing help, but he stood his ground, and after a couple of seconds, Dylan nodded.

"Get him a vest, and check your radios before you enter the tunnels."

Check the radios, definitely, Gabriel thought. It wasn't a mission, exactly, going into the basement, but if they were going to use radios, there was a little more edge to it than anything that ever happened in the Marsh Annex.

Saturday, 6:30 P.M. —the Colorado—New Mexico border

Spencer had a plan. He'd give the city of Denver two days to cough up the bracelet, two days he would spend working his network to see what he could come up with in the Mile-High City, two days putting the pressure on people elsewhere who could put the pressure on people in Denver to find him a goddamn 1968 Shelby Cobra Mustang, red with white racing stripes, and the asshole who drove it.

If he came up empty-handed, he'd head to Europe and start serious inquiries into who, what, when, where, and how the bracelet might change hands. And for every buyer he found, he'd chase down a goddamn seller, until he nailed somebody.

He hated that it had come to this. If Paul

Stark and Jason Schroder hadn't already been dead, he'd kill them tonight, just for messing up a simple plan. They shouldn't have gotten within a hundred yards of Lily Robbins. The woman should have taken the bait to Tahiti, or have been comfortably in her bed when Spencer had gone to visit this morning, instead of hell-and-gone somewhere with a house full of blood and bullet holes.

"You're not happy, Spence."

"No, Kitten, I'm not."

She started to say something, to offer some words of comfort, which was always her way with him, when her phone rang.

"Rush," she said. "Rick, how lovely to hear from you." She pulled a pad and pencil out of the side pocket on her leather messenger bag. "Yes, I know, it took a long time, all day . . . Poor baby, you had to work so hard . . . Two cars? How perfect. Yes, give me the address . . . hmmmm, the last one seems a bit far away, but I'll take it . . . yes, of course . . . always." She laughed, but Spencer didn't take it too seriously. She was a natural flirt, and in any room full of people, men would naturally gravitate to her. But he was her man, no other, and he never doubted it.

She hung up the phone and turned to face him, a warm smile curving her mouth.

"We've got it, Spence." She waved the notepad. "An address in Denver where not one but two red 1968 Shelby Cobra Mustangs with white racing stripes are registered through the Colorado Department of Motor Vehicles. The only other one is in a town named Greeley, about fifty miles north of the city."

"What's the address in Denver?" he said.

She looked at her notepad. "Seven thirty-eight Steele Street. Rick says it's in the downtown area, lower downtown."

"And who's the lucky bastard who owns two of these babies?" That was unusual, by any stretch of the imagination.

Again, Mallory looked at her notepad. "The lucky bastard," she said, "is a man named Dylan Hart."

CHAPTER TWENTY-SIX

Saturday, 11:30 P.M.—Denver, Colorado

Zach cruised through the streets of Denver, holding Charlotte to a low rumble. They'd made the run up from New Mexico without laying eyes on a cop, and now the whole damn thing was almost over. It had been one helluva day.

God, he was going to sleep for a week, hopefully with Lily right there next to him in the bed. Which he knew wasn't going to make anybody happy except him, and he hoped Lily. Maybe he'd been in Central America too long, too much on his own, to worry about upsetting the powers that be too much. If he could get a week with her, he was going to take it.

She was already asleep and had been for the last hour. Every streetlamp they passed under sent a lovely moment of light sliding across her face. They'd showered at Alazne's, and he'd helped her braid her hair, putting it in a low ponytail first and kissing the back of her neck all the while, but some of the braid had fallen out, and now she had a tangle of silken waves and dark curls framing a face whose curves were imprinted on his heart.

He was in love. He was sure of it.

He didn't know enough about love to know how long it might last, but he knew what he felt when he looked at her, and he didn't see that fascinating and complex mix of emotions fading for a long, long time.

He would run as much interference between her and Alex as was feasible, and the whole murder suspect fiasco had to be taken care of immediately. According to SB303, New Mexico had alerted Colorado that he and Lily were heading north out of Paysen, so the cops in Denver would be on the lookout for them, too.

Steele Street, that's where they needed to be. To put Charlotte to bed in the garage and just shut down for a while.

He turned north off of Speer Boulevard, heading up into LoDo. They were close now. It wouldn't be too much longer before they were safe.

Two hours' worth of staking out 738 Steele Street, and Spencer was growing restless. There had been lots of chatter about the Shelby Cobra on the radio, but no sightings since the motel in Paysen, New Mexico. It was like the car had dropped off the face of the earth, and with two states' worth of police looking for it, that was a pretty good trick.

If Rick Connelly had found this building, though, Spencer could guarantee the cops were going to show up sooner or later, probably sooner, and once the cops made it, the rest of the vultures who'd been cruising for the car in New Mexico wouldn't be too far behind. He and Mallory had been granted a small window of advantage here, given to them by superior intelligence, but that advantage was running out along with their time.

He'd driven past the three street sides of the building and walked through the alley once, following along with a group of other pedestrians, and he didn't have a doubt that Rick had found the right place. Four garage doors opened onto the narrow alley named Steele Street, and an ancient freight elevator crawled up the side of the building, servicing a whole series of garage doors, one on top of the other, for the next seven floors. At ground level, the freight cage would take up most of the alley, making it impassable.

There were no windows on the ground floor, but surveillance cameras covered every conceivable angle of approach to the building, an interesting fact he had Mallory working on, running the address through a number of databases. There was a sign advertising tires next to an iron door that also opened into the alley, and the place had the smell of cars—automotive fluids, grease, oil. None of that new-car smell people liked so much. No, 738 Steele Street had the smell of a place where cars were taken apart and put back together better, the kind of place where a couple of classic Shelby Cobras would be housed by the kind of people who had classified CIA data and needed cameras on their building—but was the classic Shelby Cobra he wanted already inside, or was it on its way?

Two days, he'd already decided. If he and Mallory lost their initial advantage, he would watch the place for two days, just like he'd planned, longer if anything happened to give him good cause. Patience was the key to a lot of his success, something those Vegas boys had never figured out.

If, after two days, nothing and no one of any interest came or went, he'd move to Europe, not because of a lack of patience, but because that was where the sale of the bracelet was most likely to take place. That's where the parties most interested in the CIA's intelligence data did most of their business. That's where Ivan Nikolevna and Arthur Kendryk did business, and until, or if, the deal closed, he still had a chance to make things go Kendryk's way, to get the information from the bracelet into Lord Weymouth's hands.

He was also rethinking his stance on the girl, on Red Dog, Gillian Pentycote. Five months ago, she'd killed Tony Royce, Zane Lowe, and Royce's whole damn crew in Denver; everyone knew the story. It had spread fast and hard and made a helluva impression on the world circuit. Now this damn bracelet had a good probability of ending up in Denver in a building covered in surveillance cameras. He didn't believe in coincidence. He believed in doing his homework, in following leads, and tonight, he'd been led here, to the scene of Gillian Pentycote's world-class takedown. Two days in a hotel room with Mallory on her computer and Kendryk's intelligence network at his disposal, and maybe he could come up with something, a connection, maybe even come up with the girl. He didn't have to leave the States empty-handed. It all depended on how big of a risk he was willing to take for two million dollars.

Pretty big, he figured, because he had something none of his competition could even come close to getting. He had Mallory Rush. She was his ace. She thought out of the box, and that's what it was going to take to capture the sniper called Red Dog. Actually, he was surprised Mallory's Tahiti-on-a-hook thing hadn't reeled little Ms. Robbins in like a suckerfish. If she'd used the ticket, they could all be doing this on a beach somewhere, and the guy with the Shelby Mustang would never have even made the cut. Mallory didn't fail often with her schemes, and she was usually especially good with women. Her mistake had been in thinking Lily Robbins knew what she had and would be looking for a deal. Mallory always knew what hand she was holding, and what hand everybody else was holding, as well.

But hell, Lily Robbins had been clueless, and look what had happened to her—death and destruction at the crack of dawn, a murder rap, abduction, and she'd been on the run for all of a long hot day, only to end up here with Spencer cocked, locked, and loaded, ready, willing, and able to take her down.

Of course, that was the hapless Lily Robbins. Even with Mallory on his side, he was hoping the success of this trip wouldn't end up depending on the capture of Gillian Pentycote. He was hoping the Cobra Mustang would show up here, in this alley, tonight.

Next to him in the Town Car, Mallory was watching the alley, too, and all the people and other cars on the street. On a hot summer Saturday night in Denver, the alley named Steele Street and its environs were obviously the place to be. There were lots of bars and restaurants in the neighborhood, and galleries and coffee shops and bookstores, cops cruising a beat, and people everywhere.

He would have preferred for things to be more isolated. Anything he did here was going to draw attention, and Spencer made a point of never drawing attention to himself.

He settled back in behind the steering wheel and watched, and waited, and in between one moment and the next, things went his way. It wasn't coincidence. He'd made the right moves and used his resources to insure he was in the right place, ready, when a red 1968 Shelby Cobra Mustang came driving down the street.

He actually heard the car before he saw it. So did Mallory. Their eyes met in the rearview mirror.

"Six o'clock," she said, and he confirmed. The Shelby was coming up behind them. "Seven . . . eight . . . nine o'clock."

She watched the Shelby draw parallel and slowly pass them by—cruising, checking the place out. Spencer didn't watch the car. He watched her, and waited.

The guy was going to drive around the block at least once, seeing what was up. He knew, because that's what he would do.

"The woman is with him," Mallory said. "Nine-fifteen, baby."

And Spencer turned his head, just enough to catch a glimpse of the guy as the Shelby passed them.

Dark hair cut short, lean face, hard—Spencer had seen a thousand guys like the one driving the Shelby. The world was full of hard-ass guys who did the kind of work where a man either came out on top or he died. This guy was one of them, and he looked to be in his prime.

Good. Great. Whatever. Spencer shifted his gaze to the woman. He had not seen a thousand like her, and she was definitely in her prime. Long dark hair pulled back, exquisite profile, creamy skin, one bare arm resting in the Mustang's open window.

His gaze followed her down the street, until the muscle car turned right, starting its circle around the block.

He had a plan; it was very simple and straightforward, and involved Lily Robbins. It also involved the Smith & Wesson .45 caliber pistol concealed in his shoulder holster. Fast and dirty, that's how it was going to go down. A gun to the woman's head and a demand for the bracelet.

"Hand me my suppressor, Kitten," he said.

Mallory reached into the gun bag he'd set between them and pulled out a silencer for his pistol. He quickly and efficiently threaded it onto his Smith & Wesson.

"Take the wheel," he said, getting out of the car with his pistol hidden inside his suit jacket. There were only two regular doors into the building, and they were all in view of where he'd parked the Town Car. All the garage doors were in the alley.

He moved quickly, using the crowd on the sidewalk to conceal his approach and wanting to be in place before the Shelby Mustang came back around. He noticed a spot close to where the alley met the street, opposite the garage doors, a wedge of deep shadows between a Dumpster and the next building's fire escape. He would stop there, facing the street. If he showed up on a camera, he'd look more a part of the pedestrian traffic than the alley. He wouldn't enter the alley until he had a target.

He was still on his approach when the freight elevator rumbled into action, breaking the relative silence of the night with its sudden clanking and clanging. It couldn't be anything else, not on this block. As soon as he broke the alley's opening, he saw it, the freight cage slowly descending with its gears squealing and its bars rattling, making a perfect racket.

He instantly understood. Whoever was in the building had been alerted to the Mustang's arrival and was blocking off half the alley. Nobody was getting past the huge iron-and-steel freight cage. He was glad he'd kept Mallory and the Lincoln Town Car on the street.

He kept moving, speeding up his gait, walking faster, knowing the Mustang had to be close and would come in behind him.

In less than five seconds, he was at the Dumpster, in place, and heard the car's headers rumbling up the street. Turning his head, he located the Mustang and followed it with his eyes, watching it pull off the street, stop for some people crossing the mouth of the alley, then start forward again. The car was moving slow, about five miles an hour; as it crawled along, one of the garage doors farther down in the alley started sliding open.

Spencer was only going to get one chance at this. The driver's attention would be on the widening rectangle of light where the door was opening. The guy would never see him coming up on the passenger side until it was too late.

The streets of Denver were packed with people, especially in LoDo on a Saturday night, and Zach was careful to maneuver around them. He'd gotten Lily to Steele Street, though, and that was all that mattered.

SB303 was opening a garage door for him. They were less than thirty seconds away from being home free. He glanced in his side-view mirror, saw nothing, and brought the car to a stop, waiting for the garage door to fully open.

"Don't make a move, or she dies."

Zach didn't make a move. He'd heard similar words and similar voices before, and in his experience, they meant exactly what they said.

He shifted his gaze hard right without moving his head and saw Lily. He also saw the suppressed .45 jammed up against her head, saw the hand holding the gun, saw the asshole's finger on the trigger, already applying pressure. He had his Para in his shoulder holster, but inside the car, even though he'd trained for it, he knew he couldn't draw faster than the guy could squeeze those last few ounces of pressure on his trigger.

"Give me the bracelet, now." The guy's voice

was cold and calm, with just a hint of impatience.

Ahead of the Shelby, the garage door was still opening.

"I dead-dropped it a couple of blocks north of here, on my way into town," Zach said, lying and buying time. "Let me leave the woman here, and I'll take you to it."

"Tell me where it is."

Zach couldn't see the guy's face, nothing above the man's shoulders, which were broad and muscular, beefy under his suit jacket.

"That'll be tough," he said. "There's a warehouse on Nineteenth, near Market, with a loose brick in its west wall. I left a chalk mark on the sidewalk a block farther north."

"Then Ms. Robbins comes with me. We'll follow you. Open your door, Lily."

"No," Zach said, fast and low, making the word a command. "She's handcuffed to the seat. She stays with the car." Even as he spoke, he took a chance, reaching down for Lily's hand. She understood completely, and in one smooth move, he had the cuff back around her wrist and was lifting it to show the guy, at least show him the illusion of the cuff around her wrist.

"So where's your fucking key?"

"Lost it. The guy in there probably has one,"

he said, jerking his chin toward 738 Steele Street. "My dead-drop buyer wants the brace-let. This guy is paying for the woman."

He heard the man with the gun swear.

"Back up real slow," the guy said. "If I lose contact with her head, I pull the trigger."

Interestingly enough, Zach had heard those words before, too, in Vientiane, on the Mekong River. He'd gotten that woman out alive. He was going to get this one out alive, as well.

He put Charlotte into reverse and started backing up very slowly. The garage door was al-most up now, and he could see Dylan coming down the stairs at the back. He hoped to hell the guy with the gun didn't see him, but he didn't speed up. He just kept Charlotte to a crawl, slow and easy, taking her back out of the alley.

"The pickup at the dead drop will take place in about fifteen minutes," he said. "We need to get over there."

"What's your name?" the guy asked him.

"Alejandro Campos."

The guy let out a short laugh. "Yeah, Campos. I heard your name from somebody else. Didn't know you ever made it this far north."

"Only for special occasions," he said, holding Charlotte to a crawl. Not an easy task.

Next to him, Lily was white-faced, and holding perfectly still. The *pendejo* had one of his hands twisted into her braid, which made Zach a little queasy, and he had that big fucking gun jammed up behind her ear, which made him downright sick. And he still had his finger on the trigger, which made him very angry and very cautious.

Once Zach got Charlotte on the street, the guy told him to stop.

"Put on the parking brake and get out of the car very slowly. Don't look back at the car, not even for an instant. Move toward that gray Saturn and put your hands on top of its roof."

The gray Saturn was parked less than ten feet away.

"Spread your legs, and wait for my associate. We're changing places. You're going to drive my Lincoln, and I'll drive the Mustang."

He got out of Charlotte and started walking, and the next sound he heard sent a bolt of sickening dread down his spine. It was a solid thump and a soft, startled cry, then silence. The bastard had hit her, probably knocked her out.

Zach took the final steps to the Saturn and placed his hands on top of the gray car. He didn't look back at Charlotte, didn't look to see what kind of shape Lily was in, and then it was too late. He heard the guy shift the Mustang into first and saw him take off up the street, cross Eighteenth, and wait in the middle of the next block. Dylan hadn't made it out into the alley yet, but he would have heard Charlotte leave. The sound was unmistakable. He was probably already on his phone, asking SB303 what was up.

Goddammit. The sonuvabitch had hit her.

He heard the Lincoln pull up behind him, and to anyone walking down the street, he knew nothing looked out of place. He was just a guy leaning on a car. The only odd thing might have been if anyone had noticed the woman coming up behind him and giving him a quick frisk—and it was definitely a woman. Her hands were small, her touch lighter than a man's. She found his Para almost instantly and slipped it out of its holster like a professional. His two knives came next. She pulled one out of his pants pocket and the other out of an ankle sheath.

"Get in the car," she said when he came up clean everyplace else. She hadn't actually shoved her hands in his pants pockets, just patted them down from the outside. She'd gotten his wallet, but she was welcome to it. He didn't keep anything important in his wallet when he was on the job, just a fake I.D. and a boatload of cash.

He was happy to get in the Lincoln Town Car and get closer to Lily.

Once he was behind the Lincoln's steering wheel, he headed northeast, along Wazee. The woman in the car with him was beautiful, very elegant, with auburn hair, and a 9mm Sig in her hand. She was wearing a black V-necked sweater, low cut, and a pair of cigarette jeans, tight, with red heels, and she was dripping in diamonds—bracelet, necklace, earrings. She looked rich and spoiled and like she could be dangerously bitchy—emphasis on the dangerous.

"What's your name?" he asked, and saw Charlotte slip in behind him as he crossed Eighteenth.

"He calls me Kitten," she said, and Zach cast her a quick glance.

Geezus. Kitten. She had a voice like twelve-year-old Scotch, rich and smooth, full-bodied, with just a touch of huskiness.

"What's his name?" It never hurt to ask.

"He doesn't have a name, sweetie, and he's not happy right now, so don't make him mad, okay?"

She was smooth, all right.

Lily had put her Colt in Charlotte's console. If she could get to it, she could even out the odds real damn quick.

The next cross street was Nineteenth, and he turned right and then parked a block up. There was a loose brick on the west wall of a small yellow warehouse on the corner, something only a street kid would know about. It had been used to stash stuff since God knew when. He wasn't worried about showing the guy the chalk mark. There wasn't one, but there was no reason to go looking for one, either. All the guy wanted was the bracelet.

Charlotte pulled to a stop behind him, and he could see Lily slumped down in the passenger seat, then saw her raise her hand to the side of her head, where the bastard must have hit her. He tried not to think about it, concentrating instead on the guy with no name. The man got out of the Mustang at the same time that Zach got out of the Lincoln. Kitten stayed in the car.

Zach only had to stall for a minute. That's all it would take. SB303 was still tracking Charlotte, and Dylan had to be on his way, especially if SB303 had gotten a look at Charlotte's new driver.

Unlikely, he realized a couple of seconds later, when the first thing the guy did was throw the Bazo out on the street at Zach's feet.

"I broke your toy," the guy said, his gun leveled at Zach's chest.

Yeah, broke. More like ripped it out by its hardwired guts and smashed the screen. So much for Dylan coming to the rescue.

"It's down here," he said, not giving anything away. He was alive, Lily was alive, and he actually had what the guy wanted, most of it, anyway.

At the side of the building, it took him a minute to remember which brick was loose.

"What's the problem?" the guy asked.

"No problem. It's just been a while." About twelve years.

"A while, like what, half an hour."

"Yeah." Asshole.

He tried one brick, then another. The guy's phone rang, and he answered it without a flicker of distraction. His gaze didn't leave Zach, and his gun held steady.

"Where?" the guy said. "Coming south or from the west?"

The guy didn't take his eyes off him, but Zach looked in both directions and saw a silver Mercedes crossing Eighteenth and heading their way.

"You're out of time, Campos."

No, he wasn't. He jiggled the loose brick free, noticed the cavity was full of junk, and pulled a classic bit of sleight of hand, blocking the guy's line of sight for a second with the brick while he pulled something out of his pocket.

Without a word, he handed the guy the macramé bracelet.

The man grinned and made his first mistake—and it only took one. He lowered his gaze to see the bracelet, and Zach nailed him, parrying his gun hand and slamming him hard up against the brick building, hard enough to hear a loud crack, hard enough for his head to bounce off. Zach twisted the gun out of his hand, and the guy fell to his knees, but he didn't fall over.

Zach didn't give a damn. It was enough. He was running for Charlotte. If Kitten was calling in a warning, then he needed to get the hell out of there.

Out of the corner of his eye, he saw the Mercedes speed up. He knew Kitten was watching the silver luxury car, but any second she was going to look to see what her partner was doing, and when she saw him on his knees, Zach was betting she was going to level her Sig out the window and go for him or Lily.

He wasn't going to give her the chance. He was only seconds from Charlotte, and then he was inside and sliding the Mustang into first and hitting the gas hard. He'd be goddamned if he got trapped between a damn Mercedes and a damn Lincoln Town Car.

He pulled out onto Nineteenth as fast as Charlotte could take him, which wasn't nearly as fast as he would have liked, not with traffic getting in his way. *Goddammit*. All he had to do was get past the Town Car before Kitten could pull her pistol and take aim. And by the skin of his teeth, he did, hitting the street with a bit of luck and a carefully controlled drift to get him heading in the right direction, which was "away."

Nothing could have gone smoother—except for the searing pain suddenly engulfing his body.

Oh, fuck. It stole his breath.

He shifted up into third, tearing down the street, getting away.

Away from that goddamn dangerous Kitten, who had just shot him with her goddamn Sig.

He felt Charlotte's right rear tire get blown out and was barely able to hold her on the road. *Goddamn. Goddamn*. That had been no 9mm. The Mercedes was on his ass and tearing into him with something a whole helluva lot bigger than that.

Another bullet hit Charlotte, something big enough to come through her trunk, slip through her backseat like butter, and scream through the interior to cut down the length of his thigh.

Fuck. He was trying to think, trying to keep his head clear, but it wasn't working. The Mercedes was behind him, gaining, and the Lincoln was tearing out after the Mercedes.

Fuck. He'd run out of time, all of his time, all at once. *Goddamn.* And he hadn't seen it coming, not like this.

No time. There was no time.

He turned the next corner, not even bothering to shift, just spinning the wheel, using the brake and clutch, and letting Charlotte ride the drift. Lily was talking to him, her voice high and agitated, but he couldn't hear a word she was saying. He had an awful lot of stuff on his mind, most of it looking like it had hit a fan, and he was having trouble piecing his thoughts together.

It was just the pain. It would pass, and then he'd be fine. It was just the initial shock of getting hit, and of course the blood, which he could feel running out of him.

Goddammit.

When he saw a squad car up ahead, cruising its beat on the street, he didn't second-guess the one complete thought he got. He slid Charlotte to a tire-squealing stop, sending up a billow of smoke and almost slamming straight into the POS.

"Get out of the car," he growled, and when she started to speak, he cut her off. "Don't fuck with me, Lily. Get out of the goddamn car *now*!"

He could take care of himself, but he couldn't take care of her. Not like this.

The two officers in the squad car were scrambling out, pulling their guns, and she must have understood—she either got out of the goddamn car, or somebody was going to get hurt. Probably him.

As soon as she slammed the door, he took off again, putting her completely out of his mind. Gone. He had one goal now. Only one.

He took the next turn, and drove through five more, weaving his way back toward Steele Street, and now he was two blocks north of it, with the cops calling him in, and the Mercedes and the Town Car still on his ass.

Perfect. He'd counted on it.

He had not been interested in any half-assed standoff with these assholes and the Denver police, with him in the middle of it, and Lily standing right next to him. For what these guys were after, shooting it out with the cops was well within their risk quotient.

Zach had taken that option away from them. If they wanted what they'd all come for, they had to come for him, or so they thought.

He tasted blood—*Dammit, this can't be good.*

Slamming down on the clutch and the brake, he pulled Charlotte to another rubber-burning stop. Then his foot slipped off the clutch. The Mustang's Cobra jet engine died, all 428 cubic inches of it, stopped dead.

Fuck.

He pushed open the door and half slid, half fell onto the pavement. Squealing tires and a flash of headlights were the last things he heard and saw before he rolled under the car and started his fall into darkness.

CHAPTER TWENTY-SEVEN

Saturday, midnight—Denver, Colorado

At least her watch worked, Cherie thought, its tiny tritium numbers glowing in the dark, showing her the time, midnight, and no doubt irradiating her, but not enough to be the end of her.

No, she thought. Her end was going to come from getting herself so damn lost in the absolute heart of Denver that she would become a trivia question in the city's history books, an urban legend, an enduring mystery. *Dammit.* She was right in the middle of the damn city, and she was nowhere, trapped in a wasteland of tunnels. Not the huge ones carrying the city's utilities. There were people in those tunnels, maintenance people, engineers, safety inspectors.

No. She was lost in the old abandoned tunnels, where all those kinds of people had worked years and years ago, but where nobody came anymore.

She slid the light from her flashlight down both sides of the next intersection of byways, and chose to go right for no special reason. She'd given up on reasoning her way out of here. The one thing she was good at hadn't been doing her any good.

No, sirree. No safety inspector was going to save her down here. There was only her in these damn tunnels, lost and all alone. Just her—*and oh, my god*. What was that?

She turned her head to the left, listening. She'd heard something, some faint echo. She took a step to the left, then another, and she heard it again—street noise. Honest-to-God street noise. If she could find where it was coming from, and if there was any kind of an opening, she would be saved.

By her watch, it took her another half an hour, not because of the distance, but because of the labyrinth of tunnels she had to negotiate to close the distance between her and where the street noise originated, where it had penetrated into the underground world below Denver. When she felt fresh air, she knew everything was going to be okay.

Propelled by sheer relief, she picked up her pace, moving faster, splashing her way through the tunnel streams, following the fresh air and the increasing noise. Her flashlight beam careened off the walls with her uneven gait over the piles of debris in the tunnels—until she came to a sudden stop.

The air was strong where she stood. She could actually feel it blowing against her cheeks, and the noise was pure, no echo, as if she could almost reach out and touch it. But there was something else, something at the edge of her sight that had stopped her cold.

She lifted her flashlight higher, and—*oh, my god*.

A dead body was piled in a heap on the tunnel floor.

A less smart girl would have run screaming in the other direction and gotten herself lost all over again. Cherie moved forward, and when she saw blood running down the man's arm and pooling in the upward curve of his palm, she moved even faster.

Oh, my god. She dropped to her knees beside him. He was still breathing. He had short dark hair and a long-healed scar running down the side of his face, and was wearing expensive clothes. She put her hands on him, one touching his shoulder, the other feeling his brow. He was alive.

"Oh, geez. Okay. I'm going to get help." She'd hardly been able to help herself. "Just hang in there, okay?" God, that sounded so lame.

She looked around, sliding the light from her flashlight along the walls—and then she saw it, an old ladder bolted to the side of the tunnel. She tilted her flashlight up. Her way out was at the top of the ladder, but she couldn't leave the man. She needed help.

Grabbing her cell out of her pocket, she was about to dial, when she heard footsteps coming her way. *Oh, God.* She froze where she was, hoping whoever had hurt the man wasn't coming back to finish him off. Just the thought was enough to get her to her feet, ready to run if she needed to run, while her fingers raced over the phone's touch pad. Then a figure came into view, and she felt a wave of relief so huge, it almost swamped her.

"Gillian." She breathed the name.

Instead of saying anything, though, Gillian raised her finger to her lips and shook her head. Then she pointed up.

Cherie looked in that direction, and heard the sound of voices mixed with the car noises coming from the street.

Silently, Gillian knelt by the man and slid the beam of her flashlight over his face. She didn't look at him for more than three seconds before she rose to her feet.

That's when Cherie noticed the other person with her—Gabriel Shore. Like Gillian, he was being very quiet. Unlike Gillian, when he knelt by the man, he started checking him for injuries.

Red Dog stood perfectly still and listened for a moment, her gaze angled up toward the street, then she slid up the ladder like a snake and disappeared from view.

Cherie's heart was pounding. Something was going on, something dangerous, whatever had been going on all day and kept everybody so busy.

After no more than a few minutes, during which time Cherie prayed the wounded man would not die on her, a huge rumbling roar shattered the silence. Her hands instinctively went over her ears. *Oh, freaking geez.* She knew that sound. It was one of Steele Street's babies, one of the cars, and someone had just started it up right on top of her head.

In seconds, the noise moved, fading to a mere rumbling purr, and Gillian came back down the ladder.

"I've got an ambulance on the way," she said,

coming over to be by the man and sliding a large folding knife between her belt and her jeans. "Gabriel, go topside and direct them down here. Cherie, are you okay?"

"Yes." Yes, she was fine. "Who is this guy, Gillian? What's he doing here?"

Kneeling down again, Gillian put her hand on the man's forehead and gently traced a long scar down the left side of his face.

"This is Zachary Prade, Cherie," she said. "Last of the lost chop-shop boys."

Cherie looked at him. She knew the name. She probably shouldn't, but like Skeeter, she did a lot of poking around at Steele Street, and Zachary Prade had been the lost chop-shop boy for as long as she could remember, for as long as she'd worked for Dylan. Three years ago, they'd lost another, and amidst a wave of grief and regrets, they'd all had to face the fact that he was never going to come home. In the jungles of Colombia, South America, J. T. Chronopoulos had been lost to them forever.

But this one was back.

Bleeding, broken, and collapsed, but still breathing.

"Is he going to make it?" she asked.

"Yeah, baby," Red Dog said. "He's going to make it."

The sound of sirens broke the night, and Cherie sent up another prayer.

Spencer normally ran a six-minute mile. He was doing a little better than that, pounding the pavement. That asshole Campos had cheated him. Even with his ears ringing, and Mallory screaming at him and blasting away with her Sig, he'd torn into the bracelet, and there'd been nothing in it, no polymer strand with microdots, just damn macramé. He'd shoved it in his pocket, raced back to the Lincoln, and Mallory had hit the gas, going after the bastard—and after a short, hot chase, the bastard had led him here, to another goddamn alley, him, and Mallory, and damn Grigori Petrov in his silver Mercedes, with the cops on all their asses.

Jesus. The alleys in Denver were fucking crazy places. Spencer knew what he'd just seen in this one, and it was so unexpected, so surreal, it had spooked the holy living hell right out of him.

Jesus. He kept his legs pumping, heading back toward the Town Car and Mallory. Petrov was on his own, and Spencer's money said he was doomed.

Alejandro Campos had disappeared. Spencer

could live with that. The muscle car had smoked to a screeching stop, the driver's door had opened, and the guy behind the wheel had disappeared. Okay, fine. Shit happened.

Petrov had reached the Shelby ahead of Spencer, and for a split second, Spencer had thought The Chechen had killed Campos, knifed him or something. So Spencer had come in fast, the Recon Tanto in his hand, ready to cut the truth out of Petrov, hurt him in whatever way was necessary to get what he wanted—the damn polymer strip with the damn microdots that should have been woven into the damn macramé bracelet—and then get the hell out of Denver.

But there'd been no Campos in the Shelby Mustang, no one behind the wheel, just Petrov tearing through the car, looking for the same damn thing Spencer wanted. Then the damnedest thing he'd ever seen had happened: Gillian "Red Dog" Pentycote had slid out from under the Shelby Cobra, right at Petrov's feet, right out from between the Mustang's chassis and the street, as if she'd simply coalesced off the pavement or something. There was no mistaking her. He knew the girl, and everyone knew she wasn't normal. She'd been enhanced, changed right down to the molecular level by some drugs she'd been given, some real cutting-edge psychopharmaceuticals out of Thailand. Everybody knew how dangerous she was, how nearly superhuman she'd become.

Everyone knew she'd killed Tony Royce, and Zane Lowe, and half a dozen of their guys in Denver five months ago. Everyone knew she was lightning fast and had deadly skills, with weapons or without. But *geezus,* nobody had said she could fucking *materialize* out of fucking nothing. No wonder all those guys had died. Kendryk was fucking nuts to want her back. Crazy to put a bounty on her.

Still, Spencer might have taken her on, if it hadn't been for the damn cops, sirens coming from all directions.

Sure, he might have risked his life for two million dollars and maybe one more chance at the damn encryption code.

But maybe not.

She'd gotten The Chechen. He'd heard the guy go down, hard and fast, heard Petrov grunt in pain. It could have been him, and the knowledge added an extra edge of speed to his final fleeing strides.

Breathless, and more unnerved than he would ever admit to anyone, he reached the Lincoln Town Car and lofted himself into the passenger seat. Mallory was already gunning the engine.

"Hit it, Kitten," he said. Whatever the hell had just happened, he was going to sort it out someplace far from Denver, Colorado.

CHAPTER TWENTY-EIGHT

Sunday, 5:00 A.M.—Denver, Colorado

"It's five o'clock in the damn morning, Dylan, and I've been working this city way too hard all night long. This better be good." The sound of a very unhappy woman came over the phone. "Damn good."

"I think you've got something that belongs to me, Loretta," Dylan said, reaching for his coffee cup. "And I'd like to get it back as soon as possible."

"You mean the woman we picked up two blocks from Steele Street," Loretta said, Lieutenant Loretta Bradley, Dylan's favorite cop in Denver. She'd been saving his butt since he'd been sixteen. "The murder suspect out of New Mexico who got all but thrown out of a 1968 Shelby Cobra Mustang GT500KR, which I'm

guessing goes by the name of either Charlotte
or Charlene."

"Yes. That's exactly who I mean." He took a
sip of coffee and relaxed back into his chair.

"You want me to give up a perfectly good
murder suspect?" the woman asked, clearly dis-
believing that he had the gall to even ask.
"What's in it for me?"

"A clear conscience."

She burst out laughing on the other end of
the line.

"Oh, that's good, Dylan." She laughed some
more. "That may be your best one yet."

"It was self-defense, Loretta, not murder,
and that's how it's going to come out. I've got a
federal agent and an unnamable bureau of bureaucracy to back it all up. This one's a no-go."

"Yes, the damn Feds have already shown up
and riffled their way through my evidence
locker."

In his office at Steele Street, Dylan set down
his coffee cup, squeezed his eyes shut, and quietly rubbed his hand over his face. *Geezus.* Zach
was freaking nuts, and Loretta was right. They'd
all been working too damn hard tonight.

"Did they get what they wanted?" he asked,
reaching for his cup again.

"Who the hell knows?" she said. "It was the
Feds. I can tell you they did linger awhile over a

scrappy little piece of plastic stuff my officers took off her, seemed to have quite a little conference over it, just between themselves."

"A piece of plastic?" Zach had told Dylan that he'd slid the polymer strand into her braid, securing it with her ponytail band, a measure that had obviously paid off. What Zach hadn't told him was why the polymer strand was important enough to have sparked a couple of international incidents, the one in El Salvador three weeks ago, and again tonight on the streets of Denver.

"Yes. It went in the evidence bag when they booked her," Loretta said, "along with her rings, and earrings, and a necklace."

Well, that's what Zach had been counting on, and Dylan had to admit that it had been a brilliant move, a classic bit of misdirection. Give the cops a murder suspect, drop her right in their laps, and there wasn't a policeman in the world who would think twice about a piece of plastic in her hair.

"Red Dog should be knocking on your precinct door any second now," he said.

"You sent the girl?" Loretta laughed again. "Well, at least you've got the brains to send somebody I like."

Yeah, he did. He knew Loretta had a soft spot for Gillian. Hell, Loretta had a soft spot for all of SDF's kick-ass women. The lieutenant might have been staring fifty in the face, but she was one of Denver's original kick-ass-and-take-names girls.

"So how is that federal agent from the un-namable bureau of bureaucracy doing?" she asked. "I heard he got shot."

"Yeah. He did, but he's going to be fine. The docs say he'll be out of the hospital in a couple of days at the most. He's tough."

"He always was," Loretta said. "One of the toughest."

Dylan set his cup back on his desk and leaned forward in his chair, his hand back over his face. *God. Goddamn.*

He let a moment pass, and then another.

"Yeah, he was," he said, lowering his hand and reaching for his coffee again. "Still is. Doc Blake is up with him now. Apparently, Zach went to see him the other night." Doc Blake ran a very unofficial free clinic out of his place up on Seventeenth Avenue. He'd been running it and taking care of street kids for twenty years.

"Good," Loretta said. "That's a good place to start, with the guy who put him back together. Geezus, he was a mess the night you found him, a bad thing to see, even for a hardened beat cop."

Yeah, that night. The night Dylan had found

a skinny fifteen-year-old bleeding to death in an alley with his face laid open, really laid open, almost peeled back. Zach was just lucky his mother's pimp hadn't killed him for trying to interfere with his business.

"Did you get Red Dog's present?" He changed the subject. It was hard for him to remember that night. The pimp had really worked Zach over, done some bad things. Alazne knew. Zach had told her everything, and she'd sent him back a little changed, a little stronger, and in a whole lot better place within himself. Dylan would love her forever for that alone.

"Grigori Petrov?" Loretta said. "Yes, that was one nice present. It's going to make me look real good. Too bad the others got away."

Bayonne and Rush had disappeared off the street while Gillian had been dealing with Petrov, but Dylan was sure their time would come. The files Gabriel Shore had brought with him from Washington, D.C. all but guaranteed it.

He looked out into the main office. Skeeter had her feet up on one of the desks and was sketching on a pad. From what he could see, it looked like one of her comic-book stories. She had tons of those things, and some pretty nice erotica she drew just for him.

And finally, some of the night's weight seemed

to lift just a bit. Skeeter and erotica were his favorite mood-enhancing combination. It had
never failed him. So suddenly, the night, what
was left of it anyway, looked a little more promising.

Except for maybe the two people sitting on
the couch playing some sort of high-tech, light-
speed video game—Cherie Hacker and Gabriel
Shore.

Dylan got the uncomfortable feeling he was
observing a computer geek date. It was odd, like
that opening mating ritual thing that had taken
place earlier in the office, and like the hand-
shake, this video-game-playing idea didn't look
like it had much potential to get the job done.

Dylan considered himself a real smart guy,
but not so smart that he and Skeeter ever played
video games.

"We'll get them next time, Loretta."

"Yeah," she agreed. "Next time."

After they hung up, Dylan watched the two
computer geniuses for a moment longer. It was
five o'clock in the morning, and they were playing a video game.

They could have it.

He was going to get his wife and take her to
bed.

Lily sat down next to Zach's hospital bed in Denver General and took his hand.

"Hi," she said, and felt him squeeze her fingers.

"Hi." He was patched, and bandaged, and had an IV pumping him full of something or another.

"You look great."

He attempted a grin, and just about made it.

"They let you out," he said, sounding incredibly tired. "Good. Don't worry. They'll never get the murder thing to stick. We're the good guys, and we can prove it."

"Yeah, we're the good guys." At least he was, the best guy, and she was so damned grateful to see him still all in one piece. When he'd dumped her on those cops, she'd been terrified she'd never see him again. "It was pretty cool the way you put that piece of plastic in my hair."

"You liked that?" He really looked like hell, but not critical. She figured the only critical thing in the room was her heart. It had been a helluva day.

"Yeah," she said. "Gave me kind of a shock to see it, but I liked how you did it. I hope it was part of your plan not to get it back, because somebody else confiscated everything they made me give up when they booked me."

"FBI," he said, and yawned. "I called my boss.

Told him to get somebody over there ASAP. The FBI is the closest Feds Denver's got."

"So all's well that ends well?" She hated to say it, but a few wild hours in a car with a man didn't necessarily add up to anything, no matter how much sex they'd managed to fit into the day.

"I hope nothing is ending," he said, still holding her hand.

"You're not a lawyer or an accountant, Zach," she said. He hadn't precisely told her who he worked for and what he did. She had a feeling his job description wasn't available for public perusal. She accepted that, and she understood what it meant.

"I'm not a fool either, Lily," he said. "Don't write me off just yet, that's all I ask." He was fading, drifting off to sleep, but his grip on her hand didn't lighten, not a bit. He yawned again. "A few things have come to an end lately, like El Salvador, and maybe more than that. We should talk . . . and celebrate."

"Celebrate?"

"We did it, babe. We won." His eyelids drifted closed for a second or two, then slowly lifted. "You should really be here when I wake up."

He'd saved the free world, and her, and thank God, he'd still had what it took to save himself.

"Okay, I'll be here."

"I mean right here." He pulled her closer. "Right here next to me. In the bed."

"I don't think they like that sort of thing," she said, holding back a smile, resisting the pull of his hand.

"We saved the free world, at least for now." He did a little better with his grin. "We can do what we want, at least in here. Come on." He pulled a little more, and even though her common sense told her not to be ridiculous, she went with ridiculous anyway, and with very little more coaxing, ended up stretched out next to him, drifting off with him into sleep.

"I . . . I don't even know your last name," she said around a yawn of her own.

"Prade," he said, and it was the last thing she heard.

CHAPTER TWENTY-NINE

Four weeks later—Chouteau County, Montana

Zachary Prade—she liked his name.

"This isn't Tahiti," Lily said from where she was sitting next to him.

"Not even close, babe," he agreed.

"I'm just about freezing my butt off."

"Hang tight. It just takes a little getting used to, that's all."

She rolled her head in his direction and opened one eye. "You have never done this before in your life, city boy."

He just grinned and settled himself deeper into the stock tank. Above them, a windmill turned in the cooling breeze, and beyond the windmill, the Bearpaw Mountains jutted up into the sky, their peaks dusted white even in the middle of July.

"Definitely not Tahiti," he said.

"I don't think we'll be seeing Tahiti any time soon."

"No, me, either," he said. They never had tracked down whoever had sent her the plane ticket and the money. It was an unsolved mystery, a loose end. He'd had his old boss, whose name Lily had never heard, from a place he'd never mentioned by name, put somebody on the whole Tahiti aspect of their day with the bracelet, and so far, Zach hadn't heard anything back.

They'd speculated a bit between the two of them, though, and the best he'd come up with was a true story about a pair of FBI agents who had worked a successful sting operation by sending criminals free plane tickets to Hawaii. There'd been a bit more to their scam than just the tickets, but the free plane tickets were what had turned the trick. They were bait, plain and simple, and people who took bait got hooked.

Of course, in Lily's instance, it had been the criminals who'd been offering the bait. The trouble was, there had been a lot of criminal elements after the bracelet. They'd get them tracked down, though, one way or the other.

"I think I like ranching," he said.

She burst out laughing. "You haven't been

ranching. You've been eating steak and biscuits three times a day, fishing in the mornings, trail riding in the afternoons, and today, lounging in a stock tank. You haven't been hot and sweaty and dirty once since you got here."

At that, he arched an eyebrow in her direction, and she burst out laughing again. "That doesn't count."

"We were in the barn, sweetheart," he begged to differ. "You and me, hot and sweaty and rolling in dust in the haymow. Trust me, it counted." He leaned over and nuzzled her neck. When he reached the tender skin just below her ear, he stopped and ran his tongue across her skin. "So what do you think of Denver?"

She leaned back and slanted him a curious glance. He was licking her neck and thinking about Denver?

"I think Denver is great."

He kissed her again, on the cheek this time, and drew her close with his arm around her shoulders. "It's also about halfway between Albuquerque and Montana."

"That's A-plus geography work." She grinned, having some idea of what he was getting at. They had hardly been out of each other's sight in four weeks, and every single day had been the best of her life. They talked for hours, and made love for hours, and somehow, with him, she felt like she'd come home, like there wasn't any other place she needed to be. There were no siren calls to exotic lands, only the call to be with him.

It wasn't a feeling she ever wanted to give up.

"If this ranching gig doesn't work out," he said, "I'm going to go live in a loft in LoDo, a really big loft on Steele Street. If you promise not to use up all the towels and steal all the covers, I think I could get you on at the loft, too. It might be a handy stopping-off place for you, when you're going back and forth between Albuquerque and Montana."

"I'm not going back to Albuquerque." She'd given it a lot of thought, and a move she'd made to please a husband she no longer had didn't seem like the best thing to stick with, and she couldn't bear the thought of going into her house again. She'd have to, sometime in the next few weeks, but Zach had already promised to go with her, and he'd promised her a cleanup crew would have the whole inside looking like new before they arrived.

"Good," he said. "Then the loft could be a handy stopping-off place between Denver and Montana . . . or you could just stop in Denver, and Montana could be a sometime thing."

She smiled, loving this conversation. It would definitely go in her diary, if she'd kept a diary: where it had taken place, who she'd been having it with, and she hoped, how it turned out. Love talk in stock tanks was every cowgirl's dream come true, even more of a dream come true than white-sand beaches, palm trees, and pink sunsets on the ocean.

She had a smile on her face, a real enigmatic Mona Lisa smile, and Zach was hanging over an abyss, declaring his love everlasting, laying his heart on the line.

And she was smiling. Enigmatically.

"You love the idea, don't you." It wasn't a question. She loved the idea.

Her smile broadened.

"You're crazy about me," he said. And yeah, he figured this was a good tactic. She could smile, naked in a stock tank, freezing her gorgeous ass off, and he'd just live in his little dream world—which, amazingly, looked exactly like his real world. Beautiful naked woman sheltered in the curve of his arm, love in her eyes, and an enigmatic, Mona Lisa smile on her face.

"Yeah, you're in love with me, I can tell."

She just smiled, and started doing some very nice things with her hand below the water.

He settled her in closer and kissed her mouth. "You probably want to marry me in this stock tank, before we go back to Denver. You know, just take a chance on me."

She just smiled, her hand never stopping its wondrous exploration of his anatomy, and so it went the way it had been going since he'd gotten out of the hospital, crazy hot sex almost every day—and yeah, that was part of the dream, too.

He didn't know what Alex had done with the polymer strand out of the bracelet, or how the U.S. government was going to leverage the information. His job had been to get the damn thing, and he'd done it. And the next job he was given, he'd do that, too, but he'd be doing it for General Grant over at the Department of Defense, via Dylan Hart at Special Defense Force, SDF. He was going back to 738 Steele Street. He was going home.

This whole little sidebar he'd worked for himself, this "saving the woman" part and fulfilling his "sex with a cowgirl" fantasy, that was the extra, that was for him.

And hours later, when they'd gotten back to the ranch house and warmed each other up in bed, when she finally said yes—yes to Denver, and yes to him. That's when he realized that from the very first moment he'd seen her, from the moment when he'd felt his world shift a bit on its axis, from that moment onward, the whole "saving the woman" part had actually been about saving him.

*Want more steamy
Steele Street adventure?*

Then Don't Miss

*LOOSE
AND EASY*

The next book in
Tara's action-packed series

BY TARA JANZEN

Coming November 2008
From Dell Books

LOOSE AND EASY
ON SALE NOVEMBER 2008

CHAPTER **ONE**

Johnny Ramos knew the sad-looking little hooker limping her way down Seventeenth Street in two-inch black patent-leather platform heels. Her fishnet hose were torn in the back, revealing the bottom curve of her ass under what could only be described as a super-micro-miniskirt. Red lace and leather that had seen better days, the skirt was barely seven inches wide from top to bottom and matched her red lace gloves. The cheap white vinyl tote bag slung over her shoulder looked like it had seen better days, too. The white Lycra T-shirt laminated to her upper body had more heart-shaped cutouts and pink sequins than material. He could see a red pushup bra doing its job under the shirt.

Esmee Alexandria Alden, he thought, East High School's valedictorian the year he'd graduated. *Jesus, how the mighty have fallen.*

"Easy Alex" hooking in LoDo—Denver's lower downtown district—it was enough to boggle the mind. Nothing about what he was seeing made sense: that sweet little size-four ass in torn fishnet; the twisted-up pile of ratted and heavily sprayed blond hair he'd only ever seen in tight and tidy braids; the smartest girl he'd ever known turning tricks.

He slid his gaze over her again, from the shoes to the French twist falling out of its pins. At seventeen, he'd have given anything to get her hair loose and falling down. Those long blond braids of hers had driven him crazy. He'd wanted so badly to undo them. Hell, he'd wanted to undo everything on the girl, from her prim little button-down shirts to her carefully tied and spotlessly white tennis shoes, but there hadn't been anything easy about "Easy Alex." That had been the joke. She'd never had a date in high school, not one, not even prom.

She couldn't possibly be a prostitute. No way in hell. Back then, she hadn't known what the word "sex" meant. He knew, because he'd gotten more off of her than any guy in East, and it had taken him weeks of pursuit and most of one hot summer night to even get to second base.

She'd been sweet. Yeah, he remembered. Sweet and scared, mostly of him, he'd guessed, and of herself, of her reaction to him. He'd been one of the city's bad boys, and she'd had the lock on the title of Little Miss Goody Two Shoes.

He'd loved it, loved the challenge of it, but she'd been too good to let him get in her pants, which is where their party had ended that night, with him aching and her panting, and neither of them getting what they'd needed.

Fifty bucks said he could get whatever he wanted off her tonight. Hell, maybe it would only take twenty, but with her looking rode hard and put away wet all he wanted was the story, the explanation.

Yeah, that's what he wanted. No way in hell should Esmee Alden be limping down Seventeenth with her ass hanging out of ripped fishnet. After graduating from high school, she'd been slated for the University of Colorado on a scholarship, full ride.

She got to the corner at Wazee and started

across the intersection, heading toward the Oxford Hotel. When she was partway to the other side, the Oxford's valet signaled her, and Johnny swore under his breath.

"Jesus." She'd been called in to service some guy staying at the hotel, and he had to wonder, really, how many doormen and parking valets in Denver had her name in their little black books?

He hated to say it, but he would have thought any girl working the Oxford would look a little classier than what Esmee had pulled off tonight.

None of his business, he told himself, not for any good reason on God's green earth, and yet he stepped off the curb from in front of the Lizard Tequila Cantina, the bar where he'd been with his friends, and crossed Seventeenth. He wasn't following her. He was just checking things out, doing recon, getting the lay of the land.

He'd gotten home from his last tour of duty, this one in Afghanistan, two weeks ago and was still waiting to be reassigned to General Grant's command, specifically into Special Defense Force, an elite group of operatives based in Denver and deployed out of the Pentagon. Until his official orders came through, he was on leave, on his own, hanging out in his hometown and looking to stay out of trouble.

Or not.

A brief grin twitched the corner of his lips. Easy Alex had never been anything except trouble for him, starting in Ms. Benson's seventh-grade social-studies class, where he'd come up with her nickname and ended up in detention. Decking Freddy Harrell for pushing her up against a locker in a back hallway in East High when they'd all been juniors had gotten him suspended for three days. He'd been protecting her honor.

And now she was hooking?

No. He wasn't buying it. Not the Esmee he knew. Something else had to be going on, no matter how much of her ass he could see— except when she got to the sidewalk, the damn valet handed her a room key.

Johnny came to a sudden halt. *Jesus, a friggin' room key.*

Okay, this really wasn't any of his business, and honestly, he didn't really want to see what she was going to be doing in the hotel, or who in the hell she was going to be doing it with, or doing it to, or any damn thing about Esmee Alden "doing it" at all.

Which was why it took him another second and a half to get moving again. *Goddammit*. Inside the hotel, he caught sight of her just before she disappeared up the stairs.

He didn't hesitate. Taking the damn things two at a time, he easily made it to the second landing in time to see which door she opened with the key—number 215. She slipped inside the room and the door closed behind her, and there he stood, like an idiot at the end of the hallway, wondering what in the hell he was thinking.

The seconds ticked by, and he was still standing there. When a whole minute had gone by, he knew he should leave—but he didn't, he just kept staring at the door to room 215 and telling himself not to go anywhere near it. Good advice he might have taken, if he hadn't heard a loud thump come from inside the room, a sound like somebody falling or getting knocked over.

None of his business—right—except it was Easy Alex in there, and he didn't want to be reading about her in the morning papers. He'd "been there, done that" with too many people in his life, so better judgment be damned, he started down the hall.

When he got to the door, he could hear

some guy spluttering in indignation and anger from inside the room.

"You . . . you . . . goddamn *schickse*. You . . . you can't do this to me."

Johnny pressed his ear closer. None of his business, absolutely none—*dammit*. He wasn't cop of the world, not here. He should be enjoying the reprieve, not jumping in the middle of a fifty-dollar trick.

"*Schickse* yourself, Otto," a cool, sweetly feminine voice replied. And yes, it was definitely Easy Alex. He remembered the slightly cultured accent, the honeyed tone, the instinctive edge of authority. *Christ*. She'd always had the edge of authority, usually with her hand in the air, fingers waggling, her arm stick-straight, going for all the height she could get—*Hey, hey, teacher, I know the answer, I know the answer*. Hell, she'd always known the answer.

"That's not . . . this isn't," the guy kept spluttering, his voice starting to sound a little strained. "This isn't what I asked for . . . I wanted Dixie. I was told to ask for Dixie, and . . . and you're not Dixie."

No, Johnny thought, a little taken back. She most certainly wasn't. Anywhere in Denver north of the Sixteenth Street Mall, the name

Dixie bandied about in that tone of voice by some guy in a hotel could only mean one thing, a diminutive forty-five-year-old dominatrix with a quirt. She'd been a permanent fixture of the city's nights for as long as Johnny could remember, which did nothing to answer the questions of why Esmee Alden was taking one of Dixie's calls, and what in the hell she'd just done to the German in room 215.

Somebody in the room let out a strangled sound of distress, and he knocked, twice, hard and solid, a pure knee-jerk reaction that clearly said "What in the hell is going on in there?"—and the room went silent. He could have heard a frickin' pin drop in the hall, and he could just imagine the two of them frozen in some sordid S&M act, their gazes glued to the door, wondering who in the hell had knocked.

"Housekeeping," he said, loud and clear. "We have your towels."

Towels?

Esmee tightened her grip on the handcuffs she'd used at Otto Von Lindeberg's request to secure his hands behind his back. He was facedown on the floor, her knee planted firmly and deliberately in his back, pressing hard. Her other hand had a strong grip on the dog collar the German had also been so kind as to provide already in place around his neck. She had the attached leash tied to the bed frame—and there was somebody at the door, somebody she'd bet didn't have any towels.

Dammit. Releasing her hold on the collar, she swiveled on Otto's back and quickly flex-cuffed his ankles, then used one of his other leashes to hog-tie his ankles to his wrists.

Geez. Germans and dogs—it was always the Germans with the dog paraphernalia. She'd seen it half a dozen times in her line of work, which despite her outfit didn't have a damn thing to do with prostitution.

Esmee Alden, Master of Disguise—yes, sir, that was her, all right, when the situation called for it, and old Otto had laid himself wide open to get taken by a hooker tonight. She'd known he would, and she'd known exactly what kind of girl he'd be looking to hire. Six months of investigation hadn't gone for naught, and fifty bucks to the parking valet had done the rest. The call for Dixie had come to her instead. She might have to make up the missed trick to the aging dominatrix, just to keep peace on the street, but a couple hundred bucks ought to cover it, which left her with the night's profit margin hitting close to a thousand percent.

And it still wasn't enough, not even close.

She rose to her feet, leaving Otto to squirm on the floor. He'd left his suitcase open on the bed, and it took her about thirty seconds to search through his clothes and the rest of his dog collars. He had a penchant for spikes and studs.

She had a penchant for fine art, the stolen variety, and she wasn't finding any packed in his suitcase. Oh, hell, no—that would have been too easy.

Reaching into her tote bag, she pulled out a knife and thumbed it open, then started in on the suitcase itself. She kept to the edges, inside and out, running the blade close to the frame and carefully pulling back the linings and fabric covering.

No art.

Specifically, no Jakob Meinhard's 1910 *Model in Blue*, an Expressionist masterpiece last seen in Munich in 1937 as part of the *Entartete Kunst* exhibit, the Degenerate Art exhibit, and believed burned in Berlin in 1939. Her father had been on the painting's trail since word of its survival had surfaced four years ago.

Four years of following the painting. Six months of following Otto, including the two months needed to set up a "sale" in Denver, and about five minutes in a hotel room to set almost seven decades of loss right—not to mention saving her dad's butt. Again.

Dammit. She let out a short sigh and thumbed the knife closed, her gaze searching the room. All Otto had brought with him, that she could see, was the suitcase and the clothes on his back.

She dropped a glance at the mostly naked man trussed at her feet. Without the black leather thong he'd strapped on with all its buckles and snaps, he'd be completely naked.

She was so grateful for the thong.

The rest of his clothes were in a neatly folded stack on the bed—except for his suit jacket.

She looked to the open closet near the door leading out into the hall. Sure enough, he'd hung up his jacket, and it was looking very tidy in the closet. Very tidy, indeed, and rather stiff.

Walking over to the closet, she opened the knife again in a single, smooth move.

"Policia." She heard the man outside the

door talking again, the guy with no towels. *"Abra la puerta, por favor."*

Open the door, he'd said, and Esmee could see her time was running out damn fast. He was obviously speaking to somebody with a key, and given his choice of language, she was guessing one of the maids. Everybody manning the front desk spoke English.

Without rushing, she didn't waste a second, taking hold of Otto's suit jacket and neatly slicing open the side seam. Her hand went in between the silk lining and the English tweed, and her smile came out—*voila!* Success.

She slipped the painting free from its hiding place, took a quick look, and rolled it into a tight tube. She was heading toward the window that opened onto the alley even as she was sliding the painting into the cardboard sleeve she'd brought with her in her tote bag.

The Oxford was an old historic hotel, and the windows did open. In room 215, where fifty bucks to the reservation clerk had guaranteed Otto would be put, the window not only opened, it opened onto an old fire escape that she'd personally checked out two nights ago. It had held her then, and it held her tonight.

By the time she heard the commotion of the no-towel-guy and the maid discovering a dog-collared, thong-clad foreigner leashed to the bed, she was in the alley, disappearing into the shadows.